PRA
THE EQUAL

"Tucker's gift for dialogue asserts itself often . . . A romantic fantasy series starter full of intriguing concepts from science and spirituality."

—*Kirkus Reviews*

"This mystical novel will have you begging for the sequel."

—Brit + Co

"In this captivating and explosive story, Skylar must make choices that will indefinitely alter her own life and the lives of everyone around her."

—Buzzfeed

"It is time for the power of women, and women's mysteries, to reclaim their rightful place in world cosmology . . . the lore behind the book came across as well researched. Enjoyable."

—*San Francisco Book Review*

SKY OF
WATER

SKY OF WATER

BOOK THREE OF THE EQUAL NIGHT TRILOGY

STACEY L. TUCKER

SparkPress, a BookSparks imprint
A Division of SparkPoint Studio, LLC

Published by SparkPress, a BookSparks imprint,
A division of SparkPoint Studio, LLC
Phoenix, Arizona, USA, 85007
www.gosparkpress.com

Published 2020

Printed in the United States of America

ISBN: 978-1-68463-040-0 (pbk)
ISBN: 978-1-68463-041-7 (e-bk)
Library of Congress Control Number: 019916864

Cover design © Julie Metz, Ltd./metzdesign.com
Formatting by Katherine Lloyd/theDESKonline.com
Map illustration by Sean Donaldson

For Kayli

Every day on the balcony of the sea, wings open,
fire is born, and everything is blue again like morning.

—Pablo Neruda

Silver wood

Ocean's House   Rosen

Beatrice's House

Atlantis

In the First Age, in the dark cave of creation, the light of knowledge was infused with the blood of compassion in the womb of earth. The heart light was born. Its power was coveted by those that knew its strength. But soon fractured, the stone could not come to light. So began a world controlled by fear, where the devil was blamed for all sin. A fractured stone meant a fractured humanity, and the dark ones were pleased. But the sands of time have waited for the moment to arrive when the extraordinary magic of the human heart will have another chance to shine again. If the stone can be healed by the pure of heart, its power will be remembered in all souls that walk the earth.

Vivienne DeClaire's apartment sat perched precariously over the lapping waves of the Mediterranean. An ancient, gnarled pine clung tenaciously to the exposed face. It hadn't yet decided to succumb to the sea. Vivienne's marble deck now hung completely over the side of the cliff. She had made Bari, Italy, her home after the First Age, when more land surfaced after the Great Flood. Good memories had soaked into the land there. She had only wanted to remember the good. But now she looked out at the stunted shore beneath her and saw the painful ones returning. Ghostly, black, crab-like creatures crawled out of the sea at a snail's pace. Their slow speed made their return that much worse, prolonging the inevitable. They had been waiting, as all painful memories do, in the churning, deep, dark water of the ocean. They were messengers from the primordial deep, and Vivienne was now faced with a choice she thought only applied to humans: act or react. She already knew she had waited too long to act.

The earth was experiencing remarkably swift changes that no scientist could explain away with global warming. Beatrice, the Great Mother of Air, was to blame for some of them. She hadn't limited her wrath to the US. Many of the shores of Europe had been coated in silt. Now a light gray color, the beaches couldn't hide their sadness. The shadow of humanity had been drawn out of the protection of the ocean and washed up like a tidal wave of beached sea life. It was forcing mankind to look at its own darkness.

Ocean, Great Mother of Fire, had to take responsibility as well. Fire was volatile, and volatile energy was escaping the earth's core through volcanic activity. Volcanoes were, surprisingly, more easily dealt with than the quiet migration of the rising tide, however. The sea was just like Vivienne, Great Mother of Water—reserved and commanding, yet lethal when necessary. Nothing could stop raging water.

But all of the earth changes couldn't be blamed on the Mothers. The greatest Mother herself, Gaia, needed to stretch and change. If a house sat where fire or fresh water must flow, so be it. Humans were required to adapt; they could no longer believe the earth was for conquering. Gaia had allowed people to live on her body, and they had proven horrendous stewards.

Natural disasters were the Great Mothers' way of healing, of purging their personal pain. Although selfish in motive, the disasters always helped collective humanity. It seemed people forgot their pettiness and self-absorbed lives when disaster struck and remembered what life was truly about.

"Beauty always emerges out of destruction," Vivienne said. "Always."

Milicent Grayer wrapped herself in her vintage Armani purple silk kimono and sat on the corner of the ornate, satin-covered bed in one of her grandmother Vivienne's guest rooms. Vivienne's grand apartment had nine bedrooms, unheard of in crowded Bari. But Vivienne had converted six apartments into one at the turn of the twentieth century, mostly out of boredom. She had admired the rich Italian décor then, but now over a century had gone by, and she hadn't the energy or desire to redecorate. She was considering leaving the apartment and relocating to Indonesia.

Milicent was slow to dress that morning as the wet heat wafted off the water through the open doors of the balcony. Her assistant, Noah Maganti, sat in lotus position on an uncomfortable antique desk chair in the corner. He was dressed all in white, his dark curls sleekly swept up in a man bun. He'd fallen off his weekly trim regimen, and it showed.

After Skylar's abduction, he'd been glued to YouTube doomsday channels until Milicent forbade the negative energy in the house.

"You love negative energy, Mil," he said.

"I'm working on raising my vibration and so should you," she said. "We can't keep feeding the collective fear. Power over others is a dying paradigm, and I'm trying to get ahead of the next big thing—power from within. Do your part to help me, Noah."

After a bit of research into the other side of YouTube, he'd discovered the world of Kundalini yoga videos and had been practicing the technology incessantly ever since. Milicent didn't know which was worse.

Vivienne walked into the room and Noah jumped to his feet and bowed. Niceties observed, he returned to lotus in the chair and resumed his alternate-nostril breathing. Vivienne chuckled quietly, but the reverberations of her laugh were felt for miles. Locals would cite a mild earthquake. Until now, she had done a queen's job of keeping herself hidden among the cliffs of Bari, but now it was her turn to be seen, and that would come with a cost. Her sisters both claimed to be the most powerful Mother, but they secretly knew nothing was greater than the power of water.

She picked up the Book of Sophia from the desk next to Noah's computer. It was barely recognizable, disintegrating by the day.

"It will return to the ethers soon," Vivienne said. "Sophia calls for its return."

"It's unfortunate," Milicent said. "It was the last piece for my library."

"Records of the past have their place, but the future will be created on a whole other level," Vivienne said. "The need for writing things down is coming to an end."

She put down the book, and the two women walked out onto the small balcony attached to Milicent's room. The high tide made the shore completely disappear.

"Grandmother, if a flood is inevitable, what's the point in trying to make the world better?" Milicent asked. "It would seem we're truly at the end of things now, and we should invest our money in that fellow who's trying to get to Mars."

"It's never the end," Vivienne said. "In the trying, help is given, timelines are collapsed, and futures change. Compassion for your fellow human acknowledges your own worthiness, and in that, worlds can be saved and crises avoided." She sat on a bistro chair and sipped a glass of something cool and sparkling. "Besides, Mars is a dusty place. You'd hate it there."

Milicent understood what Vivienne was saying. But as much as she didn't want to admit it, she liked the drama of her life—except maybe the part when her husband, Devlin, put a cord around her neck.

Vivienne glanced back inside at Noah. "I like your boy," she said. "He balances your energy."

Milicent frowned.

"You know, for someone who claims to hate men, you always choose boys to collect. Do better with this one, child."

"I've changed, Grandmother," Milicent said. "Not necessarily by choice, but even I can't deny that it's for the better."

Vivienne smiled warmly.

"And I've been thinking about something."

"Yes?" Vivienne waited.

"I want to see Diana," Milicent said. "A part of me is incomplete knowing that she is somewhere I can see her." She paused. "And I shouldn't go alone."

Vivienne sipped some more, not in a rush to reply. "I know what you're thinking," she finally said. "But this world is not mine to fix." She stared out at the sea. "It's up to humanity."

"Grandmother, we both know that's not entirely true," Milicent said with a bit of scolding in her voice. Vivienne glared at her but she didn't back down. "You know this. History repeats itself because the core issue has never been dealt with. The landscape may look different, but the energy is exactly the same."

Vivienne paused. "I am not the same," she said, quietly but firmly.

Milicent softened and took her hand. "I understand deep wounds of the past and how they color the view of things. But this is your last chance. Magus has Skylar." She followed Vivienne's eyes to the horizon. They both knew what sat underneath the ocean, waiting to be discovered. She squeezed her grandmother's hand. "It's only a matter of time before he finds a way to extract the stone and it leads him to the citrine wall."

"The stone is useless unless buried within the heart," Vivienne said. "It works its magic through human compassion."

"Magus believes differently," Milicent said. "Technology has always been his religion."

"He destroyed the world in the First Age with his technologies. Casting out love on his quest for power." Vivienne's eyes were sad but no tears would be shed. In recorded history, she had only ever shed one. She knew the secret locked within her tears and had decided long ago that no one would ever deserve that power—her vulnerability.

"Grandmother, I still struggle with finding balance between

exorcising the past and letting it go," Milicent said. "And I feel you must do the same."

Vivienne chuckled softly. "Child, you have come so far, and grown so much," she said.

"Who knew there was hope for me?"

"I did." Vivienne squeezed her granddaughter's hand.

Milicent tried to stay present but grew uncomfortable and began to fidget. "I need to go inside. This air is the worst for my hair."

Noah turned down the volume on a YouTube video about the secrets under Antarctica. He looked up at Milicent through his BluBlocker glasses. "Mil, did you know that Antarctica is fresh water?"

"There is no saltwater ice, Noah, it's chemistry," she said. "The salt is squeezed out. But don't listen to that garbage anyway."

He immediately went back to scouring the internet.

"If you care to know the real truth, the caps are melting to return fresh water to the earth," Vivienne said in the doorway. "The sleeping goddess of Gaia is waking up to restore the water to its original state. The curse will be lifted soon."

"Is that so?" Milicent asked, her cool demeanor returned. "Mother Gaia is just going to swoop in and fix your mess? After all this time, you'll just be exonerated, without any penance?"

Vivienne walked toward Milicent and stopped inches away from her. "Be careful how you judge others, dear one, for it is how you judge yourself." She turned and walked out the door to the living room.

"She looked hurt, Mil," Noah said.

"She needs to own her role in this mess."

"That's harsh," he said.

"Yes. But all of the Great Mothers have their secrets, and

they are usually wrapped around lost love. She loved Magus in the First Age. We're talking thirteen thousand years ago, but a woman never forgets rejection."

Noah wrinkled his nose with disgust. "He's all shriveled and pruny. He must have looked better then."

"He only looks that way in our timeline. He can manipulate his appearance to suit his needs. I'm sure he was disgustingly handsome in the First Age. I mean, why wouldn't he be?" Milicent sat on a round, tufted chaise tucked behind the balcony door. "She's kept a low profile ever since, perfectly happy to let Ocean run the show. But this is her karma to dissolve. The whole planet is in *Dissolution*. This is hers."

Noah got up and walked to the floor-length window. "Mil, how long do you suppose we'll be here in Italy? It's just glorious. I could stay forever. The world back home is a distant memory."

"In more ways than one," she said, staring at her cuticles. "Washington is officially dead. And Rosen . . . It's marred now that I know Devlin was playing me all those years. I spent thirty years of my life with the man while he was orchestrating some other horrible plan. It's as if he had me under the spell I claimed to know so well."

"I'm sorry, Mil." Noah bent to take her hand, forcing her to look at him. "If it's any consolation, I've loved every second of the past year. Even almost going to federal prison." He got up and walked to the balcony door. "It's probably too soon to ask *what's next.*"

"*What's next* is we have to stop Magus, once and for all. Then we can discuss a future."

2

Argan sat with his arms resting on his knees, staring out at the sea. As the small waves lapped at his bare feet, he casually let the emerald stone slosh around in the tidewater. He sat so long, the water receded and the stone was left in a small tide pool the size of a puddle. He drew a heart around the green stone, and one last wave of the outgoing tide lightly splashed it.

"Come in, child," his mother, Leonora, called from the back door. "You'll catch cold."

He shook his head. The women in his life loved to tell him what to do. All except one. Skylar balanced him, complemented him. He loved taking care of her, making her happy. Their time together had been so short. He made no effort to go inside. "It's eighty degrees out, Mom," he called back.

A minute later, Leonora took a seat in the sand beside him. Her long, black hair blew in wind. "Rain's coming," she said, looking at the sky.

Argan glanced up briefly, then returned his gaze to the horizon.

"You'll wait until tomorrow."

"Tonight," he said curtly. "The weather doesn't matter."

She shrugged and glanced down at the stone in the water. "You should keep that in a safe place."

"That is a safe place." He chuckled to himself, thinking of Skylar's haphazard care of the Book of Sophia. The light from the gem made the water around it glow fluorescent green. Argan watched the light extend from the stone and out into the sea.

"It's reacting to the silver in the seawater," Leonora said. "Most of the silver on the planet is dissolved in the ocean. That's why the moon has such an effect on the tides. It's pulling the silver around like a magnet pulls metal filings."

Argan nodded, acknowledging the science trivia. He picked up the stone and the light faded. "It's not that special," he said, unable to convince his mother or himself.

"It's half of the whole, but perfect in itself, only enhanced by its other half," Leonora said. Argan knew she was talking about more than the stone. "Come in soon. We'll eat." She squeezed his knee and stood up. As she stood there, her long hair whipped around wildly in a sudden burst of wind.

"Okay." Argan put the stone in its bag and got up to head inside. The cypress trees in the backyard still stood as protectors of his childhood home in Kythira, but the landscape had changed so much since he was a boy. In two short decades, the sea had edged dangerously close to many of the homes that had once been well protected from the water. Now it was anyone's guess how long it would be before they were in the ocean.

When he walked into the house, he found his seven older sisters all crying, holding a vigil; they assumed Argan was leaving to his death. He rolled his eyes at the drama. He hadn't missed any of them while living in the States.

His father, Giannes, sat asleep in a well-worn recliner in the living room. The chair was the one thing he'd shipped back to Greece a dozen years earlier when they'd returned from America. He said he wanted to be buried in it. Argan wasn't sure how soon that would be. His father spent most of his days asleep; if anything, death would be an improvement.

He was grateful for his father's teachings. He was an old soul and had raised Argan in the traditions of their Greek heritage. He'd instilled in him the importance of being respectful, a gentleman, a good provider. He lived by tradition and resisted changing what worked. Argan appreciated his father but now that he was older, he saw Giannes' limitations, especially with his mother. Giannes loved Leonora and gave her earthly security, but Argan could see there was something missing. A loneliness permeated his mother's eyes that he hadn't noticed until recently.

It was Leonora who'd given Argan his true schooling. From the moment she conceived him, she'd known she was carrying a boy. After seven girls, this one was different. From the time her belly started to grow, she talked to him about the Goddess, about Sophia, and about the daughter who would rise to challenge the beliefs of their time and usher in the Golden Age. Her daughters were beautiful, smart, even cunning, but she knew her son had a destiny to fulfill. Argan was to help the *daughter*—be her knight, fulfill his duty. And young Argan had loved the idea of being a knight. He'd easily become proficient with a sword. Another mother would have cringed, but Leonora had encouraged her son to excel in the art of war. She'd known what he would someday face.

She'd also taught him something more vital to his purpose—the art of love. She was determined that "Leonora's boy," as the neighbors called him, would teach his sisters about honor and integrity. She'd seen her girls and the way they conducted their lives. She'd loved each one, but she'd also seen their cattiness, watched as they threw each other under the bus for the attention of a man.

Leonora was a sybil. She'd seen the coming age of the Divine Feminine and the one who would start the chain reaction to bring balance back to the world. And she knew her boy was no ordinary boy, and would grow into no ordinary man. He had the kiss of destiny on his forehead. And she was honored to have been the one to bring him into this world.

Argan entered the kitchen. Leonora was looking out the window, lost in thought, her mind still sitting by the ocean's edge.

"I remember that summer—September came and you returned to Greece with your father," she said. "Until then, you had clung to your childhood. You'd resisted growing up the whole way. But then you came back and you were heartbroken and too young to understand why. But I knew. I was heartbroken, too, because it was my first taste of losing you. You just didn't know what it meant. A mother's love can only sustain for so long before a young man needs sustenance from another. The masculine needs the nourishment of a woman's energy. At your tender age, this was a foreshadowing of the future. And it would appear the future is upon us."

He looked at his mother with tears in his eyes. "No one can ever replace you," he said.

"I am not worried about replacement, my love, nor am I in need of reassurance," she said, cupping his face with her hand. "You are a strong man and you deserve the love of a strong woman. Skylar is worthy of you, and you will find her. It is destiny."

He hugged his mother tight and wept openly on her shoulder. She knew his tears were for her as much as they were for Skylar. They were tears mourning the loss of his relationship with his mother.

"Our bond will always be right here." She clasped his hand and held it to her chest.

He reciprocated and held her hand to his own heart. "I love you, Mama," he said through his tears.

"You will always be my one true love," she said. "Through you, I have learned my greatest joy and my greatest sorrow. Thank you for picking me as your mama."

13

He bent over so she could kiss his forehead, as she'd done before he grew a foot taller than her. They heard the wailing coming from the living room. She waved her hand in the air, dismissing his sisters' ridiculous behavior, and left the kitchen before he saw too many of her tears fall.

3

Devlin Grayer's red book sat on Ocean's bar cart next to her whiskey decanter. She looked at it and felt its charge of pure evil—or was it ignorance? She often confused the two. With a flip of her wrist, she tossed it across the porch without ever touching it. It landed on a table near the door. She lit a smudge pot and picked up a glass to pour a drink, but stopped. She didn't feel like drinking. For the first time in a long while, she felt lonely. After all the help she had given the girl, she'd refused to acknowledge how much the girl had given her. And now they were in this mess. She sighed.

Magus had a way of screwing everything up at the end of things. She'd watched him do it at the end of the First Age. She was convinced he had turned the seas red. And here they were again. The red tides were returning, just like the last time. She could no longer prevent the heating in the earth's core. She had delayed it as long as she could, waiting for humanity to wake up. A storm was coming on the horizon, just like last time—although this time, it would be without Beatrice. That was fine with Ocean; she was no help anyway.

It was Vivienne's turn now, the only other Great Mother who cared about the future of earth. Beatrice certainly hadn't. How insular she had become. Ocean wasn't sorry she'd left the earth plane. Beatrice was of no use to their cause. If Ocean were honest, she would own some of that drama herself. But there was no more hiding for Vivienne.

Ocean had to admit that Skylar had surprised her, restoring the memory of the citrine wall as she had. That had happened ahead of schedule. But the United States still needed an overhaul, and the new president was not the one to do it.

"Your lack of faith in others is your biggest affliction," Magda said from behind her.

Ocean resumed making her drink.

"You know that libation is not good for your physical or mental body," Magda said.

Ocean turned to face her. "It hasn't killed me yet."

Magda turned her attention to the vast backyard and the black tree. "You should be pleased about the political progress in this country. So much has happened so quickly. No one has had time to adjust or even completely process the enormity of it all."

"You are not telling me anything I don't already know," Ocean said. "Why are you here?"

"Mica is the one to dissolve the sins of this country. Accept her help. To do that, you must acknowledge the other Great Mother—the one deeper than the elements, the one that comes from deep within the earth."

"Right." Ocean knocked back her whiskey.

"It is time, Ocean," Magda said.

"It's always time, Magda," Ocean said flippantly.

"To bring forth the lost knowledge," Magda said, ignoring Ocean's tone.

"Skylar has done well with Sophia's book," Ocean said.

"I am not talking about Sophia," Magda said. "Her energy has saturated the ethers and is now permeating the physical plane. We must shift our focus to the Sacred Masculine."

Ocean shook her head. "That is *not* my department."

"It is that very attitude of separation that got the world in this mess. You have your own healing to do." Magda's etheric body floated gracefully around the porch. "The masculine starts with science, and we have friends that can help there."

Ocean knew Magda was talking about Joel. "I've already given him a job to do," she said. "He's very reluctant."

"And you're very persuasive," Magda said. "There are genealogical origins that now need to be uncovered." Her stare bore through Ocean's skull. "You know of Skylar's blood, where it comes from."

"Right," Ocean said. "But even if I can convince Joel, few will believe him."

"That is the desired result in the short term. You know most truths are rejected by the masses at first. Do this." Magda faded into mist.

"I like giving orders, not taking them," Ocean said loudly into the air. She shot back her second whiskey of the morning and went inside to dress.

Later that morning, Rachel and Joel sat on Ocean's back porch in the same spot Magda had occupied earlier. Rachel was alive with energy she couldn't name, unable to sit still.

"Magda was here this morning, maybe you feel her," Ocean said.

"Maybe," Rachel said, unconvinced. She studied the backyard, specifically the tree. "I can see the energy of the tree, it's Skylar's. She's not dead, but her soul is hanging precariously in two worlds." She dashed down the back steps and ran to the charred maple. She paused only briefly, asking permission, then placed her hand on its trunk. She waited with her eyes closed.

A few moments later, Ocean met her at the tree.

Rachel opened her eyes. "I can go to her," she said. "I can help her. She's in a hospital bed, hooked up to machines. She's being used as an experiment." She looked at Ocean. "Can't you go there? You can go anywhere."

"Unfortunately no," Ocean said. "I'm not the one to do this. Argan is. If I intervene, timelines could change, and not for the better."

Rachel's shoulders sank and she nodded. She breathed in the hot air of the last day of May, and her head rose to look at Ocean. "This tree *is* Skylar."

Ocean chuckled. "Yeah—she didn't recognize it as her own, but yes. She has more fire in her than she cares to admit."

Rachel looked at Rhia's and Joshua's headstones. "This really is bizarre, having them buried next to each other," she said. "He killed her."

Ocean shrugged. "In this life, yes. But if it's any consolation, they aren't enemies. They're actually working together to help us from where they are now."

"Yeah, I guess so," Rachel said, still staring at the ground.

"Come on," Ocean said, motioning toward the porch. "I asked Joel here for a reason."

The women walked back up the stairs to where Joel was sitting. He had his nose in his cell phone.

Ocean went inside and was back quicker than her usual pace. The light she carried preceded her by tenfold. Rachel made no move but Joel had to shield his eyes.

"Put these on," Ocean said, handing him a pair of protective eyeglasses.

He obliged willingly and gasped in a rare moment of surprise. "What the hell is that?" The glasses diffused the light shining off of the object so he could see it clearly. A holographic cylinder crystal tube, about the size of a microscope, stood upright, numerous reflections of rainbow light shining brightly from it. It was energy itself, condensed into one square foot of space.

Ocean cleared a few glasses off her bar cart and placed the device on its woven bamboo surface.

Rachel chuckled. "Good thing it's daytime. That thing would light up the night."

Ocean laughed. "Yeah, I take it outside when I can't find the cat. It lights up the whole backyard."

"You have a cat?" Rachel asked.

"You've seen one of these?" Joel asked Rachel.

"No, but I've heard of them," she said. "The women in my family talk."

"Joel," Ocean said, "it's time to solidify the bridge between magic and science. I need you to put your scientist pants on and report a finding."

His brow creased with immediate doubt. "Which one is that?"

"The scientific proof of the soul," Ocean said.

"All right," he said. "And how do I do that?"

"With this." She gestured to the magnificent crystal scope. "This is a piece of technology not yet invented in this world. It's unlikely to be for at least another hundred years. Those on the planet using crystal technology aren't even close. And that's a good thing. Because it's dangerous. Misuse of crystal technology caused the fall of Atlantis."

Joel shook his head. "Where'd you get it?" he asked skeptically.

She gave him a tight-lipped look.

"You expect me to believe this is from Atlantis?"

"I don't expect you to believe anything, but I do expect you to do me a favor. And this will help get Skylar back, and I know that's your priority."

"Go ahead," he said.

"Many new agers dabble in crystals. Some forward-thinking entrepreneurs are even using them in products to promote well-being. All good things, but no one in this age has truly harnessed the capabilities of crystals as communication devices. They have the ability to absorb and amplify the emotions of their subject in addition to the intentions of the observer. Think of this as a virtual reality, interactive microscope. Instead of using learned knowledge from a textbook to interpret what is happening with a specimen, with this technology, it's as if the observer becomes one with the observed. In doing so, she or he gains insight—*the sight from within*, where wisdom and answers are readily available to aid the observer in his diagnosis."

Joel dangled the glasses on the tip of his nose for a brief second and then pushed them back over his eyes. "How does this get Skylar back?"

"Is there one of these where Skylar is now?" Rachel piped in.

"Yes," Ocean said. "Her memory will return on how to use it. When it does, she'll try to contact you."

"All right," Joel said, clearly still skeptical. "And until then, what am I looking for—to find the soul?"

"The God particle," Ocean said.

"Oh." He shrugged. "Is that all? And where do you suggest I look?"

"The thymus gland."

"God is in the thymus gland?" he asked dryly.

"Not in the literal sense, but yes."

"The thymus gland shrinks in adolescence," he said. "It really serves no function after that."

"As far as you know," Ocean said. "Has the thymus gland of highly spiritual people been studied?"

"I don't know. I'd have to look that up."

"Do that," she said. "And then study them. Or, to save time, use this crystal and study yourself or anyone else you might have lying around."

"Science already uses light for many experiments," he said.

"Yes, but it's the wrong kind of light. This is pure love light from pure source energy. This crystal is blinding because of its purity. It hasn't been corrupted by the density of earth. Healthy cells turn sickly from a weakened, magnetic pull of light. Over time, this fosters disease."

"You want me to announce that disease is caused by lack of light?" he scoffed.

"It's more than that," she said. "By a lot. It's also magnetics. Push and pull is what runs the human race. The sun and moon, man and woman, positive and negative charge, they're all the same concepts, wrapped in different packages. The balance of action and receptivity is what promotes well-being. So much can be explained by being out of balance. But now, at this time in history, as I've said so many times before, our world is changing from an electric push to a magnetic pull. Nothing can remain the same, nothing. Fear held the old world in place. As humanity moves out of fear, it will step into its sovereignty and create a new, better world, one based on love and compassion."

"I have no idea what you want me do," he said. "Am I reporting scientific facts or writing poetry? There is no room in science for love and compassion."

"You'll only learn from experience." Ocean threw a blue velvet bag over the cylinder, extinguishing the blinding light, and Joel was able to remove his glasses. "Take this home and work with it. Ask it what it wants you to know. It will show you."

He exhaled loudly. "Fine, but I'm keeping these glasses."

"They come as a set." Ocean smiled.

"How is Mica settling in to her new post?" Rachel asked once the microscope was tucked away. "Is she someone we can call on to help us get Skylar back?"

"I haven't tried with all that's on her plate right now," Ocean said. "Besides, she enjoys putting me way down in the mystical pecking order. The Great Mother she answers to is much older than I am."

Rachel looked to the black tree. A vision of a great beast—half woman, half sea creature—appeared in the ethers before her. The Vodou mother appeared in her vision, the one who was cursed with the darkness when time began. She was so completely shunned by the world of light, she could only find love and beauty in the one place that remained: within her own soul. Those of the light were ignorant to the truth they had unintentionally bestowed upon her. Instead of shame, she found love of self and love of others that are thought of as worthless in the world. This discovery of the greatest hidden truth of the soul gave her the ultimate power over the world of light. She would never fear total annihilation; she knew that only beauty would emerge from the ashes.

"Yemaya," Rachel whispered in awe.

"Yup," Ocean said, knocking back her third whiskey before ten. It wasn't a record. "She makes the rest of us look like house cats. Mica may be the president of the United States, but she serves at the pleasure of Yemaya. Goddess help us all."

"But we're all fighting for the same result. We all want the old paradigm out. Surely she'll help."

"You'd think," Ocean said. "But Vivienne was justified in her disapproval of Milicent's actions. Devlin we could manage. Mica Noxx is a wild card we'll have to work around. The good news for us is that she will be heavily scrutinized and stuck in political inertia."

Rachel walked around the patio and picked up the red book on the table. She shuddered. "Devlin was a part of this darkness?"

"Yes," Ocean said.

"I'm not surprised. Milicent is pure evil. It's no accident they were tethered together."

"I would call Milicent misguided more than anything," Ocean said. "She used the losses in her life to fuel her victimhood and excuse her immature behavior. Only lately have I seen any maturity surface. And Devlin was the puppet of a clever master. We need to take down Magus."

Rachel looked back at the book, still uneasy. "How much of this is accurate?"

"All of it," Ocean said.

"But it's so scornful against the feminine," Rachel said. "How can it be accurate?"

"There are great lies in fear, but there is also great truth. Their fear of the feminine energy reveals how powerful we truly are. They covet what they can never possess, and siphon off its energy through fear—the original vampires, dressed in robes of every color. It has always burned my ass that the church uses Jesus as a control mechanism. If sins were taken away by one man, why is the world in the state it's in? I'm sorry, but the state of the world doesn't look saved to me. It's worse than ever. Did Jesus's good deed have an expiration date? Taking the power away from the individual and putting it in the church was the original sin." Ocean picked up Devlin's book and wagged it in their faces. "This mindset has locked humanity in chains for thousands of years, but the Divine Mother has returned to set us free."

"Why do you include yourself in humanity?" Joel asked accusingly. "You aren't one of us."

"That hurts," Ocean said drolly. "I've lived on the planet long enough to deserve at least squatters' rights. But apparently it's time to integrate the worthwhile parts of this thing." She waved the book in the air. "People are on the planet for different reasons, and now we are all coming together for a common purpose. Some are passing through on a vacation from another solar system. These are your Sagittariuses. They love a good party. But some are very old souls that have seen civilization end more than once. And they are back to make sure it doesn't happen again. This is Skylar. Her memory of Lemuria will return to her soon. It's been rising to the surface of her consciousness for weeks now. It got slowed down by the sheer volume of memories she acquired by drinking from the Mnemosyne. But we seem to have fixed that problem."

"Lemuria?" Joel sighed with exasperation.

Rachel studied him for a long minute, then looked out at the backyard at Skylar's tree, tears glazing her eyes. She shook them off and walked to Joel's side. "I'm sorry," she whispered. "I'm sorry I got you into this all those years ago."

"Huh?" he asked, dumbfounded.

"This life . . . this crazy life." She gestured around her—to Ocean, and to the whole magical world he'd resisted for decades, partially due to his limitations, partially due to his desire, or lack thereof, to see the world in a different way. "I knew her destiny all those years ago and here it is, playing out before us. It sat on our timeline, just waiting for us to come to it. You've been a good dad to Skylar, Joel, giving her the stability she needed to grow into an incredible young woman. Thank you for giving her that . . . for giving me that."

He stood up to meet her, concern sweeping across his face. "What are you saying?"

She took in a deep breath. "I'm saying it's time to face the truth we've both always known. We've stayed together all these years to give Skylar that stability, but she doesn't need it anymore."

He searched her face.

"You loved Cassie, not me. And if we're totally honest, we made it work for so long, but now . . . "

Joel sank into the wicker chair behind him. "You're choosing *now* to tell me you want out of our marriage?"

"It has to be now," Rachel said. "The energies of the planet—"

"Enough with the fucking energies!" he snapped. "Take ownership of this moment and stop blaming the energies. If you're out, that's it."

Her tone turned curt. "Joel, does this really surprise you? Are you really happy? I think if you admit the truth to yourself, you'll agree with me. A break was inevitable, and to do it now gives us the freedom we both secretly seek." She walked inside.

Ocean, leaning on the porch railing a few feet away, didn't move throughout this conversation. She looked at her wristwatch. "It's not even ten a.m. and already divorce hangs in the air. Crystal cylinders, life changes . . . I wonder what other surprises the day will bring." She was almost jovial.

Joel looked up at her with a pained face and she softened momentarily.

"I'm sorry, Joel. Our biggest lessons are forged in the fires of pain. At least you have a new project to sink into. It'll keep your mind busy." She followed Rachel inside.

Joel stared at the black tree. *Can this really be happening?* His mind was spinning in five directions. Should he cry? Scream in anger? He did neither. He scooped up the velvet bag containing the crystal cylinder and left.

4

S uki paced in Skylar's house, which was now her house, since her grandmother's had been sold a month earlier. Much of the contents had been donated. Suki hadn't wanted any of it, just the stuff from her room and a few boxes of mementos. She had moved into Skylar's room and Skylar had taken the loft, Cassie's old bedroom.

She wanted to do something to help Skylar, but Ocean's plan involved a lot of waiting. She hated waiting more than any fight she could take part in. She knew what the red book said. She hadn't told anyone. Milicent probably suspected that she had read it. It was most likely the reason she was so unconcerned about Suki studying in the library. She knew nothing she uncovered would be as detrimental as Devlin's book.

She wondered what would happen now that a woman sat in the Oval. She had dreamed of this for years. Each election, the country came closer, and now, by "accident," here they were. Questions ran through her mind . . . *Will we continue with greater globalization, or return to a simpler way of living? How will Mica tackle the natural disasters happening in the country? Can she?*

She stood in the kitchen in silence. Since Skylar had been taken, much of Suki's life had shriveled to miserable silence. She'd enjoyed the silence she'd discovered at Silverwood. Meditation had helped her connect to the divine spark within her, just like Skylar had said it would. But this silence was different.

This one was charged with fear. Chess pieces continued to move, and everyone had their role to play in Ocean's plan, but the waiting would age her for sure. She twirled her one gray lock of hair around her finger. She'd hated it at first and tried to dye it, but it had refused to be covered. She'd finally realized that it was her wisdom showing through, and now she wore it like a badge of honor.

She thought of her life before and after meeting Skylar. Such a brief amount of linear time had passed, just two years, but everything in her life had changed. Her guarded, insulated life had been turned inside out. The way her well-intentioned grandmother had sheltered her from everything had made her rigid and closed off. Skylar's mystical world had opened her eyes and her heart to a world she would now die for. Research had always been her magic. The faith Skylar had in the unseen, Suki had in data. Her stories were formulated by numbers.

She thought about calling her ex-boyfriend Kyle but stopped herself. She didn't need him back simply to fill the silence. Calling him would only complicate things. And dating anyone else would have to wait until her part of the plan was done.

Michael, Skylar's cat, yowled from the loft.

"Meow," Suki answered flatly. His company would have to suffice, even though she wasn't a fan of cats. He answered her again and she continued to meow in conversation as she climbed the stairs.

He sat at attention on Skylar's bed, as if he'd been waiting there since she left.

"I'm sorry, bud," Suki said, patting his head. "I miss her too. But we'll get her back." He pushed his face into her hand and purred briefly before he jumped down. He skidded across a piece of large, shiny paper before scampering down the stairs.

Suki picked up the paper and flipped it over. It was the Porta

Alchemica Game they had taken from the Salem Witch Museum gift shop. She'd forgotten Skylar had taken a stack of those. The background of the paper featured various geographical locations: upstate New York, Italy, Greece, and one muted, nondescript island in the middle of the Atlantic Ocean. Suki took one of the small paper doors out of the Ziploc bag stapled to the corner of the map and started moving it around like a Ouija board triangle. It "locked" on the island in the Atlantic. Underneath emerged a much larger island. "Of course, Atlantis," Suki said dryly. "Why not." She continued to move the paper door around. Another sticking place—Japan, her ancestry. Her heart leapt. She didn't want to give in to the flutter in her heart. *This must be what Skylar feels like,* she thought. *Connecting to the unseen outside of meditation.* More than synchronicity, this was an actual dialogue with spirit.

Suki often thought of exploring her ancestral roots. Research was in her blood, but she had resistance to it. Her father was from Japan, and his mother had raised her after her parents died. But the tragedies of her early life had left her closed off from reaching out to other family members. Learning about them would only remind her of her parents and that was too painful, so she'd locked that part of herself away. But the experiences of the last two years had cracked open that door just a bit. She'd have to give it some thought.

One last go-round of the paper door landed on the continent of Antarctica. At first she started to dismiss it. *No one cares about Antarctica,* she thought. It was just ice. Then she gasped. *Of course it's ice, and it's been melting at an alarming rate.*

What did this frozen part of the world have to do with the great story they were all involved in right now? One person might know. She tucked the map under her arm and headed out the door.

⤳

Kyle was standing in the driveway when Suki got outside.

"Hi," he said.

She took a misstep. "Hi," she said back. It was creepy—she had thought of him and he'd appeared. She briefly wondered if she'd manifested him.

"How are you?" he asked.

"I'm good," she said. "And heading out. Why did you come here?" She resumed walking to her car.

"I miss you, Suki," he said.

"Oh, okay."

"And I got a job."

"Oh, wow," she said. "Good for you."

"I'm leaving town. It's a relocation, not sure of exactly where yet. So I wanted to say a permanent good-bye."

She felt her heart actually shrink. Kyle was never a permanent good-bye. The door had been left open, but now it was shutting. She didn't like it.

"Well, I'm glad to hear you're moving forward in your life, but I will miss you," she said. "Even though we haven't seen each other in months anyway."

"Yeah, I felt the same," he said. "But I wanted to thank you."

"For what?"

"If you hadn't kicked me to the curb, I wouldn't have ever been motivated to go make something of myself. It was the kick in the ass I needed. Thanks."

She softened and Skylar popped into her mind. "Kyle, Skylar . . ."

A car careened down the driveway, cutting her short. She looked up, questioning the unfamiliar car, and was horrified to see Britt Anjawal hop out after it screeched to a halt.

"You have nerve coming here," she said angrily, moving toward Britt.

"Please wait," Britt pleaded, approaching her. "Let me explain."

Suki didn't slow her steps; she felt like she might punch the girl.

Britt, seeing the look in her eyes, started backing away. "I had to try to save my mother," she blurted. "That stone was supposed to restore a memory. My mother's is all but gone." She held Skylar's simple rock out in her hand as an offering. "If it's any consolation, it didn't work."

"No shit." Suki grabbed the rock out of her hand. "It was a decoy. But Skylar succeeded anyway, without your help. So maybe, after a little time has passed, your mother will recover." She said in a more gentle tone, "I hope she does."

"Thank you," Britt said. "Is Skylar home?"

"I guess you don't know," she said, glancing at Kyle. "Skylar was taken."

"Taken? Where?" Britt and Kyle asked in unison. Both looked horrified.

"That's the million-dollar question," Suki said. "No one knows. She went through an alchemical door with a black sorcerer. And we're devising a plan to get her back."

"No . . . shit," Kyle said slowly.

Britt's face fell. "I can't believe it. After all she went through at Silverwood, all she's done for humanity . . . she gets punished even more. This is terrible."

"Tell me about it. But this isn't the end. Like I said, we've got a plan," Suki said with conviction.

"I wish I could help, Suuk, but I've got this new job," Kyle said.

"Yeah," Suki said. "You need to go start that job. Don't worry.

We've got a lot of people working on this."

"I want to help," Britt said.

"Well, thanks," Suki said, unconvinced. "Leave your number under the doormat. If something comes up that fits, I'll give you a call." She hopped in her car.

"Sure you will," Britt mumbled, just loud enough for Suki to hear as she drove away.

Ocean opened her front door seconds after Suki knocked. "I expected you long before now." She glanced out to the circular driveway. "Did you come alone?"

"I'm not with Kyle anymore," Suki said.

Ocean moved aside and let her through.

Suki had only been in Ocean's house once before—the day Skylar was taken by Cyril Magus. She followed her into the parlor room. She hadn't noticed the incredibly odd paintings on the walls the last time she was here. They were Renaissance style. Most depicted goddess-like women in battle. One was fighting the actual devil.

Suki sat on the sofa. "Ocean, what do we do?"

"Would you like some tea, dear?" Ocean asked, ignoring her question.

"No, thank you. I really just need direction. I understand the mechanics of Skylar's rescue, but I can't help but think there's another part of this. Like we have a chance to help in a different way." She put the gift shop map on the coffee table.

Ocean looked at the map. "Witches don't want to help us."

"There seems to be a lot of information on these maps," Suki said.

"There's a lot of information everywhere. You just have to be open to it. Tuck that away for later, Suki. Maybe it will come in handy."

Suki forced herself to say the words. "The red book," she said. "I read it."

"All right," Ocean said, expressionless.

"And he was the president of this country! And now Mr. Magus is still out there, with Skylar. I can't help but think that what's going on with Skylar is tied to that book. Kyle was the conspiracy theorist between us, but I think of Joshua and his *behaviors* and the things I read in that book . . ." She winced. "I was under the impression that it was Milicent who had the control over him, but now I'm thinking it was Devlin."

Ocean sighed. "You're not far off." She left the room and came back a moment later with the red book in her hand. She tossed it on the coffee table in front of Suki. "The Freemasons are just one of the many sects over the millennia that have had knowledge and kept it hidden," Ocean said. "They weren't all bad. George Washington was a decent man. But things have deteriorated a lot since then."

Suki got up again to pace the room. "Skylar getting caught up with Joshua was no coincidence. I never understood it. He was so crass. But now I think it was all so much more complicated than we could have imagined—or, at least, *I* could have imagined. Milicent was never involved in the *dark* occult." She phrased her statement like a question. "I mean, it looked like witchcraft but it was actually more science—manipulating energy, that kind of stuff, right?"

"Fine," Ocean said, throwing up her hands. "I guess everyone is involved at this point." She went out to the back deck and Suki followed her. "Devlin had his own secrets, but mostly he was a puppet for Magus. He knew about Joshua all the years of his marriage to Milicent. She is brilliant but oftentimes blind to what is right under her nose. For every measure she took to make Joshua superhuman, Devlin countered it with occult darkness."

She studied Suki. "The heart thing?" she asked, reading Suki's thoughts.

Suki nodded.

"Yes, that came from Devlin. There are deplorable practices swirling in the world of the Freemasons I can't pretend don't exist. Unfortunately, Joshua is in the past and I'll have to wait until the next time he comes around to fix him."

"Right," Suki said. "But did Milicent know? I mean, she's always been pro-woman. How was she married to a Freemason?"

"She firmly believed in keeping your enemies closer," Ocean said. "But I know that rocked her. She thought she was the one in charge of their sham. But it turned out he was."

"All of a sudden, this is bigger than just our circle. Like, the whole country big," Suki said. "Are there other superhumans on our side to take on Magus?"

"Actually, it's more about the energy on our side. Energy fuels the universe. The original Masons were alchemists. They knew how to manipulate energy and create magic from plants and minerals. Along the timeline they were vastly corrupted and began to use the simple, neutral properties of alchemy in the darkest ways imaginable."

Suki frowned. "They've been in control for the last two hundred years. Why do you have hope to beat them now?"

"Because nothing beats an idea whose time has come," Ocean said.

The Lost Word
The Future of America
by Devlin P. Grayer

August 17, 1987

What can I say about the Harmonic Convergence? Some think it is of science fiction, but those in the ranks know better. We have foreseen this time for over a hundred years. We have known of its prophesy. We have planned for it and are ready. We will wait to harness the power of the sun, the power of the grids, the power of humanity. This igniting of the earth's energy is the fight we've been expecting. We are prepared to win.

I continue to rise in the ranks. I am prepared to do what it takes. The seeds have been planted to ensure success.

July 25, 1998

The Day out of Time. We have learned that the Daughter was born today. How precious. Her origin is clouded. She seems to be a blending of the three we can't explain. We will watch closely.

December 21, 2012

The allure of an enemy is a strong one. The idea feeds on itself so beautifully it takes on a life we only imagined would take hold. War is seductive. How we've seduced the children under the noses of the apathetic parents. Our future Americans. Our future fighters, so immune to the violence, so immune to the carnage they see in their streets, on their screens, in their hearts. How easy it is to feed the flame of rage handed down, father to son. Mother caught in the middle, powerless to change what has always been. War has always been. War is profitable. Unseen enemies are profitable.

Freedom. What does it truly mean? The original Masons had a vision for this country but they lacked the manpower fear offers. Free to live in this country yet a slave to money. Who are we trying to break free from? Should I ask what? Struggling for freedom.

Zero point will come in the year of perfect vision. The year I will take the presidency. We will have to enact the plan or perish. The light, if forged and made whole once more, will ensure the next age will remain in our hands.

The children, their energy and God presence, is vital for our success. How easy it is to harness their vitality while they sleep.

The third peril is coming, and we will be ready. I will be President. Humans will yearn for more from their existence. And we will give it to them. There must be death to have rebirth.

The Lost Word

Magic is suffered by fools who proclaim "Abracadabra." Most do not know what they speak. I create by my word. I create by my intention, combined with the science of sound. Words can change timelines because the fulcrum is the word itself. The lost word is Mother.

B ritt knocked on the door to Beatrice's house in Valhalla, New York. A For Sale by Owner sign sat in the window. She had decided she couldn't just leave the country without paying Beatrice a visit.

The door flew open. Al Unger raced out the door and smacked right into her. "You?" he said, startled. He had a panicked look on his face. "You can't come in." He grabbed her by the elbow and dragged her down the front steps.

"Hey!" She yanked her arm away. "Hands off. I came to see Beatrice." She looked up at the front door, still wide open.

"She's dead, and you need to leave. No one is inside, except—"

"Dead?" Britt asked in shock. "I didn't think that was possible."

"Well, maybe it's called something else for ones like her, but she's gone," he said. "That's why I'm selling." He gestured to the sign in the window. "Look, I gotta go. Don't go inside." He hopped into his late-model Jaguar in the driveway and peeled out down the street.

She looked back at the open door. "Wow, dead." She let out a big sigh and walked back up the cement steps. "Hello?" she asked, peering into the house. *Who could be in here?* she thought. *Pets?* She looked around the living room. All signs of Beatrice had been stripped away. The interior was sterile, ready for a new owner.

The quietness of the house was eerie. Britt had thought maybe she would feel the energy of the Great Mother of Air, but she couldn't. "Except who?" she asked aloud. "Hello?" she called again. It was listed for sale, so anyone could go through it. She decided to take a quick tour.

She made quick work of the small top floor, then headed to the basement. There were many doors, most leading to empty closets.

The last door at the end of the hall drew her attention: a red light shone out from under it. At first, she stood still. Al could be roasting a dead body in there, for all she knew. He had serial killer written all over him.

With her cell phone at the ready, she opened the door. The smell and the wet heat hit her before her eyes adjusted to the low light. Briefly unable to see, her mind told her this was a mistake. But a second later, the contents of the red room came into focus, and she wasn't surprised to find snakes. Her nose had told her before she could see.

She *was* surprised at their large size. This enclosure rivaled any zoo display. The large snakes danced back and forth, more active than Britt had known snakes to be. They all seemed to be following the lead of the great white snake that undulated in the middle of the window. Britt touched the warm glass wall and all the serpents stopped weaving to stare at her.

In her head, she heard their voices sing in unison:

You are one of ussssss.

When the time issss right, you will be back, dear one.

"What the hell?" Al bellowed from the bottom of the stairs and Britt jumped backward.

"I . . . I'm sorry," she said stumbling out of the room, "I shouldn't be nosing around down here but I—"

"But you were," he said angrily.

She regained her courage and took a deep breath as she drew closer to him. "You won't sell this house with those creatures in it."

All of Al's hubris fizzled away. "I know," he said. "But I can't get near enough to move them, and it's not like I can just call an exterminator."

"I'm surprised you didn't just shoot them," she said under her breath.

"I've had a bit of trouble obtaining a gun," he said. "Look, you've got to go." He almost appeared compassionate. "I'm sorry this isn't the family dynamic you were hoping for, but it is what it is." He turned and sprinted up the stairs. She followed him up, and when he kept going to the top floor, she showed herself out.

"One sec," he called, running to meet her on the sidewalk. "It's actually a good thing you came by. Beatrice left this for you." He handed her an antique-looking bracelet made up of three awkwardly chunky, intertwined silver doves. "I wasn't going to mail it to you or anything, so here you go." He left her standing on the sidewalk and scurried inside.

Britt looked at the garish bracelet and tried it on. It was hideous, but she told herself it would grow on her; it was, after all, a gift from her grandmother.

With nothing much to return home to, she decided to stay in the US a few more days and left to find a hotel.

7

Mica Noxx stood alone in the Oval Office with her arms folded, staring at the desk chair. It was the same one Devlin had sat in. She cringed at the slick of oil on the head cushion, left by his hair. She had yet to sit in it, having asked for a new one. But it seemed no one on staff was enthusiastic to help her. The governmental chaos hadn't subsided in the month since Devlin's death. If anything, it had gotten worse. Many cabinet members had resigned at her swearing in, leaving gaping holes in her support system. If she admitted to herself that she was ill-equipped for the job of president, no one was in line to take her place. She'd known when she agreed to the VP role that this could be one outcome. She just hadn't expected it so quickly. A year or two would have been nice.

She hadn't been the original choice for Devlin's running mate. Sara Hendricks had fit the role much better than Mica. She was in deep pockets due to a few skeletons in her closet and could be controlled like the rest of them. But as the conscious-ness of the planet grew, so had Sara's conscience. Guilt for the things she'd turned a blind eye to had started spilling out weeks before the election. She had become a liability the party had to extinguish. Without notice or permission from her family, Sara had been admitted to a mental hospital and the ballot quickly changed. They needed a woman on the ticket for appearances. Mica had not even been in the top five for choice, but after dealings even Devlin hadn't been privy to, she'd been put on the ticket.

Devlin should never have died in office. He was a biotech giant pumped with enough medical magic to keep him young for as long as needed. Even unnatural causes would have been hard-pressed to kill him. But no one had accounted for Milicent. She, with her own dark magic deep in her veins, had been a match for Devlin's technological immortality.

Mica had grown up in a large, affluent, African American family in the Northeast. Her Catholic roots had never sat well with her internal compass; she'd always believed her savior was within, not without. She despised the idea of needing a middle-man to connect with God. So it had been no surprise, yet not happy news, either, to her parents when she rebelled in college, spat on the church, and took to alternative ideology to sink her beliefs into: Vodou. She'd attended undergrad at Loyola in New Orleans and spent much of her free time connecting with locals. She'd been enamored by their raw beauty and earthly abun-dance, despite their impoverished conditions. They'd had strong ties to their spirituality and needed very little material items to be happy.

Mica had also witnessed how some took advantage of the locals' good nature and swindled them out of the very little they had. She'd turned her studies to pre-law, went on to get her law degree, and eventually served as a judge of the City of New Orle-ans. She'd made it her mission to protect those that needed it. She'd given back to the community that had given her so much. The community had taught her about the sovereignty in her own skin and given her a fierce sense of self and importance in the collective. This community had given her the roots she'd always felt were lacking in her family of origin.

After diving briefly into her own genealogy chart, she'd

begun to suspect she belonged to the bloodline of Maria Laveau, nineteenth-century Vodou priestess. That turned out to be wishful thinking; however, her research had left her forever changed. Embracing the wisdom of the Vodou culture, she'd become convinced that the world of materialism was an illusion, and life was a game she could play for as long as she wanted.

She'd remained in New Orleans until Devlin Grayer knocked on her door, requesting her presence in Washington to run on the Republican ticket. She'd known this was absurd. She hadn't voted in decades, knowing that at the root of the system of democracy, her vote meant nothing. She'd said no a half-dozen times before the fateful night the Great Mother of them all, Yemaya, came to her in dreamtime—or, more like, chased her through the seven seas—and commanded her to do this.

"It is your divine responsibility to clean house of the filth that has occupied Washington for one hundred years," she told her. "This task was assigned to you. You can not say no."

Mica sat, waterlogged and tired, on the shore of an ocean she'd never seen. "What about free will?" she asked. "I'm happy with my life. I do enough good where I am, I help enough people."

"I am not appealing to your sense of duty," Yemaya said. "You have already demonstrated your constitution. All of the lessons you have learned have brought you to this moment, to use that information for this final act. I am appealing to your sense of righteous indignation. The foundation of the corrupted state has cracked. It is time to kick their feet out from under them so they collapse. You must be at the helm to do this. There is no turning this down. Others will take over to rebuild. But you, child, are in charge of the *Dissolution*."

With that she was gone, and Mica found herself standing in the street in her pajamas, barefoot. "I have to stop drinking red wine before bed," she said and made her way back inside.

"With liberty and justice for all," Ocean said, standing in the Oval Office.

"Back so soon?" Mica asked.

"I've been in this building too many times this year," Ocean said. She picked up a small peacock figurine from the desk. It was Mica's only personalization of the room so far.

"I'm not supposed to be here," Mica said, hopping on the presidential desk as if she were in grade school.

"You can keep saying that but it won't start being true."

"I'll rephrase: I don't want to be here."

"No people can be bound to acknowledge and adore the Invisible Hand which conducts the affairs of men more than those of the United States," Ocean said.

"Don't quote George Washington to me."

"Mica, you are working for the Goddess of Liberty now, like it or not. You have to play by some of the rules."

"There are no more rules, Ocean. This place is under water."

"Not yet," Ocean said. "Vivienne is distracted for the time being. The karma of this country is finally coming due. All its tyranny, all its suppression, when it boasted freedoms. It was supposed to be liberty for all. Instead, it was liberty for those with information. Masonry lay the bricks in early America for the unity of all races. But then that fucking New Deal ruined everything. The Roosevelts were hijacked and Magus showed up. I swear he must have broken out of a pod." She scowled. "We've gotten away from the principles in the Constitution so horribly. But the truth is, it's all part of the Divine Plan. As I told Milicent, we can't appreciate light without first experiencing darkness. The division in this country is a distraction, one that we need in order to prevent the original plan of the Masons. We have to take Magus out once and for all. If he bleeds, the rest will cave."

"I love that idea," Mica said. "I hate him. But I need to do it my way."

"Why?" Ocean asked. "You can't do this alone." She handed Mica a gold amulet, an odd tree engraved on top. The words *The Liberty Tree* were inscribed below it.

"Thomas Paine?" Mica asked.

"Yes," Ocean said. "Mica, we are in the *third peril* Washington spoke of two hundred and fifty years ago." Mica stared at her. "And you know the help against the third peril comes in the shape of divine assistance, passing which, the whole world united shall not prevail against her."

"Again with the Washington quotes." Mica shook her head. "You've never shied away from asking for the moon."

"Neither of us wanted you in this post," Ocean said. "No offense. But here we are. And I hope you'll help the cause. If nothing else you can enjoy the notoriety."

"Yeah, 'cause that's always been my motivation." Mica rolled her eyes. "What is your timeline, exactly?"

"We have to be swift. We have until the solstice to prepare. Right about then, we'll need ten thousand celestials."

"Right," Mica said through pursed lips. She'd come a long way and molded herself through different decades of belief in her fifty-five years, but her faith in her own spiritual power had always been a constant. It was a good thing, too; she was going to need all the power she could muster, internal and ancestral, to prevail in her current agenda.

Ocean walked out of the Oval Office feeling unsure of Mica's cooperation. Mica was their only option if things had gone wrong, though. And they had.

With the warrior goddess energy in her blood, Mica could take down the whole damn thing and not feel a bit of remorse. Of that Ocean was certain.

8

Joel hadn't showered or brushed his teeth in three days. His mind had been filled with thoughts of Rachel, Skylar, and the last twenty years of his life. He had known they were together to give Skylar a solid life, and that had been accomplished. That was, until the last couple of years—until everything had turned on its ear. He thought back to how distraught Skylar had been learning about Rachel and Cassie and all they had kept secret. Well intentioned or not, they all had deceived her. Now he looked back on the last twenty years with regret. At the time, you make decisions thinking they're the right ones. Only looking back is it painfully obvious how wrong some of those decisions turned out to be.

He went out to his car and looked at the bundle sitting on his passenger seat. He hadn't touched it since he'd taken it from Ocean's house. Finally getting out of his spiral of self-pity, he got it out of the car. *If this can help get Skylar back, if I can somehow contact her with this insane gadget, maybe it will help undo some of the damage of the last twenty years.*

The horses whinnied and strolled toward him as he walked by, but he paid them no mind. Not even a hello. He went back into the empty house. "Time to sell," he said. The walls echoed back in agreement.

He brought the crystal down to his lab and donned the glasses. He removed the bag and stood back. It really was a magnificent piece of technology, if technology was what you'd call it. It was more like magic. He snorted.

He put his hand under the viewfinder and looked through the lens. Geometric shapes popped into view where his skin should be. He pulled his hand away and tried again. Same outcome. He raced to his supply closet and took out a sterile slide and needle. Without hesitation, he pricked his finger and dripped blood onto the slide. He placed it under the crystal cylinder. Instead of cells, he saw memories. He saw himself as a boy with shaggy brown hair, already looking into a microscope. He had wanted to be a scientist all his life. He'd always searched for the answers to the big questions.

He pulled away from the lens and stared across the room. Somewhere along his timeline, he'd closed himself off to the magic of discovery. Proof had become his religion, and only now did it dawn on him that when that happened, something in him had died. He had severed ties to mystery, and then resented Cassie for trying to bring that same sense of mystery to life in their daughter. His pride and ego and need to be right had driven a wedge into their marriage, and now he sat in the same situation with Rachel. His inability to embrace the unknown and so much of what made up his wife had ultimately driven them to opposite ends of life. They'd had a mutual desire: to raise Skylar in a stable home. But he had to admit that Rachel was right—they no longer belonged together.

He returned to his new gadget and thought for a moment. *What specimens do I have?* He remembered the one Ocean had given him, the cancer cells. They had been sitting in his car for three days in the hot sun. He wasn't expecting live cells, but he was curious about what he might see.

Nothing moved under the scope, but the moment he looked into it, he was transported within, as if inside the cell itself. His field of vision was striated, with black and gray lines webbed in very dim light. It was like being in a virtual reality of thick, dark mucus. He could feel the hatred within the cell's essence, and it affected him viscerally, as if he were being attacked. He drew back and removed the slide. He hadn't been prepared for that; he needed a minute to recover. He went to his prep sink and splashed some cold water on his face, then went to his lab freezer. It kept specimens at just below the freezing mark, which preserved them indefinitely while still allowing for a quick thaw. He took out a bag of Skylar's blood and rested it on the counter. As he waited for it to thaw, he returned the slide of his own blood under the crystal.

He held his breath as he flipped through compartmentalized scenes. When he focused on one, it grew larger. It seemed the "reality" of his view depended on his focus. He saw the day he and Cassie got married. His eyes saw the beauty of the day. It was perfectly sunny. Puffy white clouds were scattered in the bright blue sky. Nature was smiling. The scene quickly overlapped into the day he wed Rachel. It also was sunny, but there was a film over his eyes. He tried to wipe it away with his fingers, but it wouldn't budge. They had come together for a different love— one for their daughter. It was a worthy love, but one that wasn't sustainable for their entire lives. This day of departure had always sat on their timeline, waiting for them to reach it. Although painful, he understood and couldn't find blame in Rachel, or himself. If anything, he had compassion.

He sighed and moved the slide out of the viewfinder.

Skylar's blood had warmed to room temperature; he could take a sample now. He prepared the slide, placed it under the crystal cylinder, and peered into the viewer. Instantly he was transported into the awareness of Skylar's blood. He lost sight of the room around him and was consumed by red walls. It felt like he was violating her privacy. He sprang up and stepped away from the scope, the tick of the clock on the wall the only noise. *How does this help Skylar?*

He returned to the viewer, expecting to see blood again, redness. Instead, he was transported to another time. He saw Skylar as a young girl. The world was hers to create. She was happy with her horses. He saw Argan in her life.

A burst of light shone like a sunburst, and suddenly Skylar was grown. At first Joel thought it was her wedding day: She was in a white gown tied with gold trim. Her hair was fixed with gold rods that fanned out in a crown, making it seem like golden light was shining behind her head. She was standing in water. He watched her walk deeper and deeper into the sea. "A baptism?" he asked and instantly knew he was right. A tear came to his eye. His daughter was a goddess. He saw her life path. It wasn't meant to happen any other way.

"Magical blood," he said.

All blood is magical, he heard from within his heart.

Heart.

He remembered Ocean's words . . . what she'd said about the thymus gland. How would he go about extracting a sample of his? He didn't think it was possible and immediately shelved the idea.

He returned to his freezer and pulled out a few dozen vials and some Ziploc bags of things long forgotten. He homed in on one bag in particular. The sample of grayish tissue had been in the freezer for over a year.

After setting it on the counter, he paced nervously. *It's just a sample*, he tried to convince himself, but his heart knew better. He stopped pacing and stared at the bag of tissue. As it warmed to room temperature, the color changed. It was pinkish now.

He took a deep breath and prepared the slide with the tissue. He placed it under the cylinder and prepared himself to look.

He drew his breath in over his teeth. "A boy," he whispered with a shaky voice. *The boy who wasn't meant to be.* He was beautiful, with blue, saucer-shaped eyes and a mop of blond curls. *Just like his mama,* he thought. He shook off the sadness and disbelief took over. "This makes no sense," he said out loud. "This tissue is just tissue. It didn't have a heartbeat. It's not a child."

"As it is, no, it's not." Ocean appeared at the doorway, startling him so badly he fell backward. He hit his head going down to the floor.

"Shit, Joel," Ocean scolded him for his own clumsiness. She helped him up off the floor as he grabbed the back of his head gingerly, then opened the freezer and handed him the first ice pack she found.

"That's horse plasma," he said, rejecting the bag.

"It's not going anywhere," she said. "Hold it to the bump."

He obliged and walked back to the crystal cylinder.

"Having fun with your new toy?" she asked.

"I was at first. This is incredible," he said. "But now things are getting weird."

"Things have always been weird, Joel. You're seeing things you can't explain away with logic. Steiner always said, 'Material substances in different beings have secrets not dreamt of by material science.' I miss that guy."

All of Joel's conflicting emotions could no longer be contained. They spilled out in tears, and he held his head in one hand while he pressed the plasma pack against his bump with the other. "She was too young to be a mother," he said, his face still down.

"Yes, in our culture, few people should be having babies before they're thirty. Today's generation is too immature."

"But . . ." He stopped himself, unable to find words. He gestured to the sample.

"But that boy was the most beautiful creature you have ever seen," she finished his thought. "And your heart aches not to hold him."

Joel got the sense Ocean was speaking from experience. "Yes." He sobbed for just a minute, then quickly composed himself. "It's silly. It was only a brief moment that I saw him, but I loved him instantly. I don't know him, yet I completely and utterly believe he is a lost part of me I've just found."

She smiled—a rare moment of compassion for her. "I'm so glad, Joel." She touched his face lovingly. "That soul of that boy wasn't meant to enter this three-dimensional world. He had another purpose. One being today, showing you the magic of the universe. In a split second, your world has been changed forever by someone you'll never know. You've been gifted with a glimpse of the divine."

He nodded his head slowly. "I don't want to ever forget," he said wistfully.

"Then consider the crystal your perpetual View-Master," she said.

"The microscope has always been *my* portal to another world. Now it literally is," he said.

"Be careful, Joel," Ocean warned. "It can be easy to get lost in a world of what-ifs. Know that everything is perfect, and all choices lead to the same conclusion. We can believe a fetus that dies is gone forever, or we can choose to believe it's just been transformed into something else, something better—and that the love of that soul is never lost." She squeezed his arm. "How's your head?"

"Better." He removed the plasma bag, which had now thawed considerably, from his head.

"You're making me forget why I'm here," she said. "Mica is ready to support a bill. Are you ready to announce your findings?"

"Oh, cancer." His demeanor turned dark. "It was quite grue-some under the crystal scope."

"Whad'ya think, it was going to be moonlight and roses?" she asked.

He shrugged.

"Have you worked with the sound vibration technology I gave you?"

"Not yet," he said.

"What are you waiting for? You've had three days," she said. "I wanted you to come to your own conclusion, but I'll just tell you the answer. Sound waves only work on some cancers, not all," she said. "But there's something else that will work every time."

"What is it?" he asked.

"It's radical," she said.

"That's never stopped you," he said.

She searched the countertop until she found tweezers. Joel watched her intently as she took a sample of the fetal tissue and placed it on top of the cancer cells, still out on the counter.

"That's insane," Joel said.

"Is it?" she asked. "What do you think will happen?"

"I have no idea." He was quick to look through the viewing hole. "Nothing's happening."

"Give it a minute," she said.

He looked again. The tissue no longer showed Joel an image of the baby boy but rather of his pure essence, his light, the light of a soul close enough to know God in his heart. That light was enough to penetrate the dark walls of the cancer cells.

"Astonishing," he whispered.

Ocean beamed proudly.

Joel watched holes rip through the black fiber, allowing blinding light to emerge. Within minutes, all blackness was gone.

Only pulsing white cells remained on the slide. Their work done, they encapsulated the light and returned to their intended shape and size.

"I have no idea what this means," he said.

"It means the frequency of love cures cancer," Ocean said.

"That is far from what you usually teach," he said. "And I'm sorry to tell you, that's not a scientific finding."

"Then your job is to turn it into one."

9

Argan didn't dwell on long good-byes. His sisters would cry for days either way. They swore to keep candles lit until his return. His father gave him a strong hug and left the room without a word.

He looked around his house. It held good memories but also now seemed no longer useful. He was ready to let it go, to let it become part of his past.

He stood with Leonora at the threshold of the front door, one foot in each world, a small but mighty backpack slung over his shoulder. He held a chocolate croissant, Leonora's favorite, in his hand. A lit candle burned in the center.

"I'm sorry to leave on your birthday," he said.

"It couldn't be helped," she said.

"Make a wish."

"You take my wish." She pushed the croissant back toward him.

"I'll be fine." He pushed it back to her.

"Not just for today but always," she said. "I'll always give my wishes to you."

He smiled. "Okay, then . . . together. One, two, three."

Together, they blew out the candle.

"You've prepared me well, Mom," he said, taking her hand.

She touched his cheek. "There's always more," she second-guessed. "You need to . . ."

"Mom." He stopped her gently. "I'm ready."

She smiled and nodded. "I love you and I will see you when you return with Skylar."

He hugged her tight and walked down the steps to the sea.

He had decided to take the long and arduous ferry from their local port to Bari, Italy. The ride was almost seventeen hours. But he wanted to connect to the sea and detach from most of the world. The ferry was the way to do it.

He stood on the deck of the boat. The air was a brisk reprieve from the hot June weather, even under the high noon sun. He breathed in the fresh air. The boat reminded him of New Year's Eve with Skylar, although this boat was far from private. He didn't mind, though. A sold-out boat filled with economy travelers made for interesting people watching. He was among many families, some with small infants. Some looked like it had been a while since their last bath. A few carried chickens in cages. He didn't know how that would work on such a long boat ride, but he would find out soon enough.

He'd missed out on the last seat inside the glass cabin so he'd headed up top, not sure how long he'd last. The wind was considerably worse above. But he was finding it invigorating.

He put his backpack on the floor and sat back in a worn plastic seat. With the sun on his face, he closed his eyes. He had a new appreciation of the elements, feeling the Great Mothers surrounding him now. The sea, the wind, and the fiery sun. He had known Ocean for a while now, and Beatrice briefly at Silverwood and then met her once again on her last day on earth. Vivienne had long flitted in during dramatic moments in Skylar's life, but it would seem it was time for her to take center stage.

Argan had always loved the sea. It was the backdrop of his home in Greece, and he knew the magic it held. Leonora had made sure commanding the sea was part of his training as a boy. Although she had always said *commanding* was a strong word. It was more of a *cooperation*. No one commanded the sea. No one except Vivienne, whose secrets of the sea ran deep.

He'd always had the sense that his mother knew the details of Vivienne's past, but she'd never spoken one word about it. His mother had the highest integrity. It was one of the traits he admired in her.

The wind kicked up and smacked him hard in the face. He laughed. "Hello, Beatrice. Were my thoughts lingering too long on Vivienne?" It quickly died down to nothing, and the temperature became almost pleasant. "Thank you," he said. "I forgot I could ask for help with the elements." With the whole top floor to himself, he laid his head back against the seat and fell asleep in the afternoon sun.

He woke up with the sun much lower in the sky. He stretched and rubbed out his stiff neck. He hadn't slept that long, though, only a few hours; he wouldn't be to Bari until after sunrise. He reached for his backpack to get some water, but it was gone from the floor. He jumped up and looked under the seat.

"Damn," he said, with his head on a swivel. He saw a small object huddled in the corner and ran over to find that it was a young boy who was using his backpack for a pillow. He breathed a sigh of relief and relaxed. He still wanted his water but didn't want to wake the child. It was odd that someone would leave him alone to sleep up here, but people in this part of the world were more trusting than in the States. Everyone watched out for everyone else, and their kids.

He took a seat next to the boy and immediately smelled alcohol. "You're way too young," he said aloud and frowned. Argan shook the boy lightly but he didn't stir. He figured the kid was passed out and reached under him to retrieve his water bottle. He got it out without a peep from the boy.

Argan decided to spend the rest of the trip there on the floor. He had brought a book but didn't feel much like reading. He stared up at the sky and made pictures out of the clouds until nightfall. He laid his head on the other side of the backpack, and eventually fell asleep for the night.

Daybreak came quickly; the sunlight was a natural wake-up call. When his eyes adjusted, the coastline of Bari was in view, and they would be docking within the hour. He ran his fingers through his hair and decided it was time to meet his bunkmate. He shook the boy gently. He didn't wake. He tried again: nothing.

"Hey," he said loudly. "It's time to wake up!" he said first in Greek. "It's time to wake up!" he then said in Italian.

The boy jumped to his feet in one move.

"Hi," Argan said. "You were asleep on my backpack." The boy stared at him. "Do you speak English?"

"A little," the boy said quietly.

"You're too young to drink. How old are you?"

The boy looked to the side. "Sixteen."

"That can't be true," Argan said. "How about twelve."

"Eleven," the boy said.

"Yeah, that's what I thought," Argan said. "Are your parents below?"

"No," he said. "I travel alone." His accent was Italian.

"You headed home?" Argan asked.

"Yes," he said.

"Okay, well, we're almost there. Do you have money for food? Breakfast?"

The boy shook his head no. Argan nodded and put his hand in his front pocket. He pulled out a few euros and gave it to the boy. "For food," he emphasized.

"Thank you," the boy said thickly.

They docked in Bari and the port was already bustling. Argan made his way down the stairs and joined the crowd disembarking. He became one with the mass of people on the gangplank, eager to get to their destinations. He glanced to the side of him. The boy was right by his side.

"Where do you live?" Argan asked.

"Down the street." He pointed.

"Well, I'll be seeing you," Argan said, not sure if he needed to take responsibility for the kid. The boy paused and let Argan move ahead, making his way down Via Adriatico.

The city was crowded. Early summer was a busy time on the Italian coast. The weather was already hot, and a light breeze wafted in from the sea.

It only took a few minutes to arrive at 117 Via Adriatico. The ornate door was just as his mother had described it. He recognized the three doves.

He walked up the first step.

"*Signore, no!*" a voice yelled, and a hand yanked Argan backward. It was the boy from the ferry.

"What's up?" Argan asked, almost annoyed.

"You can't go in there. She's a witch. Everyone says."

Argan relaxed. "Could be, but it's okay. I know her."

The boy's eyes widened. He threw Argan's money back at him. It landed in the street and he ran off.

Argan shook his head and bent to get the money. The door swung open and he stood up. A guy his age stood barefoot at the door, all dressed in white.

"I remember you," Noah said.

"Hey," Argan said, picking up his backpack.

"Hey," Noah said. "You look like shit."

Argan gave him a look. "Dude, don't pretend you know me. I slept on the floor of a boat all night, I'm not in the mood." He didn't wait for an invitation; he walked inside.

"Where can I use the bathroom?"

"Down the hall." Noah pointed lackadaisically.

"Thanks." Argan walked down the hall, but before he found the bathroom, Vivienne appeared.

"Bel ragazzo!" she exclaimed. Argan glanced back at Noah, and saw a look of jealousy overtake his face. Vivienne enveloped him in an immense hug and kissed his face a dozen times before she let him go.

Argan was confused. He had met Vivienne two times before. Both times, she'd been very reserved. It seemed Italy warmed her up a bit.

"Thank you for the warm welcome, Ms. DeClaire," he said.

"Oh, child, please call me Vivienne. You must be hungry from your journey."

"Yes, but I'd love to clean up before breakfast," he said.

"Of course," she said. Noah was soon at her back, following her the way he had followed Milicent in the White House. He scowled at Argan.

Before he went into the bathroom, Argan chomped in the air at Noah, who startled backward. Argan laughed.

After a fair amount of cleaning up, Argan opened the bathroom door to find Milicent standing in front of him, her arms crossed over her chest.

"Hello, Mrs. Grayer," he said, almost in singsong.

"Argan," she said, all business, "when are you leaving to retrieve Skylar? Because I'm planning on going with you."

"I'm not sure. I just got here," Argan said.

"No fucking way, Mil," Noah said, now substantially more upset than ever.

"Noah, you work for me, remember?" she said. As the two of them started bickering in the hall, Argan slipped past them unnoticed.

He found his way to the kitchen, the delicious scents of bacon and fresh biscuits guiding him in.

"Are they at it again?" Vivienne asked.

Argan shrugged, assuming yes.

"It really is the most bizarre relationship," Vivienne said. "I haven't been able to make sense of it."

Argan smiled politely.

"Dig in, child," she said, and Argan wasted no time piling breakfast items onto his plate. He hadn't eaten since the day before.

He was on a second helping before Milicent and Noah made it into the kitchen.

"Grandmother," Noah said, "please talk sense into Milicent. She insists she's going to see Diana."

"Noah, stop calling her that," Milicent barked.

"What makes you think wherever Skylar is, she's near Diana?" Argan asked. "Magus can't reach Diana. If he could, he would have control of the citrine wall and all of this would be over."

Vivienne busied herself with tea making and Milicent studied her. "You're awfully quiet, Grandmother."

"No more than usual," Vivienne said.

"What do you know?"

"Milicent, you have developed a very unattractive paranoia about you," Vivienne said. "It's unflattering and, quite frankly, aging you prematurely. I would suggest you take a vacation."

"I'm on vacation," Milicent barked.

"Then go out in the sunshine and have some fun," Vivienne

said. "You are making the rest of us miserable. Better yet, take a trip to Rome or Sicily. Or Milan! You've seen none of the big cities since you've been here."

"I didn't come for the culture, Grandmother," Milicent said. "We're on a mission."

"Child, I'm sorry to tell you this, but you don't have much of a role in this mission. You've done your part, rest assured." Vivienne smiled at her. "So now maybe buy something new. Clothes used to make you happy."

"You are sending me shopping?" Milicent asked, insulted.

"Yes, and take Noah with you. He's absorbed a fair amount of your toxic energy. I can call a douser I know in Sicily to see if she'll see you while you're there."

Noah perked at the idea. "I have to say, Mil, I could use some new Ferragamos."

Milicent shook her head in protest, but Vivienne gave her a look, and she soon acquiesced. "Fine, but I have no interest in being doused."

"Of course you don't, child," Vivienne said.

"I'm going to pack!" Noah was off in a flash.

"This isn't over," Milicent said before she turned to leave.

"Of course," Vivienne repeated.

Plans were quickly made and bags quickly packed. Milicent and Noah were saying their good-byes in less than two hours.

Vivienne waved good-bye as their car pulled away. She closed the door behind them, and Argan felt the energy in the apartment turn.

"She wouldn't have left if she thought she'd get anywhere with me," Vivienne said. "She knows better. But she will just complicate things, and Noah is likely to screw up everything. It's better they're out of our hair."

Argan knew it wasn't his place to comment; he stayed quiet.

"Follow me," she said.

Her apartment was deceptively large. From the outside it looked like any other on the street, but inside, it was palatial. It had a fair amount of Italian marble and fixtures from the early twentieth century mixed with very few modern furnishings. She led him out of the kitchen and down the long hallway framed with artwork he could have sworn were original Rembrandts, but he didn't ask.

"I know you've had experience going through the Portas," she said.

"Yes, well, just the one," he said.

"Right. So you know there were six original doors," she said as they continued down the never-ending hallway.

"Yes." His curiosity was building.

"And you're probably assuming I have one of the doors."

"Yes."

"You're right," she said stopping at the last door in the hall. "This one is the closest in proximity to the one in Palombara."

Argan studied it. It looked exactly like the one in the cabin at Silverwood.

"Child, how many times have you been through the Porta?" she asked.

"Once in and once out," he said.

"That's good," she said. "It ages you when you go through."

"Yeah, we found that out." He touched the tinge of gray in his black waves.

"The Portas are magical doors," she said. "They were created by early alchemists to cheat death. It's a gateway out of mortality if used properly—or to succumb to it, if they got their calculations wrong."

Argan moved his gaze around the frame, refamiliarizing himself with the symbols.

"Masters such as Magus know how to use these doors to create their reality. Meaning, they visualize, perform their incantation, and step through to the place they intend to go."

"Suki said it had a lot to do with intention," Argan said.

"It has *everything* to do with intention," she said emphatically. "Just about everyone else knows how to cross thresholds, walk through doors, change their reality by getting in a car or on an airplane, right?"

He nodded.

"That works too but involves a lot of physical effort. The masters knew changing your environment was a matter of changing your consciousness. Change your consciousness through intention, manipulate energy, and raise your vibration, and what you see, or where you see, changes. They knew walking through a doorway could mean going outside or going to an entirely different realm of being. It was that simple to them."

"Is it that simple to you?" he asked.

"Yes," she said. "I haven't taken an airplane since the very first one. I have no interest in traveling that way. My job is to get you to see reality differently so you can walk through that door and get to Skylar."

"I've done it already," he said.

"Yes, but you went through the door with Suki, right?"

"Yes."

"It wasn't Skylar's magic that got you to the Underworld, it was Suki's. Skylar originally went in under my lake. That happens to be a direct entrance. No one can do what Skylar did to go in that way. That was her brand of magic. But you all went through the Porta because of *Suki*. It wouldn't have worked without her.

She has latent abilities in the alchemical arts. She just hasn't remembered yet."

"Wow. She's going to want Skylar to know that," he said. "Can't we just have her come here and take me?"

"I'm confident I can teach you what you need to know," she said. "It's important for your own advancement to take this on. Besides, Suki is needed in the States to do her part."

"Right," he said. "So where do we start?"

10

S kylar woke up in a simple, sterile room. Everything was white: white walls, white floor, white bed coverings. Like a hospital.

Seconds went by, and then a flood of voices filled her head. The sound was excruciating and she drew her hands to her ears, only to realize that both of her arms were jabbed with needles.

One arm was hooked up to an IV, blood pouring into her vein; the other to an IV with blood drawing out. Panic set in. *Is it my dream? About Devlin? Wake up!* she screamed in her head over all the other voices. But she couldn't wake up.

The beep from a monitor on the wall increased with her heart rate. The door opened and a young woman entered. Not quite a nurse—more like a researcher. Her presence only increased Skylar's heart rate.

"My, you're tense for seven a.m.," the young woman said. She looked about Skylar's age, an olive-skinned beauty with starkly contrasting white tresses and blindingly light golden eyes.

"Where?" Skylar asked. Her head was fuzzy; she couldn't complete a full sentence. She felt a part of herself losing an important memory. *Who am I? Who are my friends?* She couldn't remember anything about her life.

"You are in the wrong place," the young woman said, her voice irritated. "But that's not my decision." She leaned over the bed, checking the bags of fluid above Skylar's head. "I'm surprised you're awake. You're heavily medicated." The embroidery on her lab coat read Heather Emery.

Skylar stopped trying to speak. She needed every ounce of energy to figure out how she was getting out of there.

"Don't bother trying," Heather said. "Your every move is recorded on multiple devices."

Skylar's focus returned to the IVs. She wanted the needles out of her arms. She needed to save the memories she knew were being drained from her.

"Not quite," Heather said. "We already have your memories. We're using your body as a kind of filter, if you will. The blood we put in goes through your system, which is heavily magnetized. The altered blood comes out here." She pointed to a large, opaque blue cistern.

Skylar winced. She was a human filtration system.

"You should feel honored that he has taken such an interest in you," Heather said.

"Who?" Skylar managed.

"The Archer," she said. "He can't hide his fascination with you. He thinks you're very valuable."

Despite Skylar's impaired cognitive state, she could detect the jealousy in Heather's voice. Her body relaxed back into the bed and she gave up trying to talk.

The door opened again and a man walked in. He had pale skin and dark eyes. His maroon hair was cropped short, close to his head. He had full eyebrows and the rest of his face was covered in dark facial hair. He appeared to be in his midthirties. Skylar didn't recognize his face, but his energy was familiar. *Maggot*, she thought as her heartbeat shot up again.

"Magus," he corrected with a chuckle, unaffected by the insult. A look of shock came across Heather's face, though she quickly squashed it. "You can relax, Skylar. I don't want to hurt you. It would seem there is a magic greater than mine anchoring your heart light within your chest cavity. It's impossible to remove."

This didn't give Skylar much comfort. "Why?" was all she could say.

"Do I look so different?" he asked. "Appearance suits the situation. I need to age in your timeline. Here, I don't."

Skylar turned away and watched her blood draining into the cistern.

"We have been without your blood for a very long time and want to replenish our supply while you're here," Magus explained.

She concentrated on the flow of dark red liquid, staring intently. As her eyes focused, the stream lessened until it came to a complete stop. A machine beeped, attracting Heather's attention.

"Even weakened, you command your power," Magus said proudly. He turned to Heather. "Unhook her. It would seem she's all done. For now."

Heather obliged and removed both sets of needles from Skylar's arms.

"Can I go home now?" Skylar asked, still foggy.

"Home?" He looked surprised. "You are home. You'll remember before too long."

Heather widened her eyes. "But, sir, I don't think . . ."

Magus gave her a look that stopped her midsentence. "There's something else we need from you," he said to Skylar. "It'll just take a minute. Then you're free to roam around." He signaled to Heather and she stepped over to a large cylinder machine resembling an airport X-ray tube, but much more beautiful. Everything in the room, including the tube, had an iridescent quality to it. Heather flipped various switches on the tube, and a loud hum joined the sounds in Skylar's head.

"Please step in," Heather said.

"Why would I voluntarily go in that thing?" Skylar asked, already more coherent now that she'd been unhooked from the IVs.

"Because you created it. And when you come out, you will remember that," Magus said.

"I have no reason to believe anything you say," she said.

"True, but if you want to kill the voices in your head, you'll do it," he said.

She scowled at him, even more annoyed because he was right about the voices. "Will I come out with two heads?" she asked flippantly.

"Only if you want to," he said.

She approached it cautiously in her bare feet, figuring she didn't have a choice. She could fight this, but he'd just get his way in the end. She stepped in and Heather shut the panel door behind her. Magus stepped to a control panel and pushed a few buttons. Nothing happened. Heather opened the door.

"Nothing happened," Skylar said, stepping out.

"On the contrary," Magus said. "Everything happened."

Skylar listened. The voices were gone. "You owe me an explanation."

"Sound waves," he said. "They can do just about anything, including stun the part of your brain receiving those transmissions. It won't last, so you'll have to go back in once a day or so."

"Why did you need me in there?" she asked. She didn't remember anything about this place, though all her other memories seemed to be returning. Argan, Suki, Ocean . . . everyone she loved rushed into her mind.

"For this," he motioned to a holographic screen that now showed her complete self in slices. Her life-size body, including her internal structure, appeared before her. Everything was shown in vivid detail, layer by layer. And at her core, her green heart light, right in the middle of her chest cavity.

She wasn't terribly impressed with the technology. She knew it existed back home. But she was captivated to see her insides on the outside. "You cloned me?" she asked, horrified.

"Not completely," he said. "But it gives me an internal makeup to work with."

Clearly, she was a science experiment on multiple levels and needed to get the hell out of there.

"I'll give you a few minutes to compose yourself, and then we'll give you a tour," Magus said, almost congenial. He turned and walked out the door with Heather, leaving Skylar alone in the room.

She felt the sting of tears stir behind her eyes. But she would not cry today. Instead, she directed her energy into the anger that sat in her belly. Her last moments at the Quine crystalized in her mind. All she'd wanted to do was give the Book of Sophia to Milicent. Everything had turned upside down so fast. She thought of the book. *Where is it now? Hopefully Milicent has it. And Argan? Does he know I'm gone? Is time passing? Will I return to the Quine, to my waiting book, and pick up the pieces?* She couldn't answer these questions. She sat back in the bed for just a moment.

She got out of bed with renewed energy. The room was quiet, not even a hum from any of the machines. She snuck out the door to a long, bright hallway. "I know this place," she said. She hurried down the corridor straightaway and stopped in front of a familiar door. Her heart swelled. "This is it." This was the fourth floor. She took a deep breath and opened the door to the cheerful waiting room. Plush animals and toys littered the floor. Toddler-size chairs every color of the rainbow lined equally bright wooden play tables.

"Pamela?" she called.

"Welcome back," Pamela said. She wore her same drab gray suit. Her clipboard had gotten an upgrade to a holographic tablet, as best as Skylar could make out. "I had you down for next week, but that's all right. We'll squeeze you in."

"In to what?" Skylar asked. She had her head on a swivel, hoping to see her baby again.

"The schedule," Pamela said. "You came here to meet your baby, right?"

"Yes, yes I did," Skylar said assuredly.

"Which one?" Pamela asked, and the wall opened up to a vast room of cribs lined in perfect rows. Terror overtook Skylar's heart. This factorylike setting was far from idyllic.

She started running between the rows of cribs, sure she would be able to know her son. A mother would know her child. She ran up and down a dozen rows. When she got to the last baby, sound asleep in the last row, Pamela was there to meet her.

Skylar put her hand on the back of the sleeping child, his little bottom high in the air. He was perfection; she felt his energy. He was pure love, pulsing like one coherent cell of love and purity. As much as she was amazed, she was still disappointed. This bundle of love wasn't hers.

"I don't know which one," Skylar said. "I didn't see him."

Pamela paused. "Him?"

"My son that I met last time I was here."

"Ahh, no." Pamela shook her head. "You won't see him here. This is the next batch, ready to get their souls. Your son had his chance on earth, but due to certain circumstances, his time there is over." She looked at Skylar with a scornful look.

A physical pain as real as an arrow shot through Skylar's heart.

"Mama," a little voice said.

She looked down and found that the voice was attached to a boy who was tugging on her pant leg. He was about six now. She kneeled on the floor and he gave her a huge hug. *She wept big tears of love, love that came from the core of her whole being. She knew this love was all that truly existed in the world.*

He nuzzled her. "It's all right," he said. "I just wanted you to know I'm still with you, you just can't see me. I will never leave you until it is your time to leave the planet. Then we can be together like this all the time."

He was so happy and effervescent. Skylar didn't want to ever leave him.

"Just remember I am in your imagination, Mama. You created me, and as long as you hold me in your heart, I exist." He looked out at the sea of children, asleep in their cribs. "They exist in your heart too. As pure potential. You can't have them all," he said playfully. "But your heart is big enough to love them all."

Skylar sprang out of bed from the adrenaline running through her system. She had returned to the nursery of souls. She didn't think it was possible. She had always thought it was a dream but *it's here*. Wherever *here* was.

"I'm glad you're up. There are some things you need to see," Magus said, entering without knocking. "You can put these on." He handed her simple leggings and a T-shirt, both white. They were made of the most comfortable material, like the softest cashmere. He, on the other hand, was dressed elegantly in a maroon suit that matched his hair. Skylar thought of Milicent and wondered if she'd ever considered dying her hair purple. Nuggets of gold studded Magus's collar and cuffs.

She quickly dressed behind a curtain, thankful to be more covered up. She knew better than to try to read her captor's energy, but she didn't get the impression that her life was in danger at the moment.

Outside the door, Heather took the opportunity to speak candidly with Magus.

"How could you bring *her* here?" she asked cautiously, treading lightly with her mentor.

"We need the heart stone," Magus said.

"I understand that, but it's only a matter of time before she remembers all of it."

"She's already remembering. I should have the stone soon. I'm not worried about it," he said confidently.

Skylar emerged from her room, ready to take action. "What did you want to show me?"

Magus got close to Skylar, and lifted his hand as if to touch her face. She reared her arm back to punch him, but he backed off, chuckling.

"I see so much in your eyes," he said. "I see your grandmother. I see our vision, what we had desired to create in the First Age. We were gods then." Skylar sensed regret in his voice. "But it was short-lived. I *am* sorry it didn't work out the way we planned."

Skylar caught Heather's eye and she quickly looked away.

"Grandmother?" Skylar asked. "Which one?"

He ignored her question and walked through the high-tech laboratory. Heather trailed a safe distance behind them. Technicians were busy studying at various stations. Some had their eyes buried in geodes formed into microscopes. Others were studying complex molecular compositions on translucent screens. The one thing that made Skylar take pause was a holographic globe suspended in the air. Rotating on a mysterious axis, it possessed magic that stood out in the room full of technology. This globe was an organic being representing Mother Earth, intricately detailed and alive with the essence of nature. Skylar was drawn to this magical orb, and she felt a pulse within her chest she'd never felt before as she approached it. She wasn't sure if these technicians were studying the globe, or trying to control it.

"Let's continue," Magus ordered, and Skylar pulled herself away from the globe.

The laboratory was both foreign and familiar. None of this technology was shocking to Skylar. Yet it seemed her presence was shocking to those in the lab. All men, they turned in her direction as she walked by. Most tried to contain their excitement, but it was obvious that her presence was interrupting the flow of work.

While she was still processing her surroundings, a familiar voice rang out. "Hey, Skylar! The guys in the break room said you'd arrived. Long time no see."

She turned around. "Kyle?" Her mouth hung open. "What the hell?"

"This is my new job," he said, as casually as if announcing a fast-food gig. "I'm head custodian."

She took a step back and looked at Magus. "I didn't realize you had a sense of humor," she said.

"Mr. Andrews, return to your post please," Magus said, without a trace of humor.

Skylar watched Kyle walk away and knew there was a good reason for him being there.

"Let's continue," Magus said, leading her down the familiar hall of the fourth floor. Awake, Skylar couldn't tell which door belonged to the nursery. There were many. The ceiling was all glass and nothing could escape being showered with intense sunlight. It felt stiflingly hot on the back of Skylar's neck.

The hall spilled out into a massive opening as big as an airplane hanger, with one giant water tank that filled the room.

Again the ceiling was all glass. There was no respite from the hot sun.

They walked down a carpeted ramp toward the tank, and a fast-moving creature caught Skylar's eye. It was too quick for her to discern what it was. With a twist of his hand, Magus slowed the movements, as if it were recorded and being played back at half speed.

It appeared to be a woman with unusually long hair, swimming on the back of a dolphin. Magus motioned again. They came back around, and Skylar was astonished by what she saw. There was no dolphin; the woman had a tail.

"A mermaid?" Skylar quickly looked at Magus for confirmation and then returned her focus to the glass. "It can't be," she said with childlike wonder, momentarily forgetting her hostage situation. She rushed the glass and her motion attracted the creature in the tank. As she came closer, Skylar lost her breath, mesmerized by the beauty staring back at her. She was everything the imagination could dream up and more. Long threads of light ran through her dark hair, lighting up the water around her as she spun gracefully in circles. Gold flecks shimmered over the greenish hue of her extremely long tail. Everything about her was long.

Skylar put her palm up to the glass, but the mermaid, startled, swam away in a flash.

Three others came over to see her, all female. Skylar was delighted to see them. It was like every one of her childhood fantasies had come to life.

She touched the glass and one mimicked her. Her face was completely different from that of the one that had swum away, but her tail was the same. All of their tails appeared to be identical, in fact.

"Hello," Skylar said.

The mermaid didn't respond, only stared at Skylar with sad eyes.

"These creatures are your captives," Skylar said to Magus. "Why do you think you deserve to hold power over any of us?"

"These creatures aren't captives," Magus said. "They are creations."

Skylar's attention swiveled between the mermaid and Magus. "I don't understand."

"Mermaids exist in the human fantasy world because they remember them. And they remember them because we created them here, in our laboratories, during the First Great Age. In present day they are hidden from humanity except in myth, where many truths are kept safe from the uneducated." He gestured at the tank. "A rare few are seen in the waters of earth when they happen to cross timelines into current reality—the Triangle, for one. But current reality is so shrouded, any who see them swear them off as hallucination or a trick of the eye. Except children, of course. They aren't blind to the truth yet."

"Am I in Atlantis?" Skylar whispered.

"No," he said. "We rarely use that base anymore. Too many know about it and it's constantly bombarded with tourists. This base sits atop the old continent of Mu. Science is even further behind on Mu."

"Why am I here?" she asked.

"That light you carry was forged here," he said. "And only here will I be able to release it from you." He took a step toward her and she pressed her back against the glass. The mermaid in the water drew closer with interest.

"You have been to the Underworld," he said. "You have seen it."

"It?" she asked. "I've seen a lot of things."

"The citrine wall," he said. His eyes glowed yellow for a moment before returning to their deep chestnut.

"Oh, yes, I've seen it. It's quite beautiful." She instantly knew what he wanted with it. It contained the ideas of humanity, past and future. Diana had said that if evil were to find it, it would control the imagination of men. All ideas of humanity would have a middleman; direct connection to the Akasha would be lost. Lucifer had been there as well, confusing Skylar's understanding. But she'd later learned that Lucifer was neutral—that he was knowledge without heart. It was up to each individual to use that knowledge, combined with their heart, to make their choices in life.

Magus stepped closer still. "You were powerful once, and now it would seem you have gained additional magic. We wanted access to that wall in the First Age but it was denied us. The portals of time are open again. What we once desired can finally be ours." He reached out his hand to touch her chest, which contained the stone, and the mermaid rushed the glass, her face full of fury. She slapped it with her tail and the reverberation traveled the wall of the entire tank. Instantly, Magus snapped his fingers and a wave of high frequency sound shot through the water. The mermaid covered her ears in agony and swam off.

"You could just release the stone," Magus said. "Then you could return home and your old life."

"Something tells me that's a bad idea," Skylar said.

"I will get it either way, and there is only one scenario where you will survive," he said. "It would be a shame to die for this cause you were thrown into unwillingly, don't you think? This is someone else's battle." He waved Heather over. "I'll leave you to think about it," he said to Skylar.

"I need to leave for the afternoon," he said to Heather. "Keep an eye on her."

Heather started to object but stopped herself when Magus turned his gaze on her. He left them in the hallway.

Skylar walked slowly around the glass, hoping to catch sight of the mermaids again. Their speed returned and she was left only to see the bubbles in their wake.

"So extraordinary," she said.

"Not very," Heather said coldly. "No more than you or I."

"You have no tail," Skylar shot back. "Not extraordinary."

Another technician walked by, openly seeking out Skylar. Heather rolled her eyes. "You are not special!" she burst out. "They all think so, but any one of us could have carried that light. We're all equipped." Heather's appearance seemed to morph; her face changed, almost aged, in the different light. Skylar was unsure of what she was seeing. The next moment, Heather composed herself and her face returned to normal.

"How so?" Skylar asked, daring her warden to spill the information she was so obviously seething to tell.

"All of us who originated here, we all carry the bloodline. The term *blueblood* has been lifted and used for the wrong reasons, linked to aristocracy. It should be credited to the ocean creatures, those with high concentrations of copper in their veins. The Rh negatives that walk among you. So much of the crap on your—*internet*, you call it? It tells you that you're from another planet when you're just from a different part of this one . . . the ocean. Those glowing eyeballs of yours? Before that happened, you had glasses right? Astigmatism? It's a classic symptom of those who once lived in the sea. It has to do with the developing eye adjusting to the fractured light under the water. You are no more special than me. The same blood runs through my veins. It should have been me carrying that stone."

Conflicting emotions ran through Skylar's heart. She didn't appreciate Heather's jealousy, but she understood it. She could see the adulation in her eyes for Magus, misguided as it was. And if she were right about these facts, any one of them could have been in her shoes. She really wasn't that special.

"You think you can just show up here and I'll accept you as the missing piece we've been waiting for," Heather said. "I won't do it. I see the damage your presence can cause, even if he can't."

"I didn't show up here," Skylar said. "I was dragged. And I'll be leaving first chance, so don't worry."

"I don't think you fully understand," Heather said. "The Archer won't let you leave still holding the stone, and there's no way you'll release it willingly. So either way, I don't see you leaving here." She was cold with her words.

Heather had said too much; Skylar could see it. But she could also see that the temptation of cutting her down to size was too great to resist.

"Why the animosity?" she asked flippantly. "You don't know me enough to judge me." She read Heather's aura quickly. It was a light blue, but it had dark patches around her heart, to the point of blocking her heart chakra completely. "Ahh, you love him," she said. "Good ol' reliable jealousy. It spans the sands of time." Skylar walked around the water tank. The reflections of the sun were iridescent because of large geode-shaped crystals in the corners of the room. They reminded her of Ocean's grotto. The crystals and the sunlight made the room pulse with energy, but she had no problem handling the intensity. She'd come a long way from throwing up in Ocean's house.

"You don't understand," Heather said, turning her face away.

"Okay, well, I guess I still have some things to learn," Skylar said. The light reflected off the water just right and Skylar saw why it made Heather's face change. It revealed a scar. On her cheek was the familiar symbol she knew too well. It was mangled, but Skylar recognized it nonetheless. She gasped. "You . . . the three doves." She stumbled over her words. She reached out to touch Heather's face but was swatted away. "Who are you?"

Heather turned her back and shook off a truth that was

closing in on both of them.

"Well?" Skylar demanded. "Your scar is like mine." She lifted her shirt to expose her iridescent doves. "Who did this to you?"

"I don't know which one did it," Heather said. "I was an infant when it happened. I have no memory of it. You can see it in the light that reflects from the water. So can anyone like us. Before, you could see it all the time." Her expression turned shameful and almost childlike. With tears in her eyes, her voice turned desperate. "Why would they put it on my face?" she asked in horror. "With my whole body to choose from, they scarred my face as an innocent child."

"I . . . I don't know," Skylar said, her tone turned sympathetic.

"When I got older, around the time I started to notice boys, I tried to remove it with a basic spell, but I made it so much worse. But the Archer, he's a master alchemist. He fixed it for me the best he could. It still shows in the refracted light. In the water, I see what I once was. But those times are few. For most of my waking day, it's hidden." She dashed the tears from her eyes. "I owe him my recovery. I don't love him the way you think. It's more of a gratitude for his help."

"And your mother?" Skylar asked, dreading the answer.

"I was told she died giving birth to me," Heather said. "All I've ever known is the Archer."

"I see," Skylar said. "But now, all grown up, will you be a part of the heinous acts he commits? Do you owe him your conscience?"

A look of revelation came over Heather. A piece of a puzzle clicked into place, and Skylar heard it. "Conscience?"

Skylar continued to probe. "Yes, conscience! You know in your heart, where your truth sleeps, that this life is no longer right for you. Listening to your true voice takes immense courage, but the cost of ignoring it is much greater."

Heather froze, staring at the large tank of water. One flash of an iridescent tail went by and she lowered her head. When she looked back up at Skylar, it was with blank, dead eyes.

"I know you hear me," Skylar said. "None of my words resonate?"

Heather looked into the water and placed her hand on the glass. "The water holds memory. You know this?"

"It would seem everything holds memory," Skylar said, sighing loudly.

"Water is the earth's blood, running through the veins of our planet, through the rivers into the oceans, through the roots of the trees, cycling the oxygen for life. We owe everything to the water. It is our blood."

"Yes, I agree with that," Skylar said.

Heather seemed to get lost in her thoughts as she stared at the water in the tank. The creatures within slowed and gathered where she placed her hand. Skylar sensed Heather had a greater power than she had originally thought. The first mermaid Skylar had seen earlier put her hand up to Heather's. Skylar felt the great compassion coming from the sea creature. A song could be heard through the water and the glass. It was haunting and soulful. The sea maid had connected to the pain within Heather's heart, and she was letting it out through her voice.

Heather closed her eyes and the waves of the tank behind her burned away like paper on fire. Skylar was left standing in the same spot, but Heather looked much younger. Magus was there and looked the same.

"I'm through with being held back," he said. "Too much time is wasted on unnecessary processes."

"These steps are hardly unnecessary!" an angry woman's voice replied. Skylar knew it was Magda. "We have to slow down and find the source of the energy fueling these capabilities. Do you know?"

He didn't reply to her question.

"Our technology is ballooning out of control, to a point where we don't know what the consciousness is that animates it. This is dangerous. We must consider how this affects future generations."

Magus was done listening to reason. He spun in a circle and cast a ray of red light toward Magda. She had little time to react; she managed to lift her hand to deflect it, but only partway. She was gone.

Magus recited a command as the light over the land glowed red. "Seven times seven generations will not know their sleeping power. The world will be managed by those worthy of the Akash. Men sworn to uphold the knowledge of Lucifer will hold the key."

The scene faded, and Heather was left standing there. The mermaids gave her one last look and swam away.

"I've shown you too much, I'm sure, but"—she looked sky-ward—"something's changing, everything's changing and I just . . ."

She ran off. Skylar let her go.

She was now alone—completely alone. A faint echo of voices tried to return in her head, but she commanded them away. It seemed to work. She thought for a moment about trying to find Kyle. It wasn't even strange to see him here. She'd given up on strange years ago. But he could wait. She knew the nursery was here, she felt it. Now she would have to find it.

She left the water enclosure and went back down the hall toward the lab. With each step past each door, she experienced a replay of her short time there like a bad movie. All that she'd said to Heather; Magus leaving; waking up in that bed attached to those needles—it all came at her at once. She braced herself, holding the wall for support. A couple of deep breaths in, and she regained her bearings.

The more she walked, the more doors she encountered, and

the more her memories overtook her mind. Her pace quickened until one door charged her memory and she stopped short. The familiar door on the fourth floor stared back at her. She had found it. The nursery of souls.

11

Mica looked out the window of the French door of the Oval Office onto the patio in front of her. There were guards at every station, keeping her in. For so long she had been on the other side, with them keeping her out.

A knock on the door brought her back to the room. "Madam President, Cyril Magus to see you," Wren Riddle said. Wren had landed on her White House feet yet again, this time as personal secretary to the president.

"Not now, Wren, I'm busy," Mica said, staring out the glass.

Seventy-five-year-old Magus pushed his way through the door, past Wren, who did her best to stop him. He was freakishly strong for his age.

"That can't be true," he said before slamming the door in Wren's face.

"You should be careful, Cyril, your crazy is leaking all over the place," Mica said, staring him in the eye. She walked to the desk chair and sat down gingerly. She'd rather assert her authority than stay attached to her animosity toward the chair. "I'm not planning to run things the same way as Devlin did. I have an alternative point of view."

"The country has collapsed, Mica," he said. "You're too late to fix it."

"What you see as collapsed, I see as an opportunity. Your phantom reign is over. From where I sit, we have an enormous opportunity to create the New Atlantis America was meant to be."

He laughed. "You don't belong in that chair. I will enjoy watching the country blame you for its problems."

She smirked. "I won't be your scapegoat. You had Devlin for that. Leave it to Milicent to unknowingly put a wrench in your plan."

Her expression shifted only for a fraction of a second, but that was long enough for Cyril to catch it.

"You didn't tip your hand. I knew it was her," he said. "He was heavily monitored for health and there was no way a stroke got him. You were never supposed to become president."

"Yet here we are," Mica said. "I have no interest in being the last casualty of this divine comedy. I am going to govern this country and try to right the wrongs to the best of my ability. And you won't be in my pocket, or invited to dinner or to anything involving a tuxedo, so find a new hobby, Cyril."

He started to speak, but seemed to reconsider and closed his mouth. He opened the door to leave.

Wren stood in the doorway. "Madam President, Milicent Grayer is on the line," she said, staring at Magus as he walked out.

"Of course she is," Mica said. She picked up the office phone. "Milicent, is your witch radar going off?"

"I beg your pardon?" Milicent said on the other line. "You called me."

Mica glared at Wren and put her hand over the receiver. "Don't go anywhere."

Wren nodded and shut the door behind her back.

"Milicent, how are you holding up?" Mica asked.

"Holding up?"

"You know—you're a grieving widow. Your dead husband?"

"Oh right, well, I've been in Italy with family," Milicent said. "I'm touring the cities right now."

"Magus was just here," Mica said. "He sends his best."

"He's gloating and flaunting, two things I like to do," Milicent said. "He has Skylar."

"Who is this Skylar?" Mica asked. "You're the second person today calling about Skylar! Somehow her father got my phone number. He's insane, talking about love and cancer. I've had to block his calls."

"Skylar is our last hope," Milicent said.

"I have a few hopes left," Mica said. "And so do you. You've never seemed to be the type to put a last hope in someone else."

"I tried to be the chosen one and it got me nowhere but the White House, which was beyond dreadful. I guess it's your turn to restore the *feminine*."

Mica grimaced. "I've never believed in the return of the Divine Feminine. My goddess never left. She just had a different way of existing among the patriarchy. Slithering between the cracks like smoke, never able to be caught."

"I know your goal is to revive the red blood by denying the blue blood," Milicent said. "Hold on . . ."

Mica heard her murmuring to someone else, clearly distracted. "Milicent, don't keep me on the line here, I'm the president now—very important things to do."

"About that, how's piecing the country back together going? Should I return?" Milicent chuckled.

"You know I could use your help. Your expertise getting things back in place around here would be valuable. It's a mountain to climb. This country is captivated by shiny objects."

"The only way I'd come back to DC is if I were vice president, and this country can't handle two women at the helm." Milicent snorted. "You need a man."

"I never thought I'd hear those words from you, Milicent."

"Men do what they can to make themselves necessary," she said. "Do you have any candidates for your VP?"

"Not a one," Mica said. "You could help me first, then maybe I'll see about your Skylar."

"I'll consider it, but I have a bit of travel to attend to first," Milicent said.

They disconnected and Mica turned her attention to Wren, who stood waiting at attention.

"Tell me all you know and don't spare any details," Mica said. "Details are where the secrets are hidden."

Skylar turned the knob of the nursery door. It was locked. Her distraction allowed the rush of voices to return to her head, now seemingly amplified. She was so inundated, it was hard to focus on one thing. She needed to create space in her mind so she could hear the softly spoken answers being trampled by the other, louder noise in her head.

It was surprising that she had been left alone. She assumed Heather was shirking her duties. She kept turning doorknobs, but all were locked. There were many. She touched one knob and it triggered an awareness in her body, like muscle memory. The door itself was smaller than all the rest, and Alice in Wonderland flashed in her mind. Her blue smocked dress, her shiny black shoes . . . the white rabbit, the rabbit hole of the meaning of existence. The images turned over in her mind like the pages of a flipbook.

She turned the knob and it opened.

The door creaked loudly and then . . . silence. Skylar was astonished and actually took in an audible breath. The chatter in her head vanished. *Relief,* she thought. She played a game; if she set one foot into the hall, the noise returned. After trying this a couple of times, she went inside the room and shut the door. She vowed to never leave the tiny space, though even as she did she knew that wouldn't be possible.

She had walked into a peaceful sanctuary. One wall was

lined, floor to ceiling, with jewel-toned books. She'd never thought about how precious and meaningful books had been in her life until that moment. She had always believed in the magic of books—ideas put on paper, so many forgotten. But the written word, once captured in form, remained for eternity. That was the essence of the Akashic Records, and Skylar felt its presence here so profoundly. Here in this land where no veil existed, she could feel the energy signature of the people that had written these books. She felt their intentions, self-serving or otherwise.

She was drawn to a book with a rich orange cover. She reached out and pulled the book toward her. *Ocean's Fire* was the title. "Hmm," she said, chuckling. "She certainly is fire." She returned it to the shelf and perused along, thinking, *Suki would love it here.* She ran her hand along the spines of the books at chest level.

A large window was built into the far wall. Skylar walked over and, looking out, saw a city below, its occupants scurrying around. She backed away from it. She wasn't interested in being discovered.

A small indoor water fountain sat in the corner closest to her. The golden goddess statue had water pouring from her outstretched hand into a miniature pool of cloudy water that lapped like waves at the edges. Skylar studied it and dipped her finger in. She didn't know what compelled her to taste it—salt. Every third wave cascaded over the edge to another basin below it, to catch the spill. The fountain was calming, like everything else in the room, and she felt her own connection to the ocean in this sculpture.

In another corner sat a stuffed bird, perched on a small trapeze that was hung a few feet from the ceiling. She thought it was odd and a bit disturbing to see taxidermy here. The bird was magnificent, and its tail feathers swept so long they almost reached the floor. *This was some magical bird,* Skylar thought. *Nothing like this has ever existed on the planet.* Upon closer examination, she saw that the bird was a blend of avian and serpent, bird and snake. It was the balance between air and earth, having both wings and roots.

She took in a deep breath, still reveling in the silence and the opportunity to focus on one thing at a time.

An antique diagram hung on one wall above a small desk. The title at the top read, *Alchemical Table of Elements.* Mystical symbols flashed around the parchment in lighted sequence. Skylar saw the geometric shapes that morphed into the reality seen by the eye. "Trippy," she said. The table reminded her of Joel. He must be so worried about her. She hoped Ocean was helping him.

On the desk sat a gorgeous green plant with large, thick, waxy leaves. Hundreds of tiny white flowers were beginning to open from their buds. Skylar had never seen so many buds in such a condensed space.

In the last corner was an altar of candles in the colors of the rainbow. They were the largest candles she'd ever seen, all about two feet around. They sat in various stages of wear, the tallest about three feet, the smallest still big at over a foot tall. When she focused on one, it came to life and lit up. The first one, red, startled her, but once she understood what was happening, she relished in lighting the rest with her mind.

After the candles were lit, a movement caught her eye. She turned to see the bird shaking its tail feathers, and intuitively knew it was an invitation to sit in the one chair in the room. Despite being captive here, she felt safe in this room. She was finally able to hear her own voice, and she welcomed the help from this beautifully odd bird—who, she was happy to realize, had merely been asleep.

She took a seat in the oversize striped chair and was instantly transported to a place she'd seen among the many in her head.

It was the end of the First Age. The three Great Mothers were kneeling above the baby Sophia as she disappeared in a flash. Skylar watched Ocean pick up the stone, and she knew this was the moment before the end of the world. *Where did Sophia go? And where is she now?*

She rushed to stand up, her heart pounding. Could she really witness the end of the world? And what would it look like? Would it change anything about now, or would she simply be an observer, like watching a movie? Why was this the scene the bird was showing her?

She looked at the bird, which was now motionless. "Thanks," she said anxiously. She took a deep breath, sat back down, and closed her eyes. She waited, but the scene didn't return. "Damn," she said to the bird. "I lost my chance." She took another breath in and waited, this time just feeling grateful for the silence, not expecting anything in return, and another image came to her mind. It was a similar scene, but Beatrice was missing. There was a baby girl, but it wasn't Sophia. Vivienne was enraged, and for the first time ever, Skylar saw fear in Ocean's eyes.

Skylar watched quietly as Ocean emblazoned the circle of three doves on the face of the wailing infant. Skylar was horrified, and the scene hit her in the gut. The eyes of the baby were so trusting of the women above her, and one had just inflicted immense physical pain on her. Overwhelming sadness welled in Skylar and she sobbed, feeling the trauma inflicted on this baby girl. She felt Vivienne's rage as she walked to the water's edge and summoned great energy from the waves at her feet, and she sensed her thoughts as well.

Vivienne knew what this would do to the planet, to Gaia, but she was a woman scorned. She loved Magus but he had betrayed her. She wanted to punish him for choosing wrongly. One drop of her blood into the water would kill everything he'd created.

His world needed fresh water to exist. Her blood would carry for miles, around the perimeter of his island, enough to choke the life out of his world.

She stood at the edge of the quiet water and cut her middle finger. The drop of blood shone bronze from the copper running through her veins. She flicked her finger and the drop flew slowly through the air and hit the blue sea. She watched as it expanded outward, growing, picking up speed and overtaking the water. It did as she commanded: it choked the life out of everything it touched. A few fish rose to the surface, dead.

"I'm sorry, Gaia," she said, staring at the water. She held back her tears as best she could but was instantly stricken with regret for having hurt innocent life with her revenge. As she looked down, one tear escaped her eye. She tried to catch it, knowing the irreversible effect it would have, but it slipped past her out-stretched fingers. She watched the tear land softly on the wave, like a feather, and then fall into the water.

Her blood was one thing; it only stretched so far. Her tears were a different story. They were far more potent than her blood—one drop was enough to make the whole planet's water supply undrinkable.

Down her tear fell into the sea, saturating the water with salt. It was a curse she hadn't planned on.

Skylar sat in shock. She had always held Vivienne in the highest regard, although she hardly knew her. It seemed the Great Mother of Water stayed hidden for a reason. These Mothers, who wielded such power, were fallible and susceptible to the pitfalls of love, just like the human race. She thought of Beatrice and her convoluted relationship with Arthur. For the past two years, she had let the Mothers mold her and had accepted them as her mentors, yet she'd lost sight of her greatest authority: *herself.*

"Others will always disappoint you somewhere on your time-line," she heard Magda's voice say. "It is inevitable."

Skylar opened her eyes but didn't see her.

A heavily jeweled mirror on the wall by the door called her attention. She got out of the chair and walked to it. She saw her current appearance reflecting back for just a moment. Then the mirror showed her who she'd been in the First Age. Her eyes widened. *She was Magda.*

The goddess smiled back at her. "The mermaid's mirror shows us our true selves, under the shell over our hearts. You see your-self here in all your own glory, your own capabilities, your own wisdom. I am so pleased."

Skylar let out a laugh, incredulous.

"Would you have believed your own voice in the beginning?" Magda asked. "You needed the appearance of authority. Now you know in your heart and mind and belly that you are your own authority. Only through experience could this become true for you . . . that I am *you*. How powerful you really are. All your journeys have led you here to this moment of truth, of embracing the wisdom within."

"What wisdom is that, Magda?" Skylar asked the mirror.

"We all must go through our own journey to discover we were enough all along. There is no *becoming*, we already are all that is. Your job is to simply *be you*. Having the experience, no matter the outcome, is fulfilling your purpose."

Skylar knew in her heart that Magda's words were true. And she accepted that her own words were true. She smiled and turned away from the mirror. She walked to the other side of the room and looked out the big window to the busyness below.

"Magda, I remember why there are no women here," she said, watching the men go about their tasks outside. "He banished me . . . you . . . us to the ethers. I was no longer in human form, but

I was too powerful to be destroyed completely. So I lived on just beyond the realm of humanity. The rest of the women here were not so fortunate. They were cursed." The imagery ran through Skylar's mind like movie film. She wished she could stop it but she couldn't.

A team of men harpooned and slaughtered vast amounts of giant fish in the very tanks of the Great Hall. In the darkness of night, they entered the living quarters where the women were staying and rounded them up with force. Some died in the fight along the way. Those that survived were dragged and thrown into the great tanks where the fish had been slaughtered. Their whole bodies were submerged in the blood and flesh of the fish. Magus stood atop a platform, wielding great light with his hands, and struck the tanks with a wave of dark energy. The women were paralyzed from the waist down, all frozen in fear.

Skylar whirled around and looked at Magda in the mirror. "Soon after, the women grew their tails." She covered her mouth in horror, her eyes shining with the memory. "Their beauty emerged out of something so horrible. He could remove their influence from the land, but not the sea. Their rebellion was to retain their beauty and their voices and mesmerize the men of generations to come. They became mermaids."

"Yes," Magda said. "The myths portray them as vixens, bent on ruining men. This is not entirely untrue, but now you see the origin of their plight. Women were cursed for having heart, for being true to their humanness, for caring about those that walk the planet in the future. Magus wanted power and didn't care that he was channeling it from dark entities he had no business conjuring."

Skylar was aghast. The mermaids in the tanks *were* his creations, by the darkest means.

Her memory grew fuzzy. "All women of the age were turned into sea maids?" she asked, hoping to come to her own answer.

"A few escaped—those who had men in the secret circle who knew of the plan and cared for their safety. They fled to other parts of the globe. Most landed in Egypt. It wasn't long before Magus's plan imploded and the volcanoes erupted, turning all the land red. The time of the First Age was over."

"Men?" Skylar asked, seeing strong mermen with beards and long hair swimming with the females.

"Those that couldn't leave chose to stay with their women, and become sea dwellers. Once they made their choice, Magus cast them out anyway. Very few are left in your current time. But the impending Golden Age is for their evolution as well. As the vibration of your planet increases, the merpeople will be finally set free from the curse that has imprisoned them for millennia, and they will return to their rightful place in the stars."

Skylar looked back out the window below. All the buildings were white, luminescent, shining like a crystal city. They were the epitome of beauty except that everything seemed hollow, unreal, lacking heart. The men walking below all wore familiar gray uniforms. She saw one white lion walking among them.

In the distance, she saw a cathedral.

"Is this part of the Underworld?" she asked herself aloud, letting the surroundings sink in. "This doesn't feel right." The familiar silver and gold rivers ran through the open courtyard. A holographic image of a beautiful woman appeared by the Lethe. She scooped up the silver liquid in her hand and took a sip. The image disappeared and the woman appeared again at the great fountain farther down the pathway. It was beautiful, iridescent water cascading down multiple levels of ceramic tiles embedded with white stones.

Magda spoke. "The Mnemosyne is the predominant river in the Underworld. Those there choose to remember, to confront the past, forgive and move forward. Here, the Lethe is the drink of choice. Here, the rulers prefer to forget, deny, and hide their wrongdoings, cultivating an underlying shame that hangs in the ethers."

Skylar watched the image as the fountain's water slowly ran dry.

"It has sat dry for thirteen thousand years," Magda said.

As Skylar studied the fountain, snippets of memory entered her mind. This land of Magus's was a mirror to the Underworld, fabricated from technology but missing what was hidden, the heart. The city outside this window was shiny and bright and crystalline, yet it lacked the grit of truth, of soul. Just beyond the fountain sat a mammoth yellow crystal, a replica of the citrine wall, but Skylar could feel that the frequency of the rock was much lower than that of the true version in the Underworld.

"This *is* Atlantis," Skylar remembered. "Magus lied. And I'm not a prisoner here."

"No, you are not," Magda said.

"Why would he bring me here?" Skylar asked. "It's as if he unknowingly did me a favor, bringing me back to correct something that should have never happened."

"Oh, he knows. His arrogance runs deep," Magda said. "He will gladly take on the challenge you pose, if he can secure another thirteen thousand years of rule. You were part of this world in the First Age, but this is where you will fix the wrongs of history."

"I already did that in the Underworld," Skylar said.

"Yes, that was grand—but it was only one part. The Underworld needed its memory. Atlantis needs its heart."

Skylar looked down at her chest. She couldn't see the heart light, but she knew it glowed beneath her skin. She'd never really entertained the idea that it would one day leave her. She looked up at Magda with an unspoken knowing. Her heart light wouldn't be returning with her when she left. Skylar saw a gaping hole in her chest, her heart light gone.

"Your wound is where the light enters," Magda said. "Rumi is my boyfriend."

"A joke?" Skylar asked in desperation. "Now?"

Magda's face was serious. "What joke?"

Skylar looked around this room. It held peace she hadn't seen outside its door. "This room has such magic in it. There was heart here once, to create such beauty."

"Use this room as your sanctuary," Magda said. "You, and all you bring here, will be safe."

Skylar took a deep breath and stepped out into the hall. No crashing voices yet. She returned to the lab and looked around at the technicians. They were all men. Heather stood reading from a holographic pad of scrolling information. Skylar approached her.

"You are the only woman here."

"I am," Heather said proudly.

"Why didn't you get thrown into those tanks? Why were you spared?"

Guilt replaced the pride on Heather's face. "Because I'm his daughter."

"Of course you are," Skylar said. She walked in a circle, trying to put the pieces together. Heather was the baby; she was Magus's daughter. With which Mother? The scene she'd seen in the library—Vivienne was so angry, she turned the sea salty.

"You're Ocean's daughter," she said.

Heather stared at her blankly.

"These Great Mothers are a pain in my ass!" Skylar blurted. "With their secrets and lies . . . I am so over it! Here's a piece of advice: Live your life. Stop being a prisoner of someone else's game and go be free. It's as easy as making a decision."

She ran out of the building and out into a courtyard. The air felt electrified, like it had extra oxygen, energetic and clean, much different than the air of earth. She knew it was simply pure air, free of pollutants. She breathed deeply, nourished by its potency. She slowed to a hurried walk and kept her head down, but it was no use: everyone noticed her. Heather wasn't far behind her, and Skylar saw her motioning for all the men to keep their distance. They all obliged.

Skylar passed the great crystal fountain, no water flowing from it. She passed the wide, silver river Lethe and diminished gold Mnemosyne. She followed them with her eyes. They snaked, side by side, and flowed down the hill toward a distant shore. She looked out to the edge of the sea, knowing that was where she was supposed to go. The rivers hugged the shore of the sea, but never reached it. She followed them with her eyes until she couldn't see them anymore. She stopped and turned to Heather.

"Where do these rivers lead?"

"To hell," Heather said.

"Is that so." Skylar was piecing the puzzle together quickly. She sprinted along the edge of the Lethe, gaining on the horizon.

Heather ran behind her. "I'm not kidding!" she yelled, fear in her voice. "The Archer forbids it. You will be incinerated by the heat. It's the one place we are never to go!"

"Then that's where I'm headed!" Skylar yelled over her shoulder. She hurried down to the edge of the shore and searched for a boat or whatever the equivalent would be there. In all the foreign lands she'd visited in the past two years, this was by far the creepiest. Everyone had a deadness to them. Even the people of the Underworld had souls. These men were soulless, like shells of humanity.

"Shells!" she exclaimed. She remembered that shells held directional information. She dove into the water but Heather didn't follow. Fear of the forbidden unknown seemed to stop her.

Skylar dove deep to the seabed to find a shell. The ocean floor was abundant with them. She had never seen such large conch shells. They were vibrantly colored—pink, lilac, periwinkle.

Skylar had always admired the beauty of sea life, sensing a connection she could never explain. For a moment, she let herself enjoy the water. It reminded her of being in Vivienne's lake, yet a thousand times more intense. She looked along the ocean floor, searching for the shell she knew would give her the answer she sought. But before she found it, she came eye to eye with an unfamiliar creature. It resembled a horse, but instead of having a coat of fur, it had a coat of flowing sea leaves. Its gigantic head nudged her own.

She drew back, then laughed, sending bubbles into the water from her mouth. He wasn't dangerous. She touched him gingerly. His leafy coat felt like the wet strips of newspaper she'd used for papier-mâché as a child—not overly welcoming—but he was so happy to see her, his enthusiasm made up for the unpleasant feel of his coat. He nudged her again with his nose, swooped underneath her, and, in one flick, tossed her up out of the water, ten feet in the air.

She crashed back down, her heart pounding. She knew he meant no harm, but his size made him formidable. He was like a giant horse-shaped dog, and she had just become his play toy. She grabbed on to his coat on his next attempt to toss her and hung on. He spun in a circle, then leapt out above the water like a dolphin.

"Woohoo!" she yelled, enjoying the moment. She grabbed two leaves of kelp as if they were horse reins and tried to steer the creature—and it worked. The next moment she was riding him as fast as she could go, away from Atlantis.

⚴

From shore, Heather watched Skylar ride away on the back of a kelpie. She sighed, full of conflicted feelings. The Archer would be angry, but he was too blind to see that Skylar's presence was dangerous, rock or no rock.

13

With Milicent and Noah gone, Vivienne began smudging the apartment with cedar. "Sage has become endangered so I don't use it anymore," she said. "And you have a lot of wood energy. Cedar can only help us."

"Great," Argan said.

She waved the smoking stick around as she spoke. "I know your mother has laid much of the groundwork, so I will skip Consciousness 101 and go right to the master class. You need to energize your meridians with breath work. Once we raise your Kundalini to your celestial gate, you can command entrance to the portal you want to enter."

"Do we know what portal I want to enter?" he asked.

"We do. But first you can practice with this cedar essence. I've added myrrh too. Sit."

They sat on the floor of her parlor and she ran him through drills that were familiar, but amplified by a factor of ten. When his body was buzzing, they stood up and walked to the center of the room. In it was a circle of purple crystals; the flower of life patterned the floor beneath their feet.

"Step into the circle with intention," Vivienne said. "Where do you want to go?"

He looked to her for the answer. She stepped in with him and filled their circle with the incense. He noticed that the effervescent smoke stayed within the perimeter of the drawn circle.

"Close your eyes," she ordered. "And count backward from five."

Argan was able to slip out of his body with the slightest intention. He felt it was too easy; perhaps Vivienne's presence was heightening his abilities. He followed her directions, and when he got to *one*, he opened his eyes.

They were sitting in the park not far from Vivienne's apartment. The sun was warm on his face and the air smelled like the sea.

"I am helping show your nervous system what it's like to let go of your body and travel on the astral," she explained. "Once we do it a few times, you will be able to do it alone. Each time you close your eyes, follow the countdown and set the intention to go somewhere else. You must picture it in your third eye. But these first times, I will guide you."

They practiced for the afternoon and into the evening. Each time, Argan was able to "fly" anywhere Vivienne commanded. With their bodies planted on her parlor floor, they were transported to the Pyrenees Mountains, Provence, and Rosen, all within an hour. "Some of my favorite places," she said. "Except Rosen. But I thought you'd like to see a familiar place."

He handled all of the reality jumping reasonably well. Back on her floor, he glanced in the mirror. "No additional gray," he said.

"No, astral travel won't cause aging," she said. "The Portas have transitional energy associated with them. When you pass through one, it 'thinks' you are dying. That's what causes the aging."

He nodded. That sounded plausible, magically speaking.

"Let's give you a break for the night. Get good rest, no dreaming." She placed her hand on his forehead as if to seal in the request. "Tomorrow we will practice with the Porta. You are one step closer. You will leave on the New Moon. Worlds are thinnest then."

Argan returned to his room with his head on a swivel, looking at all of the mysteries in Vivienne's apartment. Sprinkled within the historic architecture were small touches most wouldn't notice that hinted at the magical nature of the lady of the house. Stones marked with Janarric runes sat in a wicker basket on the floor. Next to it was an indoor gardening table filled with dried herbs. One live plant sat among them, its tiny white buds opened wide to reveal hundreds of mesmerizing flowers. Having been in the Silverwood greenhouse, Argan was used to odd plants, but this one unexplainably drew him in. The tiny flowers seemed to each hold their own reality, their own world, within. He found himself gazing for far too long.

"The udumbara flower only blooms every three thousand years," Vivienne said behind him. "I so love it when it does."

She followed him on his trip upstairs. He peered into the various bedrooms as they passed them, noticing stuffed cats in most of them. He counted at least a dozen. He gave Vivienne a questioning look.

She shrugged. "I've kept all my cats."

That night, he didn't have any trouble with *not dreaming*, because it was impossible to fall asleep. He lay in bed as the moonlight streamed in, hitting him in the face. He got up to draw the curtains but there weren't any. He pushed his bed out of the way of the window and climbed back in.

His heart rate now elevated, it was no use. He got back out of bed and went into the hall. The door next to his bore the familiar symbols of the Porta. He was no stranger to the supernatural. He had gone with Skylar back to Silverwood and to the Underworld; he could handle wherever this door led. He reached out a hand . . .

"It leads to the attic," Vivienne said, startling him out of his thoughts.

"Good evening, Vivienne," he said respectfully. "I hope I didn't wake you."

"I rarely sleep anymore," she said. "They say that's a sign of age, but that can't be my reason."

"I thought this was the death door?" he asked.

"It's amusing that you've named it that," she said. "But no, not the death door. Come with me." She led him down the spiral stairs to the main level. They walked into the kitchen and toward the restaurant-size refrigerator. Next to it was the pantry door. She gestured toward it. "Here you go."

Without hesitating, he opened it. Nothing but blackness in front of him. It was just like the alchemical door in the cabin at Silverwood. "I want to go now," he said. "Every moment I wait, Skylar suffers."

"I wouldn't be so sure," she said. "If anything, the divine plan is going along as it should. She has grown immensely in the last two years. She can handle herself."

"Can we at least practice now?" he asked, glancing down at his pajama bottoms.

"Yes, we are within the three-day window of the New Moon," she said. "Energies are favorable."

She fixed two cups of tea. She sipped one; the other she immediately poured down the drain. She studied the remnants left in the porcelain mug. "Where shall you go? Silverwood? The Underworld? You're familiar with those."

"Yes, either will do," he said.

"Silverwood it is," she said. "Very well. Remember all we went over yesterday, and I will help you."

He took in a deep breath and counted backward from five. She put her hand on his back, and when he reached the count of one, she pushed him through the door.

He dared not open his eyes until he landed on hard ground. When he finally did, he was relieved to find himself in the alchemist cabin. "Wow," he said. "Not hard." He took a few deep breaths and walked around the room. It was quiet, but not peaceful. The energy seemed sucked out of the space, or dead, as if no life had been there since they'd left.

"You animated this place with your life force," he heard Vivienne say.

He looked back at the doorway, now black space from the other side of life. "How long do I stay here?" he asked, now realizing he didn't have her to push him back through.

A hole burned through the blackness, and he saw her face on the other side. "Come now," she called and reached out her hand.

He grabbed it without hesitation. She pulled him through the doorway and he was back in her kitchen.

He caught his breath. "Any grays?"

"You weren't there long enough," she said. "Expect a few when you go to the First Age."

"Underworld now?" He was anxious to try it again.

"Let your energy settle for a few minutes at least," she said. "I would be remiss if I didn't warn you: this isn't as carefree a process as you feel it is."

"All right," he said. He sat still and did a round of deep breathing, relaxing his nervous system as much as he could.

After a few minutes of this, Vivienne touched his shoulder. "Let's try now."

"Great." Argan leapt to his feet and they repeated the whole process.

This time, he arrived at the door of Diana's cathedral.

"Back alone?" she said. "How unexpected."

"I had help," Argan said.

Vivienne appeared behind him. "Hello, Diana."

Argan stepped aside.

"Grandmother?" Diana looked shocked. "To what do I owe this visit?"

"We are getting Argan ready for his own portal travel and wanted to visit those places he'd already been, as a primer. I took it upon myself to follow him on this one, to see how you're doing."

Diana was suspicious. "You would never come here for such a small reason."

"Diana, you know the Golden Age is trying to anchor itself. The energies of Lemuria are resurfacing and can't be stopped, but the Archer will try. There could be great casualties. I would like to prevent those—this time with Lucifer's help."

Diana dismissed her words immediately. "You know how he works."

"I would like to speak with him," Vivienne said.

Argan took a step back. The last time he'd encountered Lucifer had been less than pleasant.

Diana shrugged. "Of course, Grandmother."

No fanfare needed; Lucifer's light came into the room as its own horn of arrival. Argan was the only one who needed to shield his eyes.

Lucifer was incredibly tall, yet when he approached Vivienne, she was his equal in height. "Great Mother of Water," he greeted her and kissed her hand. "A pleasure. Thirteen thousand years already? My, how time flies."

She chuckled politely. "Lucifer, it is time. Portals are opening, paradigms are crumbling, and you have been trapped here long enough. We must work together to free Mother Earth."

"I've grown to like it here," he said smugly. "It's quite amusing."

"We aren't going to make the same mistake this time," she said. "Different choices will be made."

"Ahh, you've seen the error of your ways, have you?"

"I don't understand," Argan said.

"You again?" Lucifer snarled. "Vivienne, do tell your boy the truth."

Vivienne made no motion to speak.

"Well, if you won't tell him, allow me," Lucifer said, clearly chomping to tell the story. "You see, boy, that stone you've been bequeathed . . . that was mine. It belonged to me. And these Mothers felt they had a right to take it, and they infused it with love and compassion and all the things I didn't want clouding the purity of my knowledge. They wanted to take all of the gifts and keep them for themselves, give them to that baby. Serves them right, the stone couldn't take the pressure and cracked. So for thirteen thousand years it has been fractured, seeking its other half. It is the basis for every twin flame story spun in your world. So syrupy and stupid. It is a manipulation by those who know the truth. And now these Mothers want to heal the stone and hurl me back into the stratosphere from whence I came. But guess what? I'm not going. You can go on your quest and heal that hunk of glass, but I don't want it back." He left in a flash and the room darkened substantially.

"I told you," Diana said.

An audible huff came out of Vivienne's nose. "Let's go, child," she said to Argan. "We've been here long enough."

"No hug?" Diana asked as Vivienne and Argan went back through the alchemical door.

Back in her apartment, Vivienne touched Argan's hair. "A little grayer, I'm afraid. And we didn't stay that long."

"Well, that was insightful," Argan said.

"I'm sorry to say he was telling the truth," she said. "We had good intentions. We thought if we infused the stone with the pure love of a child, it would negate Cyril's darkness. But it didn't. It's up to every individual to master this part of themself. We couldn't do it for them."

"This is all very heavy," Argan said. The sun was starting to rise, and his growling stomach echoed in the kitchen. "Maybe I'll eat before the next one?"

Vivienne wasted no time; she began preparing eggs and toast. Before she could finish cooking, however, the quiet of the kitchen was accosted by a loud banging in the parlor.

"Stop talking right now!" Milicent's voice boomed.

"This is not my fault and I won't let you blame me," Noah said, just as loudly.

Vivienne quickly closed the pantry door and returned to the eggs, now firing up the oven to make a strada. She made no move to greet her granddaughter.

Milicent and Noah stormed into the kitchen. A suited driver trailed behind them, carrying shopping bags.

Vivienne, forced to acknowledge them all, scowled. "Child, it is barely six a.m. What are you doing?"

"Grandmother, I know your boondoggle was to get me out of the house and out of your hair, and I don't appreciate it. You could have just sent Noah away. I know he's the one that doesn't belong here."

"That would hurt if I still cared, which I don't," Noah said like a prepubescent boy. "And you can't blame me for getting booted out of here. She doesn't want you messing up their plans with your wayward scheme to see Diana."

"I've given up on that idea," Milicent said, directing her response toward Vivienne. "I am letting the past go. It's time to move on and get my life back. I've spent too much of it stuck in old patterns that have gotten me nothing but misery. I need new goals."

"You decided all of this before six a.m. today?" Argan asked, eating toast.

"Not that *you* need to know," Milicent said. "But I decided this last night after *Noah* ruined my meal, informing me that our shopping trip was a ruse to get me out of here. Honestly, Grand-mother, you've never resorted to lying to me before—why start now?"

"Child, relax," Vivienne said. "I didn't lie to you. Shopping in Milan is one of the great pleasures this world has to offer. Couldn't you just enjoy it for the sake of enjoyment?"

Milicent said nothing.

"Did you get your new Farragamos?" Vivienne asked Noah.

His face lit up. "I did! They are as soft as butter." He started ripping through his bags looking for his new treasures. "And the cashmere!" he said, cuddling a new sweater close to his neck. "I'm now addicted to Aperol spritzes."

"You see?" Vivienne said to Milicent. "Joy." She put her strada in the oven and set the timer. "I'm going upstairs to dress. Are you awake for the day? I thought we could all head to the beach. There's something you need to see. Meet me outside at quarter past the hour."

She waited until Milicent and Noah were out of earshot before adding, "Argan, bring the stone with you."

At six fifteen, the foursome stood on the steps of Vivienne's apartment, staring at the bay. It was too early for crowds. A single man walked his dog along the rocky coast. A fishing boat was coming in with the night's catch to sell to the locals for their upcoming day's meals. The air was heavy with humidity, yet

Noah was wearing both his new cashmere sweater and a plum pashmina, wrapped around his shoulders, that Milicent had thought she'd bought for herself.

Argan chuckled at Noah. His own attire was the absolute opposite. He had replaced his pajama bottoms with a well-worn Rosen T-shirt and athletic shorts.

Milicent, still fancying all things purple, kept on her velvet tracksuit and wore her hair swept up in a high bun similar to Vivienne's pile of braids.

Vivienne's flowing caftan mirrored her flowing personality. They followed her down to the cold, packed sand, not yet warmed by the sun. The wind carried the scent of the sea mixed with that day's catch from the fishing boat. Noah wrinkled his nose slightly.

Argan inhaled deeply. The briny scent gave him a dose of energy that pulsed through his veins in a way he'd never noticed before. As they got closer to the edge of the water, the energy within him increased and he felt an excitement build within his belly. Vivienne glanced at him; a slight smile turned up her lips.

Milicent and Noah were oblivious, too concerned with their footwear.

"I told you not to wear your new shoes on the sand," Milicent scolded.

"I can't do this," Noah said, shaking sand from his loafers. He turned back toward the apartment. He got halfway up the bank and looked back. "Mil, come with me," he whined.

"Fine," she said. "The sand isn't really my thing either." They quickly disappeared back into the apartment.

Argan looked at Vivienne. "You knew they would bail."

"Yes," she said. "They are worthy, but so predictable. They will get there in their own time and not a second sooner." She turned back to the water. "Hopefully they'll take out my strada. Let's keep going."

They stepped into the warm, foamy water. The edges of Vivienne's dress lapped up the waves as they walked farther and farther into the sea. They never appeared to get any deeper, although they walked for quite a while. Argan looked down at the edges of Vivienne's dress. The water was being absorbed as they walked. The sea had filled in behind them.

They walked a bit longer, and when they were a hundred yards out from shore, the sand dipped down and they walked on a slight decline. All the while, only their feet got wet. The water parted before them as they went deeper and deeper down.

Vivienne eventually stopped and Argan's eyes widened. In front of them stood a luminous tree. Its leaves of flowing kelp, exposed to the breeze, fluttered gently. The delicate-looking tree stood majestic yet feminine, a secret under Bari's sea.

"Wow," Argan said in amazement. "The last tree of the Great Mothers." He took a step closer. "It's the most beautiful of them all. I feel her energy." He looked at Vivienne. "That's what I felt walking over here, a stirring of excitement, like a memory of her return. Sophia's return?"

Vivienne nodded. "Yes, child, she is so close, waking up her children here on earth. This tree gives illumination to humanity and connects to the Akasha through the water." She motioned for Argan to get nearer. "She is the last tree, the last secret. She is the scribe of the Akasha. All of the Great Mothers' trees serve a vital purpose on the planet. This is mine." She reached out and touched the strands of kelp. Her hand blended with the leaf and it was impossible to discern where one ended and the other began. "Through their root system, they connect to every other tree on land. The water in the roots trickles down into the streams, ponds, puddles, rivers, and oceans of the world. The one planet comes alive with light seen beyond this galaxy." She looked to the sky, now full of sunlight.

"All water on the planet holds consciousness. The record of all life experiences is imprinted in the water everywhere. It finds its way to this tree and she filters it and it gets recorded into the citrine wall."

"This is incredible and perfect," Argan said.

"The four trees are us, the guardians of the elements—fire, air, water, and earth. We are also the four directions—east, west, north, and south. These trees are precious but strong, steadfast, eternal. The seasons come and go, there is death and rebirth, and they remain, ever watchful."

Argan counted on his fingers. "One in Ocean's backyard, one in Beatrice's, one in Silverwood, and one here." He nodded and stared at Vivienne's tree. "She is magnificent."

"We are so close to the end," Vivienne said. "Only one final piece of the puzzle."

Argan waited.

"You," she said.

"I'm sorry?"

"You," she repeated. "The Divine Feminine can not complete her mission without her counterpart, the Sacred Masculine. Lucifer was correct to bring up the Twin Flame paradigm. You, Argan, embody everything the masculine should be in our world and in the world to come. *You take inspired action from the directive of your heart.* That is what is needed from the hero of the next age."

She smiled with the warmth of a mother, and Argan thought of Leonora.

"Yes, your mother has prepared you well. We owe her our eternal gratitude. There's just one last step. Yours." He looked to her for explanation. "This is where you will walk through to the First Age, to reunite with Skylar. This is the door you're looking for."

"The tree?" he asked, eyes wide.

"Yes, and the time is now."

"Now?" He looked down at his clothes. "I'm in shorts."

"Pay no mind to your attire," she said. "It will be transformed when you transition."

"What about the strada?" he tried to ask, joking, but he choked on his words.

She smiled. "I'll keep it warm for you."

"What do I do?" he asked.

"Hold out your stone and walk toward the tree. Step into her," she said. "She will do the rest. When you emerge on the other side, turn left. When you start interacting with people, you will recognize the one that will help you."

He looked down at a glowing bed of oysters surrounding the tree. They all slowly opened, each one revealing a perfect, glossy pearl. In his greatest act of faith to date, he did as directed and walked toward the tree. He turned back to look at Vivienne. She smiled with encouragement. "Left!" she called through cupped hands. Her voice reverberated through the waves and he felt the sound ripple through his body.

He took one more step toward the warm, inviting light of the flowing kelp leaves. He felt his body release his soul, and he became one with the light.

14

Suki sat in the Quine library, exasperated. She had exhausted all the resources at her fingertips. "It's just not here," she said to the empty room.

She looked at the cartoon map, as she had done many times. She was looking for the alchemical doors, the Portas. There was one at the Quine, one in Silverwood, one in Italy, and one in the Underworld. Where was the last one? Ocean said there were six. The original still stood in Palombara and four others were accounted for. Where was the last one?

She didn't have the answer, but she knew who did. She grabbed her things and ran out of the library.

Suki called Ocean as soon as she exited the library.

"Where is the last door, Ocean? Is it at your house?"

"God no," Ocean said. "I have enough magic swirling in my house. The grotto is plenty."

"Then where?"

"At the home of the other Great Mother," Ocean said.

"Beatrice?" Suki was horrified. "That house is being sold! What's being done about this? I've got to get there. I'm sure there's information we need that'll be lost if it goes with the house. Why the hell is it being sold, anyway?"

"Beatrice's son is an asshole," Ocean said.

"I'll call you once I get there," Suki said.

"No!" Ocean commanded. "You're needed somewhere else soon enough."

"But—"

"Britt can go to Beatrice's," Ocean said. "In fact, she should go. Yes, Britt." She sounded only half engaged in the conversation.

"Britt?" Suki objected. "No."

"Suki, we all make errors in judgment. It comes from a lack of awareness. You have no right to sit on your high horse, looking down at Britt. This is her story too."

The Great Mother of Fire had a gift for inflicting instant guilt. Suki sighed loudly. "Fine."

"Do you know how to reach her?"

"Unfortunately, yes," Suki said. "So where am I needed? I've wrung out all I can from the Quine library."

"You're going back to the White House," Ocean said.

"I'm sorry, what?"

"That building needs an original alchemist, so I lined it up. Pack your bags. You have to start before the solstice."

Suki froze. "But . . ." She looked around the empty halls of the building. "What about Michael? Who'll take care of him?"

"Suki, you are using the excuse of pet sitting to get out of this opportunity? You don't even like cats. Stop hiding behind an old life and step into the person you came here to be. I'll ship him to Joel's."

Ocean disconnected, and Suki dialed Britt's number before she could change her mind.

"Suki!" Britt exclaimed. "I'm so happy to hear from you."

"Looks like you'll be getting your wish," Suki said. "You're being called to help."

15

The world of the ocean was nothing short of heaven on earth. The kelpie zoomed along, the power of the waves propelling him effortlessly through the water. Skylar felt the energy of the current as she rode on his back. It wasn't unlike riding a horse, and she thought of Cheveyo. For a moment she thought her new friend might be her favorite horse from back home, but this creature seemed too jovial. Cheveyo was much more reserved than this.

As they passed above the luminescent plants lighting up the ocean floor, she connected with the ocean. She felt her body lose its boundary and merge with the water. She felt the cold, dark sea course through her veins.

The kelpie slowed as they approached a light that grew steadily brighter as they neared it. When they got closer, Skylar saw it was a tree with leaves similar to those of her affable ride.

The great sea horse circled the kelp tree. A seabed of open oysters lay in tight concentric circles around its base. Shining pearls dotted each one. Skylar was amazed. She moved as if to dismount from the kelpie, but he quickly dashed forward. She turned back to see the tree fade behind her.

The kelpie picked up speed and Skylar had to work to hang on. The last thing she wanted was to be left in the middle of the ocean by an erratic sea horse. She let him lead through patches of dark water. With nothing to see in the dark, she closed her eyes, but became amazed at the world within the darkness. With her eyes shut, she saw the schools of fish, the coral reefs, the tubular plants swaying to the tune of the deep. This land truly was the origination of magic.

The kelpie slowed his speed and came to the surface of the water. Skylar opened her eyes to see a shoreline in the daylight. She couldn't see the sun, as above them was a wall of carved rock. The kelpie had taken her into a large cave; only slivers of sun shone through the cracks. Before them, on the shore, stood the ruins of a temple that seemed vaguely familiar. Half of the stone ceiling had been crushed in. Broken statues of marble goddesses flanked steps long gone. The statues were overgrown with greenery that came out of their trunks.

She was greeted by the cave's dwellers on the threshold. At first glance, they seemed horrid in appearance—their faces misshapen, their clothes tattered and bloody. They approached her as she hopped off the sea horse and waded in the water.

At first, Skylar thought these phantomlike creatures were sylphs, but then she remembered that this was not their domain. She remembered her experience in the arena when she went through the portal she thought led to the Underworld. These creatures resembled those souls—crying for help, sorry for their wrong deeds, looking for redemption that wouldn't ever come. They were sentenced to live an eternity of suffering. This was a true hell.

"Heather was right," Skylar said. She had newfound pity for these souls.

She looked at the kelpie, who waited patiently behind her. He nudged her forward.

"You want me to go in there?"

He glided forward.

"Of course you do."

The dwellers swarmed her immediately. The kelpie circled Skylar, keeping her just out of reach. "Why am I here?" she asked, not sure whom she was posing the question to.

All at once the creatures began to speak, all clamoring for a voice. They shifted from trying to keep her out to helping her get in.

"You can set us free," one said.

"You are the one," said another.

"You have the answers we need," said a third.

"You, you, you . . ." they all said at once.

They continued to circle her; a few reached out their translucent hands, but none had the capacity to touch her.

"Stop!" she commanded and they quieted. "I appreciate your situation, and your misplaced allegiance, but I can't help you." She swept her arms forward to clear a path to the door. The dwellers fell in line behind her and watched curiously.

She touched the stone door. It had no knob, so she pushed lightly. Nothing. She pushed harder. Nothing. She leaned on it. It wouldn't budge.

"Maybe she's not the one," one whispered.

"Oh, I'm the one," Skylar said airily. She gave it one last shove with her whole body, but it didn't move.

Many of the dwellers lost interest once her attempts failed. As they wandered away, she stepped back and walked off around the temple, in search of another way in.

On the other side of the building, she found an opening, a crack in the foundation that had widened considerably. She hopped through. The dampness gave her a chill. The difference between the climate of the cave and that inside the walls was curious.

She looked around the abandoned relic, worse inside than out. It took a few minutes to get familiar with her surroundings, but she knew exactly where she was. The walls were hollowed-out rocks, the floor dirt. A crevasse holding two long, empty, trough-like structures snaked through the large room.

As she looked around, she felt Sophia's presence. A feeling of excitement grew in her belly.

"Welcome to my home, Divine Skylar," a voice said.

"Thank you," Skylar said. "Sophia?" She searched the room for the goddess, but found nothing. "Hello?"

"Hello," the voice said, again behind her.

Skylar turned faster this time. Still nothing.

The voice chuckled. "You can't see me, Skylar," she said. "You have to go on faith."

"This is your home?" Skylar asked. "It doesn't seem fitting for you."

"Sometimes the idea of something is better than the actual something," Sophia said.

"Can I look around?"

"Of course."

"Thank you, Sophia," Skylar said, feeling the presence of the Great Queen Mother. Her voice echoed off the cold walls.

She explored for a few more minutes, and then something in the air suddenly made her eyes burn, stronger than an onion. She wiped the tears away continuously, but the burning only got worse. She closed her eyes, hoping for relief—and relief came, along with a shift in perception.

In that moment, the temple came roaring to vibrant life. The walls were no longer made of simple rock but a sparkling white crystal. Massive plants, dotted with exotic flowers of fuchsia and purple, filled the room. But the most breathtaking sight was the bookcase, stacked unimaginably high, beyond the scope of Skylar's vision. The entire temple was filled with luminescent books—each containing its own magic, its own energy. The troughs were now overflowing with familiar liquids, one gold, one silver.

"The rivers of the Underworld!" Skylar was excited to see them. She followed them with her eyes until they reached the far wall and disappeared underneath it.

"Finding your way is as simple as making a decision," Sophia said.

Skylar turned toward the voice. This time, she was able to see her. Sophia was more beautiful than Skylar had ever imagined she could be. Her hair was braided to her knees, brown, blond, and red. Her skin was a dark olive color; her eyes glowed green.

"Ahhh, you've found your sight." She smiled.

Skylar opened her eyes and the temple returned to the shell of age, worn by time. She closed them again to see Sophia return.

"Your home looks like this because of the state of the world, right?" Skylar asked.

"Yes," Sophia said.

"And once I fix everything, it will be transformed?"

"You're describing Cinderella," Sophia said. "This isn't quite a fairy tale. Have a look around. It's all coming back to you quickly." Skylar opened her eyes. The cold stone walls seemed slightly more inviting now, still standing after centuries of disrepair.

"This temple was grand once. It stood above the sea, in the land of air. It was everything you'd imagine it would be. But when the First Age ended, the Great Mothers did their best to protect the wisdom that was being wiped away by the Archer. When the stone was fractured, the wisdom was forgotten, replaced by the quest for power and possessions. Those back in Atlantis were free to do as they wished, with no moral compass to guide them. They lost all connection to their hearts. The Archer committed heinous crimes against the women left behind, and once they were all gone, he gained ultimate power."

Skylar couldn't help but gawk at Sophia's indescribable beauty.

"It is legend, what happened to that baby Sophia. Some said she took her place among the stars. Others said she returned to the ethers, the sacred mist of the gods. The truth is, I became one with the sea, the primordial ocean—my birthplace. And I have remained here for thirteen thousand years. *With my books.*" Her voice lifted when she mentioned her books. "These stories breathe life into this place. These are the stories of humanity, past and future."

Sophia's words clicked like numbers in the tumbler in Skylar's mind. "This?" she couldn't find the words. "This is the great library of the Akasha?" She closed her eyes to see the magnificence again. The books were more vibrant now than they had been minutes before. The ceiling seemed limitless; the shelves stacked far into the sky. They were individual books but also a collection that blurred into one, like individual waves of the same ocean. There was a connection between them all: the unity of all of humanity. Skylar was humbled. The burning in her eyes vanished, and was replaced by tears of humility.

The room buzzed with a vibration that also buzzed in Skylar's chest, and she felt her heart open like a hundred-petal lotus. She had connected to Sophia's wisdom. This was different than drinking the Mnemosyne. There, she'd seen experiences in her mind. Here, she felt them in her heart. She felt the last bit of armor around her heart crack and fall to the floor of the temple.

The overwhelming feeling of love was too much and she opened her eyes.

"You are not alone, divine one," Sophia's voice rang in her head. "That is the plight of all of humanity. They are able to endure the violence, the malevolence, even seek it out, but they cannot withstand the love. The cracking open to love is too much for most to bear. So they recoil. That is the Archer's doing."

Skylar looked at the bare walls; there were no books to be seen with open eyes. She closed them again, and the magnificence returned. "This is the manifestation of the great crystal from the Underworld."

"Yes," Sophia said. "On the physical plane, it appears as a giant rock at the earth's core. But its true essence can only be seen with the purest of heart."

Skylar's eyes widened, revealing all her impure thoughts.

"Don't pay those thoughts any of your heart space," Sophia said. "You are pure of heart simply by being human. That's what this library has proven to me for millennia. Ignorance clouds human judgment but the heart remains pure, no matter how buried. Even the Archer, the source of all human ignorance, has the capacity for redemption within him. The secret is to return to the childlike innocence that sits at the core of your heart. Most are afraid to look, as it's covered by lifetimes of abuse. But look they must if they wish to receive the treasure that awaits them."

This library, the greatest living library that ever existed, was like a candy store of happiness, and Skylar wanted to find one book in particular. She scanned the shelves for the familiar leather-bound book. Its energy called to her louder than the rest. Way up high, it sang a song in the language of the birds, as if calling to her from the treetops.

She pushed one of the dozen library rollers toward the book and started to climb. With each step, she became more excited. An inkling of being a child, excited to open a surprise, filled her heart. She laughed out loud at her own enthusiasm. Her steps quickened until she reached the shelf with the book that was calling her name. Her eyes grew big. This book had been a part of her world for three years now, and yet it was completely new. It felt like another secret was about to be revealed to her. She was so grateful for this quest, this adventure, no matter its outcome. No matter what this book said, she was so thankful to be the *one*.

She touched the book and its energy pulsed in her hand. Forgetting how high above the ground she was, she leaned back on the ladder and almost fell, but caught herself with one hand. She placed the book under her arm and quickly climbed back down the ladder.

The book was more beautiful than it had ever been in her world. Its leather cover was now an iridescent green, with a nautilus shell in the middle.

She grinned at Sophia and opened the cover. She turned the translucent pages, and they hummed a beautiful song in her ears. Symbols floated up off of every page. Some were familiar alchemical symbols, but others were gloriously unfamiliar. They spoke to Skylar's heart in a long-forgotten language from a faraway place she was now waking up to. She couldn't read them with her mind, only with her heart. And one page spoke louder than the rest—the last one.

16

Argan felt like a warm bath had engulfed him. Memories of his mother when he was a boy filled his heart. He was instantly comforted, instantly peaceful.

That peace was cut short, as he was soon discombobulated, tossed under water, not sure which way was up. He held his breath. Should he step forward? Or step left now? His mind and body were confused.

"Stillness, child," he heard Vivienne's voice say, and he stopped moving. "Take a breath." He trusted her but also knew he didn't have a choice. He was out of air. He breathed the warm liquid into his lungs. He didn't sputter or cough. It gave him life, like amniotic fluid. With each breath, he felt more alive, more energized.

He peeked open one eye. All around him was light. In his next breath, he was propelled forward, as if the tree was pushing him out.

He expected to be underwater, but he wasn't. He was in a subterranean cavern. Now was the time to sputter. He put his hands on his knees and coughed the liquid out of his lungs. He took in a few awkward gasps before he started to breathe normally.

When he regained his breath, he looked around. The walls of the cavern were made of red clay, and deep green pools of water dotted the ground. It wasn't damp; the temperature was warm, as if the sun were out, but there was no sky above him, only rock.

The shore stretched out in front of him to another part of the sea. He took a few steps and noticed that his clothes had changed. He was now dressed in a gray uniform-like suit, fitted but with no buttons. It was comfortable and dry. He was barefoot, but it wasn't unpleasant; the floor of the cavern was cool and smooth.

This side of the tree looked very similar to Vivienne's side. There were large circles of oysters at his feet. They had all opened, revealing the most luminous pearls. He bent to look closer but thought it best not to touch. They seemed too pure and magical to be ruined by human hands.

"*We accept your wishes,*" he heard them say in his head. "*But they must be selfless wishes.*"

"Good to know, thanks," he said out loud.

He walked in the direction of the brightening light. Vivienne hadn't given him many details; just to turn left. The sunshine led him out of the cavern like a flashlight. When he got out, the sky was gray. The beam of bright light was focused on a small city of white buildings out in the middle of the ocean. He looked right. In the opposite direction, the same city appeared. But this one was simpler, more humble . . . familiar. And it had no bright sunbeam. "Could it be?" he asked.

"LEFT!" Vivienne's voice boomed out of the shaking tree behind him. Argan chuckled and turned toward the *left* city.

He had been carrying the green stone in the velvet pouch on a cord around his neck, but here he had to take it off. It felt like a noose. He took the stone out and held it in his hand. He knew it would lead him to Skylar if he trusted it. He put it back in its pouch. Since his new clothes had no pockets, he tied it to his ankle.

He was going to have to swim to get to the city. He hoped it wasn't as far as it appeared. He was a strong swimmer, but this would be a test. He waded into the warm water and dove in.

ᥫ᭡

A short time before he reached the shore of the white city, Argan came to a dome-shaped energy field. Its green hue was visible to the eye. He had no trouble passing through it. Once he did, the sun was shining over him.

He was thankful to reach the shore; he wouldn't have been able to go much farther. His clothes dried quickly, and he tried to stay hidden until he could figure out where he needed to go. He scoped out the area. All the buildings were similar: white, dome-topped, many with glass windows. The architecture reminded him of parts of Greece.

He walked among the others in the street unnoticed, despite being barefoot. They all wore the same uniform. He didn't want to make eye contact but did glance at a few passersby. They didn't look much different than he did. They were all young to middle-aged, physically fit. It didn't take him long to realize there were no women.

He came to the largest building in the small city. It seemed to be made of marble or quartz crystal. The stone pulsed through his pouch, sending a jolt through his ankle. He was in the right place. He walked through the large, triangular doors unnoticed. A scrolling holographic directory floated in the air. Its language was in symbols, not text. He was amazed at the technology; it was something he'd only seen in movies.

He spent a few minutes walking through the hall. All of them led back to the entrance. The whole building was a circle.

"Hey, man."

Argan's eyes lit up when he saw that the words had come from Kyle. "I was not told I'd be seeing you here," he said, containing his surprise.

"This's my new job," Kyle said proudly.

"Doing what, exactly?" Argan asked.

"A variety of things." Kyle leaned in close to Argan. "Mostly custodial in nature. I wait around a lot and I have to tell ya, I can't remember most of it. But they're paying me well. Couldn't pass it up."

"Well, it's good to see you, Kyle. Have you seen Skylar?" Argan remained breezy.

"Not since yesterday. She was in the lab near the aquarium tank."

"Where's that?" Argan asked.

"Upstairs, fourth floor."

"Thanks man." Argan left him standing there.

He thought about the elevator but opted for the transparent stairs. There really was no hiding here. He took the stairs by twos and got to the fourth floor.

Heather stared at Skylar's lifeless body. The blood around her chest wound was already crusting over from its contact with air. She put on a pair of latex gloves and picked at the dried blood with tweezers. Knowing no one was watching, she tapped the exposed green stone with the tweezers. It still shone brightly, even among the mess of an open wound. She looked at Skylar's face, so peaceful, and for a moment she forgot her rage.

She heard a commotion outside the door and asked the universe for a bit more time before the Archer returned. She didn't have the answers yet. But the disruption in the hallway drew closer, and Heather realized today wasn't the day for a breakthrough.

"Skylar?" she heard a man's voice. It wasn't the Archer. "Skylar," she heard right through the door.

She looked up as a beautiful man burst through the door. Horror overtook his face when he saw Skylar. "No!" he gasped.

"No." He stumbled backward, stopped briefly, and then rushed toward the table.

"Please stop," she said. "You're making this worse."

"Worse?" he said.

She used her knowledge of energy manipulation to hold him back. "You are not listening!" she said. "This isn't Skylar. It's a hologram of her. The Archer thought this might work but it didn't."

He was relieved, but only slightly. "Hologram?"

"Yes, an etheric clone. It's part of her existence but not her physical body," she said. "Wherever she is, she'll feel a twinge but it won't kill her."

"She's not here?"

"No," she said. "She hopped a kelpie yesterday. She's probably under China by now." She turned to put down her tweezers.

Argan stepped closer to Heather and she took a step back. He took another step and she retreated one step. "You're familiar to me. Do I know you?" he asked.

"I don't think so," she said. "I would remember you." She returned to the body on the table. With a push of a button, Skylar's image faded and the table was empty. "We have more."

"More bodies?" he asked.

"Yes," she said. She gave him a curious look and then turned away, busying herself at a technical workstation. "You carry a light just as strong as Skylar's. I can feel it. Everyone else will feel it too. You're not safe here."

"You're the first woman I've seen here," he said.

"Yes," she said. "I'm the only one."

"Why?"

"I don't owe you an explanation."

He looked back at the empty table. "You said she's gone. Do you know where?"

"I don't," she said. "The Archer will be back soon and more upset than ever, but I'll deal with that."

Argan stared at Heather and his intense eyes made her blush.

"I know we've met before," he said.

"That's probable," she said. "We are very near the central crossing point of all timelines on earth. If our paths have crossed in another timeline, you would feel it now."

He stepped dangerously close to her. "Do you feel it?" He was close enough that his cool breath landed on her face, turning it bright red.

"No," she said and audibly swallowed.

He stepped back and looked around the lab. "I came from outside the city," he said.

"Of course you did," she said. "Everyone is accounted for here. I'm sure you've already been noticed." She watched him walk across the room and look out the window. "Did you see the great tree?" she asked with wonder. "It sits just outside the city. No one from here is permitted that far. I've always wanted to see it," she said wistfully.

"A city of grown men follows such a limiting rule?" he asked skeptically.

"It's more like an electric fence," she said. "The Archer insisted on its creation to keep everyone in. I have a feeling you might be stuck here now too."

"No, I'm not," he said. "I'm finding Skylar and we're heading home." He touched the empty table.

"Okay, well, I hope you get what you want," she said.

"That can't be true," he said. "You work for him, this is your world. You want Skylar back on that table. The opposite of what I want."

"I don't want that," she said.

"Then what do you want?" he asked. "A young girl here

126

in this messed-up place. You don't belong here. What are your dreams for your life?"

Her face hardened. "Why are you asking me such intimate questions? You don't even know my name."

"What is it, your name?" he asked.

She relaxed slightly. "Heather."

"Heather, I'm pleased to meet you." He kissed her hand in an old-fashioned way. "I'm Argan."

She tried to cover up her awkwardness but failed.

"What are your dreams?" he asked again.

"I don't have dreams," she said.

"Sure you do," he said. "You dream of seeing that tree. I heard it in your voice."

She hid her face with the embarrassment of someone much younger than her age of twenty-two, more like that of a ten-year-old. She pulled her hair over her scar and turned back to him. "Are you hungry?"

"I'm always hungry," he said, dazzling her with his smile.

"I could get you something," she said. "Before you go."

"That would be nice, thank you. I don't know where I'm headed," he said. "I thought my end game was this place. Now you're telling me she's out there in the sea. I can't just go out blindly trying to find her. Even with the other half of the stone."

Heather scanned his body and located the stone around his ankle, but she didn't make any move to take it. "I don't know where you could hide that the Archer won't find you. He knows everything about what goes on here. Nothing is hidden from him. Except . . ."

"I don't want to hide," he said.

"While I get you some food, you should remain *unseen*. Follow me," she said.

They walked down a hallway of doors, as bright rays of

sunshine cascaded through the windowed ceiling. The last door in the hall was smaller than the rest, so easily missed that it practically blended into the wall.

Heather touched the door and it opened inward. "It's small, but you'll be safe here."

"Why?" he asked.

"This room was created by the original high priestess of Atlantis. It contains all her magic, all her heart. It's called the Sanctuary. It sits in plain sight to the Archer but he's blind to it. Only the worthy can even see it. I had a feeling it would open for you."

"This is Atlantis?" he asked in disbelief.

"See, you don't even know where you are," she said. "You're stupid."

"Wow, thanks," he said.

She shrugged. "Wait here. I'll get you something to eat." Heather left him alone.

For the first time since arriving in this strange land, Argan could relax. The room had the same feeling as the tree. Safety. The oddities in the room made him laugh—the stuffed bird, the fountain. It was all so bizarre and made perfect sense at the same time. He looked at himself in the mirror. "Dude, you could use some sleep," he said, running his hand through his hair. Stubble smattered his face. He bent over and took the pouch off of his ankle. He slid the stone out into his hand.

The door opened and he jumped up, fumbling to hide the stone. He rushed to put it in the drawer of the small desk. He shoved it in and closed the drawer just as Heather came in carrying a tray of exotic fruits and cheese in one hand, a pair of black loafers in the other.

"These should fit you," she said.

"Thank you," he said earnestly. He slipped them on.

"Tell me why you're doing this," she said as she placed the tray on a small pedestal table. Argan wasted no time diving in.

"Doing what?" he asked, his mouth already full.

"Why you're here, risking your life with this stone you don't quite understand the value of," she said. "You love her, Skylar?"

"I do," he said. "We've been connected forever, in more ways than one."

"Mmmm," Heather said. "But are you willing to die for her?"

He cocked his head. "Why are you asking me such an intimate question?"

"Because I know your name," she said. "And it's no more intimate than *do you love her*. You answered that one just fine."

His hackles rose and he put down a hunk of cheese. "I'm willing to do what it takes to get her back."

"Mmmm," she mumbled again. "Sounds like a grown-up fairy tale to me."

"What's that supposed to mean?" he asked, instantly defensive.

"You love her, yes, but why put on the knight-in-shining-armor routine?" she asked. "I mean, you don't even know where you are, or what you're doing. It sounds like you're taking orders."

"You're one to talk," he said.

She quieted and turned to leave.

"Sorry," he said. "You're not totally wrong. It's a long story, but I've been training for this my whole life. I guess it's bigger than Skylar and me. We're entwined, but my job is to get this stone back where it belongs."

"Where's that?" she asked.

"I thought you'd know," he said.

"You took this on without any directions?" she asked incredulously. "Again, stupid."

He rolled his eyes and resumed eating.

"Don't leave this room," she said, opening the door.

"Staying in here doesn't get me where I need to go," he said.

"Seeing as you have none, I have to come up with a plan," she said.

"You're going to help me?" he asked.

"If it means getting *her* out of here, yes." She walked out the door.

He finished the food and was getting antsy. He hadn't come here to hide. *But what did I come here to do?* He retrieved the stone from the desk and held it up to the light of the window. Sparkles of light reflected around the room like a disco ball. As beautiful as it was, he hated this thing. It represented a life he couldn't escape from. He didn't want to admit it, but Heather was right. He had lived someone else's life up until now. He wanted to be done with it and figure out what truly made him happy. He didn't like the idea of leaving the stone behind but figured this room was the best option. It had a maternal energy that felt safe. And he was more vulnerable outside with it on his body. He tucked it back in its pouch and returned it to the desk. "Sorry, Heather," he said quietly as he opened the door and stepped into the hallway.

"Hey, man," Kyle said, walking by. "I'm headed to the mermaid tank. Care to join?" The words rolled off his tongue like he was headed to get coffee.

"Sure," Argan said. He donned a lab coat from a nearby row of hooks and walked in step with Kyle. "Kyle, what's your role here, exactly?"

"It's kinda like Sea World," Kyle said. "And I'm in charge of maintaining the tanks—keeping things clean and at the right pH."

He glanced at Argan, who could tell Kyle was off, more than usual. His eyes were bloodshot beyond anything Argan had ever seen. "Are you feeling all right?" he asked.

"Yeah, why?" Kyle asked. His breathing seemed elevated; Argan thought it might be amphetamines.

"Your eyes are bloodshot," he said. "Getting enough sleep?"

"As you mention it, no," Kyle said. "That's probably it."

They walked down the ramp to the tank room.

It was bigger than any aquarium Argan had ever seen. "Whoa," he said.

"Yeah, isn't it great?" Kyle said. "I can't believe this is my job."

"I can't believe it either," Argan said, fully aware that this was not what it seemed.

"You haven't seen the best part," Kyle said, leading him to the glass. A whirl of bubbles swam by, its source unseen.

"Wait for it," Kyle said.

"Holy shit." Argan's mouth fell open. A mermaid had slowed to investigate Argan.

"There's six of them," Kyle said. "They're super mean, so if they get out of line, I have to use this." He pointed to a button on the wall. "It sends out electricity."

"I'd be mean too, being trapped here like an animal," Argan said. "This is cruel on a supernatural level. Who's your boss, Kyle?"

"The Archer," Kyle said. "I don't see him all that much. Which is fine with me, he's a weird dude."

"How so?" Argan asked.

"He just runs hot and cold and some of the guys I started with aren't here anymore and I don't know what happened to them and there's only one girl here and . . ." He spewed out this information in one long run-on sentence, but none of it was new to Argan. He assumed this "Archer" was Magus. He knew Kyle was just following orders and was drugged up on top of it.

Argan approached the glass and a mermaid with long brown hair greeted him. "She doesn't look that mean," he said. He put his hand to the glass and she reciprocated. He felt the heat from her hand through the glass. "Odd," he said. Through the heat, an image of Skylar standing in this same spot came into his mind. A jolt ran through him and he smiled at the mermaid. She slightly smiled back. It was short-lived, as her smile quickly turned fearful and she swam away.

"Mr. Andrews, who is your guest?"

They both turned around to see Magus standing in front of them.

"Hello, sir." Kyle seemed to be doing his best to be respectful, but he was very fuzzy. "This is Argan Papadapoulous. It's a mouthful, I know. He's a friend from . . . back home."

"Is that right," Magus said. "Well, Mr. Papadapoulous, welcome." He extended his hand in greeting. Argan hesitated, but accepted it. Magus held the handshake for an extraordinarily long time. "Where do you hail from?"

"The Boston area," Argan said.

"You're a long way from home," Magus said. "You're here because?"

Argan knew it was useless to tell him anything but the truth. "Skylar is missing," he said. "And I've come to bring her home."

"Ahh, how valiant of you," Magus said. "She's not ready to leave quite yet, but when she is, we'll let you know."

"She's not here anymore, anyway," Argan said.

"Not here?" Magus asked. His face contorted quickly. "How do you know that?"

"I have a feeling." Argan didn't want to cause problems for Heather.

This explanation relaxed Magus a bit. "I see, you . . . have a feeling," he said. "Let's find out for sure, shall we?" He touched Argan's back, guiding him up the ramp toward the lab rooms. "Mr. Andrews, please return to your post."

"But Argan's a friend—"

"Mr. Andrews, that's all," Magus said quietly.

"Yes, sir." Kyle gave Argan a look of apology and walked on.

Magus led Argan past the small door, down the long hallway, and back into the lab he'd entered when he'd first arrived. Heather was busy at a microscope, but looked up when they walked in. Her eyes widened in surprise.

"Oh my," she said.

"Oh my, indeed." Magus gave her a look. "You've seen him before, you knew he was here?" His anger rose.

"Sir, I hadn't had a chance to tell you," she said, fear in her voice. "You've been away."

He studied her, then relaxed his tone. "Well, it would seem this unwanted visitor has been looking for Skylar. He says she's not here. Do you concur?"

She hesitated, then lowered her head like a child. "Yes," she said, looking at the floor.

"It would seem you are full of secrets today," Magus said, again in a soft voice.

"She has magic of her own and was impossible to stop," Heather pleaded.

Magus walked to the back of the room and Argan followed him, compelled by an unseen force. Vivienne had told him Magus was a black magician.

"Vivienne?" Magus read his mind. "She sent you. This is starting to make sense. You must have the other half of the heart light. Where is it?"

Argan froze. Magus could clearly see inside his head. He forced himself to think of a school trip to Santorini when he was a boy.

"I'll find it soon enough," Magus said. With a flick of his

hand, the room filled with a blinding light, more powerful than a million light bulbs. Argan shielded his eyes with his arms for the split second the flash lasted. He felt the heat on his skin and then a stark cold contrast. He opened his eyes. Magus remained there, as did Heather.

"You were illuminated by the light that should have killed you," Magus said. He stepped closer to Argan and scanned him with his eyes. "You've been through a purification. This is Vivienne's work." He stepped away and invisible energy bands cuffed Argan's wrists and ankles. They were bound so tight, he couldn't move.

"If you bind me here, she will come," Argan said, referring to Vivienne.

"I certainly hope so," Magus said.

Heather stood in the background, wringing her hands. Argan looked at her for help.

"Sir, keeping him here is not without its own problems," she said. "His energy field is . . ." She studied the hologram of Argan on the suspended crystal screen.

"Is what?" Magus asked.

"Expanding," Heather finished.

Magus watched as the outline of Argan's pixelated aura grew. "Make it stop," he said.

"How?" she asked.

He paused, seemingly stumped. "We can counteract it with sound frequency. Get into the sound chamber," he ordered Argan, gesturing toward a contraption that looked a bit like an airport X-ray machine.

"I can't move in these shackles," Argan barked.

Magus released him and pushed him toward the chamber. Argan struggled a bit but was not able to match the strength of Magus's energy. He resumed his position, hands shackled above him and spread apart, his feet wide and also tethered with energy chains.

Heather stood watching, pitching back and forth where she stood. Argan convulsed as he endured the high-pitched sound waves running through his body. His blood was being boiled from the inside out, like he was being cooked by a microwave oven.

Just before the point of killing him, Magus released the wave and Argan slumped over, the chains holding him in position. His breath heaved his chest up and down, and Heather motioned to release him.

"Wait!" Magus ordered. "He's not dead."

"That isn't your goal!" she shouted back and opened the tube door. She released the energy bonds and Argan fell to his knees, catching his body with his hands.

He looked at his reflection in the glass next to him and gasped; his eyes glowed bright gold.

Heather gasped as well as he turned his gaze on her, and she took a step back. "Archer, what frequency did you use?"

"350 Hertz," he said.

"You wanted to emblazon a hologram of his body but instead you electrified his physical one. You've switched him on, so to speak."

"That frequency would have killed an ordinary man," Magus said.

"I am not an ordinary man," Argan said, standing upright. He walked out of the tube and tried to focus on Heather, but couldn't see her body. She was a mixture of color and light. "I see your aura," he said. "You have goodness in you. Don't let him take what's left." He looked at Magus. Only a gray cloud reflected back. "You have no goodness in you," he said. He trained his stare on the rest of the people in the room. Each of the technicians had their own energy signature, but Argan could see that they were very dim. These men were astral shells of humans long dead that Magus was using as an army of workers.

Magus tried to restrain him again with the energy bonds, but they didn't have any effect, thanks to Argan's new strength.

"I will enjoy taking you down," Argan said. "But I have other things to do first." He turned his back on Magus and walked out the door.

Argan made his way outside. Standing in the intense sunlight, he now saw the men in the streets for what they were: soulless creatures attached to human shells. He spotted Kyle and saw that his energy field had been either shattered or dehydrated, he couldn't tell which. Like his bloodshot eyes, his field was a dry landscape; the life force was being sucked out of him and he didn't even know it.

"Kyle!" Argan called across the street. "You've got to get out of here."

Kyle shook his head. "I just started this job, man. And I really like it."

"Why? Can't you see what's going on here?" Argan looked all around Kyle. All of these men had gone through the same process, only kept marginally alive to be energy sources for the astral demons attached to them. He swept the area around Kyle to "kick off" those surrounding him.

"Mr. Andrews, it would be in your best interest to detain your friend," Magus said from behind them.

Conflict swept across Kyle's face. "Dude, I'm sorry," he said, stepping toward Argan hesitantly.

Argan shrugged and backed away toward the sea. He had no problem fighting off those who tried to stop him, and he didn't stop running until he reached the shore and dove into the water.

His new power lit up the crystals in the waves as he swam

toward the tree. He didn't have a plan. He couldn't return to Vivienne's. Or maybe he could. Perhaps she could come back with him and help. Either way, he had to get the stone back from the Sanctuary.

"Mr. Andrews, you prove to be less useful than originally intended. For your sake, I hope that changes," Magus said.

Kyle didn't respond.

Heather stood at the shoreline with a slight smile on her face.

"You shouldn't be happy he escaped," Magus said.

Her smile faded. He retreated toward the building. When she didn't immediately follow, he turned back to her. "Are you coming?"

She turned from the water and followed him inside.

Argan swam toward the luminous arbor. He'd have to go back to Vivienne's. He had no choice. He was almost to the tree when a disturbance in the water caught his eye.

He sped up his stroke, hoping to get to the tree before whatever it was got to him. He was no match for the water creature that was upon him in seconds—which, he was relieved to see, was a dolphin. He'd never experienced a dolphin so close and knew they weren't entirely benevolent, but of all the sea creatures to encounter, he figured this was the best.

The dolphin quickly introduced himself to Argan and any residual fear melted away. This creature was friendly. He circled Argan numerous times before nudging him with his nose. Argan picked up speed and was surprised at how much his own abilities had ramped up. He thought of swimming with Skylar under Vivienne's lake and how he'd love another chance at it. He needed air much less now.

At first he tried to lose the dolphin, but when he realized that was impossible, he decided to catch a ride. He reached out and grabbed on to his dorsal fin.

When they reached the area near the tree, Argan let go, but the dolphin circled back and nudged him to keep going.

"This is my stop," he said.

The dolphin shook his head and circled him again. He rose underneath him and started swimming, this time carrying Argan on his back.

After they'd traveled above the water for about a mile, Argan started to worry. "You are going to dump me in the middle of nowhere," he said. He had just enough time to take a large gulp of air before the dolphin dove deeper, returning to the depth of the tree.

When the dolphin pushed Argan back up into the air, he saw that they had reached a cavern similar to the one he'd arrived in. With what little energy he had left, he waded to shore and landed at the broken steps of an old relic that looked like it had once been a temple of worship. He turned back to say thank you to the dolphin, but it was already gone.

Quickly, Argan was swarmed by a crowd of unfamiliar creatures.

"You can set us free," one said.

"You are the one," said another.

"You have the answers we need," said a third.

"You, you, you . . ." They loomed closer.

"Hold up!" he said to the group, putting up his hand. "You've got the wrong guru."

He walked up the broken steps to the stone door. A bright light shone around the doorjamb, framing the stone with beams of light. He pushed the stone and it moved effortlessly.

The group gasped in unison. "He *is* the one. The girl couldn't do that. She's definitely not the one."

"Girl?" Argan asked.

"Yes, that silly girl," one said. "She wasn't very nice to us and she couldn't get the door to budge. She went around back and we haven't seen her since."

"Maybe a whale ate her," another said.

"Serves her right," another said. "She wasn't the one, you are the one."

Argan could see this circular conversation was a waste of time. If the *girl* was Skylar, he'd know soon enough.

He tried to step through the door but an invisible force kept him out. He tried twice, with both feet, jumping once. No luck.

The group shook their heads. "Tsk, tsk," one said. "He was so close."

"When will our savior come?" they pleaded, fists raised to the sky.

Argan took a step back and retreated down the steps. Before heading around the side of the temple, he turned back to the group. "You'll all have to be your own saviors. No one else is coming."

They looked at him, all expressionless.

A trail of gold specks led him around the wall to an opening in the stone. The wide crack was large enough for him to hop right in.

His hands were dusty from trailing his fingers along the old stones. How ironic: under the ocean, he couldn't find water to rinse his hands. He clapped them together to shake off the dust. The sound echoed in the hall, carrying upward to the top of the soaring ceiling.

He walked in a circle in the great hall. It reminded him of Diana's throne room. There was a chair made of old, broken stone and a large rock that could pass as a primitive podium. A sound came from the interior doorway and he glanced up. Skylar stood there, her arms crossed over her chest.

"You're late," she said calmly.

"I . . . had issues with the death door," he stuttered in a moment of uneasiness.

"I had to fix this without you," she said.

"Things don't look fixed," he said. "In fact, they look worse than ever. I was electrified by some maniac, for starters. I wouldn't be surprised if I glow with the sea life around here."

She stepped quickly out of the doorway and rushed him, stopping short of touching him. Her prickly demeanor faded quickly and she gave him a fierce hug. After a moment, she pulled away slightly, yet kept her arms around his waist.

"You're different." She squinted slightly.

"I'm sure I am," he said. "I wasn't kidding, he electrified me."

Skylar looked concerned. "I'm wondering what else he did."

"Hey, do you know Kyle is here?" he asked. "I mean, here as in there, as in Atlantis. Did you know that was Atlantis?"

"Yes," she said.

"He acts like it's completely normal to be working for that *Archer*," he said.

Skylar released her hug and kept hold of Argan's hands. "Archer is Magus. He's a black magician, on the planet since the time of the Great Mothers. He's been one of many manipulating events and timelines to control the population. He set the stage during Atlantian times, cursing the women, replacing their consciousness with jealousy and low self-worth. But the timelines are overlapping, all of the cycles we've talked about for two years have ended. It's all happening now and there is a window to lift his curse and release humanity from the control it's been under since the First Age."

"Oh, is that all?" Argan asked.

"No. Heather is his daughter, and Ocean's."

"Wow, that's huge," he said.

"I know." She sighed. "And he wants the heart light."

"I got that. I brought Ocean's half with me but hid it in the Sanctuary."

"Oh, good thinking. It'll be safe there." She pulled him by the hand. "Come, let me show you around. But you have to close your eyes."

He obliged and laughed softly—then gasped. "This is Sophia's library."

Skylar beamed. "It is." She couldn't hide her excitement. "Do you see the room?" she asked. "Come to life?"

"Yes." He opened his eyes and looked at her chest. "And I see the light shining within you, clear as day. Any idea how we . . ."

"Get it out?" she finished. "I have no idea. Part of me thinks I have to die to get this thing out, but I'm hoping for another answer."

"There is always another answer," Sophia said from behind them.

They both turned.

"You have to close your eyes to see her," Skylar said.

"No," he said. "I see her." He smiled wide and pure joy overtook his face, as if he were seeing an actual angel.

"You do?" she asked, disgruntled. "What the hell?"

Sophia chuckled and revealed herself to Skylar with open eyes as well. "This isn't just your imramma, Skylar."

"But apparently you can make it as hard or as easy as you'd like," Skylar said. "If that's the case, can you please heal the stone? I'd like to go home."

"Is that so?" Sophia asked. "It seems to me that you like challenges. You always find yourself in one. Follow me, I want to show you something." She moved quickly, and was almost through the archway on the opposite side of the library before she'd finished speaking.

Skylar hesitated, not wanting to leave the brilliance of the library, but reluctantly followed, tugging Argan along with her.

Sophia led them to the next great hall. "Keep your eyes open here. You have to see this in its truest form. Not what you wish it to be."

This room was even more primitive, an ancient rock cave, again dim and damp. When Skylar's eyes adjusted, she saw the empty troughs continued into this room from the library.

A faint pink glow drew her attention. As she got closer, she could see that the glow was coming from inside a stone well. She bent over the well to see the glow of an incredibly small flame. "The cave of creation," she whispered. "This is the chamber of the heart, where the eternal flame sits. This is where the heart light was forged." She looked at Argan. He beamed with joy.

"It is one half of the altar of the heart," Sophia said. As her words echoed in the hall, a silver cord snaked its way out of the well and connected to Skylar's chest. It left through her back, spiraled around her waist, and flowed into Argan's heart. Sparks of gold and silver flew out like stardust between them. Skylar chuckled.

"This is the spark of fire from the creator's own heart," Sophia said. "This flame is kept here, in the exact core of Earth, in this unassuming relic of a building, because it needs no fancy worship hall to exist. It can survive in its smallest essence, where no one can see it. But it is felt. You felt it. How do you suppose that happened? You just wandered here? Or were you directed by some . . . internal compass that knew the way, even if you didn't?"

"It was this homing beacon of disaster lodged in my chest that brought me here," Skylar said.

"You can tell yourself that but you know different," Sophia said. "Have you ever felt, this whole time you've carried the heart light, that it was calling the shots?"

Skylar knew the answer was no. This whole time it had sat dormant in her body, not doing much of anything except acting as a target for those that wanted it. It definitely hadn't given her guidance.

"My words resonate," Sophia said. "It is what lies underneath that guides you. It is your true altar, the sun of your very being."

"A dolphin dropped me to your door," Argan said from behind her. Skylar was unsure if it was a joke. Sophia laughed, and Skylar breathed a sigh of relief.

Sophia approached Argan and reached out her hand. She caressed his stubbly cheek lightly and he bowed his head. "You, my dear one, are our one true prince. You belong here just as much as Skylar. She is divine, and you are sacred. The Divine Feminine and Sacred Masculine together in union, represented by the stones you carry. One in your heart." She looked at Skylar. "One in your hand." She looked at Argan. "It couldn't be more perfect if I had planned it myself."

"I don't have the stone with me," Argan said. "I hid it for safekeeping."

Sophia took his hands in hers and studied his palms. "Odd, you hold the energy of one that carries the stone, despite not having the physical object. You are more powerful than I had thought."

Skylar closed her eyes. The large rocks of the well transformed into glowing orbs of quartz crystal, perfect and smooth. The light from the depths of the well grew before her, like the light of a distant fire raging upward. It roared toward her and out through the top, spraying the sky with brilliant stars and knocking Skylar to the floor. For the first time since she'd carried the heart light, she felt the pull from it, like an urge, a yearning for wholeness. A switch had turned on. Her chest tightened and she choked up from the intensity.

"Skylar, you carry the wisdom of women in your heart. Argan carries the power of men in his mind. Together they form the whole, the secret to life, the balance of masculine and feminine in the one, joined in love."

Skylar opened her eyes to get relief from the immense force of the light. She leaned on the now-cool rocks and took in a deep breath.

"This is a lot, I know, but you came to have a dynamic lifetime, Skylar, and so you shall. Each trial of your life you've faced thus far peeled a layer from this core you buried until the bonds suffocating you became so weak, they broke free. That is true liberation, true freedom. This has been your price to pay for carrying the light. You are celebrated, Skylar! You've never looked back, never given up when you didn't see the road. You have proven your faith. Now it is time to enjoy the bounty of your work."

Skylar looked at the well with open eyes. The light had returned to the dim glow far down below.

Sophia walked slowly back to the hall of books. Skylar and Argan followed.

"I'm far from done," Skylar said behind Sophia. "Magus . . . um . . . *the Archer* is still walking around, still after this stone." She pointed to her chest. "There are still many loose ends to tie before this story will be over."

Sophia stretched out her hand and the great book floated down to rest in her open palm. The pages opened to a scene. "Skylar," she said, "Gaia's lodestone glows within your chest. It represents the tear between the masculine and feminine. When the world was ready, the stone surfaced from the sea and was born again to woman—coming back into the earth plane through the purity of a girl."

"Rhia," Skylar whispered.

Sophia nodded. "That stone was then transmuted to you. It is that power that has been coveted by those in your life."

In her mind, Skylar thought of Joshua, Milicent, and Devlin. And now Magus. She saw the true identity of the stone—all human consciousness as one, the whole represented as the twin flame, the love between sun and earth, man and woman. She saw her own light shining as Argan approached her. When he drew close enough, his dazzling light joined with hers, and they became one complete, undying flame of creation, together to give the world . . .

A small, blinding orb shone between Skylar and Argan.

"Our baby?" Skylar asked. "Argan's and mine? A girl?" She looked to Sophia for confirmation.

"There's one miracle left to be revealed to you," Sophia said. "You must go back." She released the book and it returned to the shelves high above.

"A baby, I know it's a baby. But . . ." Skylar's vision of a child with Argan clouded with guilt over her baby boy. She glanced at Argan. She had never told him about her brief pregnancy.

Sophia's face held great compassion. "It's all right, Skylar. Hold him in your heart but let him go from the grip of guilt in your mind. He is eternally safe in your heart, not your mind."

Skylar felt a loss of connection from the energy of the room. The childlike lightheartedness she'd felt only moments before lessened.

"I can't stress this enough, Skylar: keep him in your heart, not your mind," Sophia repeated.

Skylar nodded. She shook off the creeping feeling and looked at Sophia with wonder. A small smile curled up her lips. Her whole journey seemed to be coming full circle.

"Almost," Sophia said. With that she vanished, leaving Skylar and Argan alone in the aged room.

The silence echoed in Skylar's ears. The happiness she had felt in Sophia's presence vanished.

"We have to go back, Argan," she said. "We'll find more answers there."

He nodded. "And get the other half of the stone."

They made their way to the open front door.

"We can't pass through," Argan said.

"You moved the stone?" Skylar asked. "I came in the back way."

"I did too. The energy was impossible to walk through here," Argan said. "Maybe if Suki were here . . ."

"Why Suki?"

"Apparently she's the alchemist among us," he said. "Story for another time."

Skylar pursed her lips. "But we've gone through energy portals before."

"Yes," he said. "With Suki."

"So?" She was confused for a moment, and then it clicked. "Nooooo! Get out!"

A smug smile spread across Argan's face. "Yup, I knew you'd find that interesting."

Skylar tried every manner of energy manipulation she had learned to date but was only met with intense static electricity.

Argan grew bored and sat on the dusty floor. "Can you hurry up?" he asked. "We have our impending doom to return to."

She conjured a few sparks of light and a faint orb in front of the door, but nothing. Her last attempt landed her on her butt next to Argan. She blew air out of her nose in exasperation. Then she looked at Argan—*really* looked at him.

"What?" he asked.

"You came for me," she said, letting the realization sink in. "That's hero work."

He dismissed the compliment. "We're not in the clear yet, Sky."

"I know, but it doesn't matter," she said. "Whatever we'll face, we'll do it together." She leaned in and kissed him softly on the lips.

He intensified the kiss and held her shoulders tightly, then pulled back slightly and leaned his forehead to hers. "I've missed you."

"How did you get here?" she asked. "I mean not just here, but *here*."

"Vivienne," he said.

"Really?" Her surprise gave way to understanding. "I guess this is her turf." She got up and dusted her behind. She reached out a hand to help Argan up. "The interesting thing is, I feel this is my turf too. I feel so comfortable, even though the places are foreign."

"You are *Sky of Water*," he said, grazing her face with his hand. "My beautiful mermaid."

"Oh, Argan, mermaids!"

"Yeah, I saw them," he said. "Like nothing I'd ever seen, and we've seen a lot of crazy stuff."

"We have to help them while we're here," she said. "I mean, why wouldn't we, when we can? I know we can." She looked at him. "We can, right?"

He chuckled. "Yes, we can."

They gave up on leaving through the door and made their way back to the crevasse in the back wall. Soon, they were back at the shore.

The dwellers on the threshold were waiting.

"Now what do we do?" one asked.

"There's two of them?" asked another.

"Are they both the one?" asked a third.

"Two can't be the one," the first said condescendingly.

"Maybe two can be the one," said the second.

"Yes, two definitely can be the one," they all said in unison.

"Then can three be the one? Or four? How many can be the one?" a fourth asked.

That question apparently stumped them all, because they stopped talking as Skylar and Argan walked down to the water's edge.

Skylar looked to her right, just beyond the temple, and saw a familiar sight: the city of the Underworld. She now recognized the outward similarity to the city on the left. They were mirrors of each other.

"You rode a kelpie here?" Argan asked.

"Yup, you?"

"Dolphin."

"Right, you said that earlier. Well, now what?"

Argan let out an ear-piercing call and waited. "Someone's gotta show, right?"

They only had to wait a minute or so before the back of a large creature floated toward them.

Skylar's eyes widened. "No way."

A beluga whale popped her head up and let out a sound Skylar had never heard before. Instead of the familiar clicks and squeaks she knew as whale communication, it emitted a beautiful song—wistful, with a touch of sadness. Strikingly similar to the mermaid's song.

"Well, this is our ride," Skylar said. "Ready?"

"Yeah, sure, why not," Argan said.

They waded into the water and the whale came close enough for them to touch her. They each patted her side gently, like they were petting a dog for the first time.

"Amazing," Argan said.

Skylar smiled. The touch of the whale's skin was cool yet supple. She felt tiny hairs on the rubbery surface, like a short coat of velvet. She looked into the great eye of the whale and touched her forehead. The creature's energy pulsed through her like a heartbeat. This whale was ancient yet retained a child-like exuberance that made Skylar smile. Never in her life did she think she would become so intimately connected to such a foreign creature, but the whale was a connection to the wisdom of the water, the memory of the ocean.

They hopped on the whale and set a course for Atlantis.

17

"I'm leaving, Grandmother," Milicent said. Her royal purple designer bags were packed at the front door. "There is nothing for me here and I've grown bored."

"You've stayed longer than most of your visits," Vivienne said. "It's been lovely."

"I need to go reinvent myself," Milicent said. "What does a First Lady do after the White House? The most vivacious of them all, Jackie Kennedy, married a billionaire. I've already done that." She waved her hand in the air. "I need to figure something else out."

She opened the front door. Her car had arrived. She hugged Vivienne and looked at Noah. They'd continued to be cool toward each other since their shopping excursion. "Are you coming?"

"I'm staying with Grandmother," he said.

"She's not your grandmother!" Milicent started to lose her composure but regained it quickly and snapped her mouth shut.

"Well, that may be true, but Italy is good for my soul—and my wardrobe," he said.

She covered her hurt feelings and slammed the door without another word.

She'd returned to the States during a rainy week in June. Harsh thunder had rolled across the sky every day since she'd been back. The rain seemed odd, almost iridescent, and she knew things were shifting again. The beauty in the colorful rain made her cranky.

She'd spent a few days getting reacquainted with her massive estate, the place she had named Neshoba. Most of the six-person staff spent their time with the horses. The horses seemed to accept handlers much easier with Milicent off property.

She was avoiding Rosen, but she quickly grew bored at the house and couldn't even drum up interest in riding. On her fourth day home, she ventured to the carriage house that had become a storeroom. All of her East Wing office furniture from the White House, the furniture that had taken Noah months to obtain, now sat in piles. Among the furniture sat a coffin-like contraption she hadn't seen in years.

"My hypobaric chamber!" she squealed. She removed its tarp and spent the greater part of the day clearing the area around the chamber. Twenty years earlier, it had been her first foray into the world of eternal youth. Oxygen was vital to keeping skin looking young.

Her cleaning done, Milicent peered out the door of the carriage house to see if any of the handlers were around. When she thought she was alone, she hopped in and quickly fell asleep. It was her first good nap in decades.

The chamber quickly became her new obsession; she was in it constantly for over a week. She would have brought it into the house, but it was impossible to move on her own and she didn't want to ask for help.

After she had sufficiently indulged in the rejuvenation sleep brings, she admitted to herself that she needed a job. She'd have to go to Rosen.

She dressed in her finest purple linen suit and sauntered into the Quine, ready to resume her post as head of Equine Management at Rosen. The dean was eager to have her back.

Her first day, she spent most of her time staring at the computer screen or out the window. She was alone. Her husband was gone; her son was gone. Noah was gone. Everyone she'd thought she loved was gone. She didn't know what this feeling was that had nagged her since she'd been back in the States. As she stared out the window, a small voice inside her named the foreign feeling . . . loneliness.

She shook it off and sat back down in her purple leather chair. She didn't make any movement toward working.

She stared at the ornate features decorating her office. "It's overdone," she said out loud. She got out of her chair and started taking down the artwork and removing the pillows from the settee and chairs. She opened the closet. It was already stuffed with spare pillows for seasonal updating. She slammed the closet door. Her heart was beating faster than she'd ever felt it, and the thought of a panic attack entered her mind. "Anxiety is a fallacy," she said to herself, now mad at her bodily reactions. She swung open her office door and tossed all of the pillows into the hallway.

"Redecorating already?" Noah asked, catching the last one in his hand. He looked around at the bare walls and the curtains lying on the floor.

Her heart leapt to see him but she refused to show it. "I thought you were making Italy your new home?" she said, her back turned. She headed toward her chair of command. She felt in control in that chair.

"The rainy season started," he said. "It was dreadful. On the fifth straight day of no sun, I decided to pack it in." He glanced toward the window. "Although I see I brought it back with me."

"Ah, well, do you expect to just come back here and be welcomed home like the prodigal son?"

"Face it, Mil, I'm all you've got," he said.

"Fine," she said. "You can have the office next door, but truthfully, Noah, I don't know how long I'll be here. It's boring as hell."

"That's because I haven't been here," he said. "Everything's looking up now. Except the weather."

She sat back in her chair and folded her arms. "No, it's just a small life here. I feel this is a step backward."

He thought for a moment. "Maybe it's just a pause. You're a full-throttle kinda gal, and maybe this is a forced respite before your next chapter."

Milicent pressed the intercom. "Suki!"

Seconds later, Suki appeared in the doorway. "You barked, ma'am?" All visible fear of Milicent seemed to have vanished.

Milicent ignored her comment. "I need a debrief of all the goings on since I've been away."

"Yes, ma'am, and then I have some news," Suki said.

"Debrief first," Milicent said.

"Truthfully, it's been quiet—almost boring, actually. I've tried to keep myself busy since Skylar's been gone. The staff is pretty on top of the stable. The horses are thriving. I've been through the whole library, did some organizing and tidying. Haven't seen the dean much."

Milicent studied Suki as she drilled her fingertips on the desktop. "Organizing?"

"Yes, many of the scrolls and manuscripts were out of order, so I fixed them."

"How could you tell?" Milicent asked.

Suki didn't answer.

Milicent bounced out of her chair. "Come with me," she said to them both.

The three of them rode the elevator to the basement in silence. Suki opened her mouth twice but no words came out.

The dim light of the Quine library gradually grew brighter as they entered. "Why did you ever care to dig into the National Archives when you had all this at your fingertips?" Noah asked.

"There's always more secrets out there, Noah," Milicent said. "And they're scattered all around the globe." She turned to Suki. "Show me what you've done here."

"I didn't remove anything, just reorganized," Suki said. "You had some manuscripts in the wrong location, wrong time frame. I put everything in chronological order within each geographical location. And I created an index. It will be much easier to find things now."

Milicent gave her a hard look. "The majority of these are incomprehensible. How did you read them?"

Suki shrugged. "At first I couldn't read anything and just enjoyed looking at them, but then it was as if I was remembering them, not as documents but as living things that I could understand without actually reading the language. I know that sounds crazy." She walked over to Ancient Egypt and pulled a papyrus tied with a thin braided rope. She unrolled it and placed it on the research desk. "This is the actual original of the Egyptian Book of the Dead. The proper name is *Book of Becoming*."

"Yes, I know that," Milicent said. "It's one of my favorites."

"You can read this, Mil?" Noah asked.

She frowned. "No, I've had a translated spell book since I was a teenager. I've always been searching for immortality. I'm counting on curiosity to keep me young, because I certainly haven't found it any other way." She brushed at the loose skin on her neck with her manicured fingertips. "And I've spent the last thirty years diving into many things that almost worked. But it's always eluded me."

"Well," Suki continued, "I found that if I sat with the works for a bit, I could hear them, feel their energy, absorb what they were trying to tell me." She took Noah's hand and placed it on the parchment. "Close your eyes and feel the paper. Listen and tell me what you hear."

Noah obliged and waited for a second or two, then opened his eyes. "Nothing." He pulled his hand away.

"You have to be open to it," Suki said. "It's irony at its best. This is Skylar's domain, not mine."

Milicent wandered over to the Freemason shelf and ran her hands along every spine of every book. "Let's see what I get from these," she said with anger in her voice. "Devlin still burns my ass, even after death. I was so mad when he found that genome. Science isn't supposed to find it first. Immortality belongs to the spirit realm." Her hand rested on a large volume and she got lost in thought.

"Mil," Noah said, trying to bring her back to the present moment, but she held up her hand to silence him. Information was descending from the ethers upon Milicent's brain and she wanted to pay enough attention to catch it.

She started to pace. "Noah, why did Devlin's lab find that genome?"

He stood confused. "He was a billionaire and had the funding to dig deep."

"Yes, or . . . he knew where to look because he had Magus feeding him information not from this world. From *my* world, my magical world!" She was angrier than before. "Science didn't find immortality first. He had supernatural help. I knew it!" She pushed aside the sliding bookcase and stared at the alchemical door.

"Ohh, where are we going?" Noah asked with childlike enthusiasm.

"Not sure yet, but it's high time I used this thing," she said.

"You've never walked through it?" he asked.

"No, I'm not certain I can. It only works for true alchemists. I never considered myself one of those."

"With all the magic you've done?" he asked.

"True alchemists look to transform their inner being," she said. "I've never been interested in inner transformation."

"Yet here you are," he said. "I'd say you are very transformed from the day I met you."

She shrugged off his comment and opened the door. Blackness awaited. She leaned in and reached her arm across the threshold. "Yeow." She pulled it back. "Terrible static electricity." She rubbed her arm to get it off. "I'm going to need a plan and a set of directions for this thing."

"I've been through it," Suki said quietly from the front of the room.

Milicent turned and looked at her with a gaze that bore right through her skull. "What did you say?"

"I've . . . been through it. More than once." Suki cringed, expecting Milicent to be angry at such a breach.

"Tsk, tsk," Noah said.

"Shut up, Noah," Milicent said, angry with him, not Suki. "Where did you go?" Milicent asked with pure curiosity.

"Well, I went back in time to Silverwood, and returned from there. Then I used the door at the cabin to go with Skylar to the Underworld."

Milicent walked toward Suki, her eyes wide. "Did you meet my sister?"

Suki's face turned bright red, which was a feat given her naturally olive complexion. "Yes, she's quite lovely."

"Why haven't you told me this?" Milicent asked.

A whoosh of air came out of Suki's mouth. "There's been a lot going on."

Milicent closed the distance between them and studied Suki's face. She grabbed her chin, opened her mouth, and peered inside. "I don't see alchemist in you." She pulled the skin down under Suki's eye to expose her inner eyelid. "No." She shook her head. "No sign."

"Well, I did go through with Skylar once. I'm sure she's the alchemist."

"All the times or just one time?" Milicent asked.

"One time," Suki said.

"Then no. It's you. So interesting."

Noah took the liberty of poking Suki's cheek with his finger. She swiped at his hand.

"It appears we have a way in," Milicent said, walking back to the door.

"All due respect, ma'am, why do you want to go?" Suki asked.

A mix of emotions flooded the older woman's face in a matter of seconds. "I have unfinished business with my sister, that's all."

"I understand," Suki said. "Loss severs the timeline we think we have with those we love. I'm happy to help you get there."

Milicent paused. "Thank you," she said curtly and nodded once. She closed the door and covered it back up with the bookcase. "I need to prepare for this. Let's plan to go in a few days."

"Well, that's my news, ma'am," Suki said. "I have to give my notice. It would seem I've been offered a job I can't turn down."

A look of betrayal came across Milicent's face. Before she could open her mouth, Suki blurted, "I've been called to the White House. Again."

"By whom?" Milicent asked, so close to Suki's face she could feel her cool breath on her skin.

"Mica Noxx."

A huff of breath poured out of Milicent's nose. "Is that so?" She shook her head. "I opened my library up to you, my private library! And now you'll be taking all of this knowledge with you in that photographic memory of yours." Noah stood behind her, scowling at Suki. "Well, I guess I can't do anything about this. When are you leaving?"

"I have to be settled there by the solstice," Suki said.

"Of course you do," Milicent said. "Well, that speeds up our timeline then. Be ready to do this tomorrow."

That took Suki aback. "I need a bit of time as a refresher . . ."

Milicent continued to scowl at her.

"Yes, ma'am."

"What should I wear, Mil?" Noah asked, breaking the tension.

"You are not going," Milicent said.

Noah took one step backward, a horrified expression on his face.

"Don't give me that look. Suki will have enough to handle getting me to the right place. She can't be burdened with you too."

This was the closest thing to a compliment Suki had ever received from Milicent.

Noah pursed his lips but said nothing.

"Tomorrow it is," Suki said optimistically. "I may stay here to get myself reacquainted with the door, if you don't mind."

Milicent waved her off, already heading for the exit. She stopped at the simple metal research desk near the door. The Book of Sophia sat upon it. "It's in worse shape than ever," she said. "I don't know how to fix that." She opened it. The Sanskrit words shone brightly, as if hovering above its pages. "Still can't read it, either." She sighed and looked at Suki.

Suki nodded apologetically.

"Of course you can," Milicent said.

Noah looked over Milicent's shoulder and she let him. "It's beautiful," he said.

Suki suspected he was just trying to be relevant to the conversation.

Milicent shut the book and she and Noah walked out of the library.

"I'm going to walk through that door and see Diana," Milicent said in disbelief as she and Noah stepped onto the elevator. "I've been trying to do this for decades. And it's really going to happen."

"I am compelled to remind you that Grandmother made it seem like this was a bad idea," Noah said.

"She thinks everything is a bad idea," she said. "I had hoped for her permission, but instead I will ask her forgiveness."

"Hmm," Noah said. "Mil, why do you want to do this so badly? I know she died and all, but that was so long ago, and not to be harsh but everyone has death in their lives. Devlin died. Do you want to see him?"

"God no," she said. "I just . . . loved her more than anyone else on the whole planet, and she is eternally nineteen in my mind. And I feel like there's so much left unsaid between us. I've had no peace for all these years."

"Gosh, Mil, I get it," he said. "I'm sure that's how most people feel when they lose someone too early. But the rest of the world doesn't plan to visit their relatives in the Underworld. They find other ways to cope. I think you just need some tools to deal with loss."

"If you haven't noticed by now, Noah, I'm not the rest of the world. These *are* my tools," she said. "I've found my new project." Her mood lifted instantly as they stepped out into the executive offices. "Leave me be. I'm meeting the dean in ten minutes."

18

After returning to the shores of Atlantis on the back of their new whale friend, Skylar and Argan made their way to the lab. Once inside, they saw technicians busy at instruments that vaguely resembled microscopes.

Joel should see this, Skylar thought. They were holographic cylinder tubes of light. The techs wore shields over their eyes. At first glance it looked like the eyewear was protective, but as Skylar observed the techs, she recalled this technology from a memory she'd forgotten she had. The glasses were a communication device. The tech could interact with the matter being examined—ask it questions with their eyes.

Skylar got closer. A desire to know more stirred in her stomach. "Hello," she said to the tech.

He stood at attention. "Hello, ma'am," he said. He appeared older than she was.

"What are you working on?"

He lifted his chin and smiled proudly. "Perfecting cancer."

Her stomach dropped. "Excuse me?"

"What are you doing, Sky?" Argan asked. "We've got to go."

"In a minute," she said.

"Here, I'll show you," the tech said, motioning for her to put on the glasses.

She obliged, and once she did was transported dimensionally

into the matter being examined. She took off the glasses immediately and returned to the room.

"Is this virtual reality?" she asked.

"What's that?" he asked.

"Never mind," she said. "Continue." She put the glasses back on and braced herself. The ugliness of her surroundings was brutal but she wanted to get to the truth. She breathed out her mouth to steady her nerves.

"Are you filling this matter with fear?" she asked.

"Kinda," he said sophomorically.

"Why?" she asked.

He paused for a moment to think. "Those were my orders," he eventually said.

"That's it? You never thought to question those orders?" she asked.

"No one questions the Archer," he said.

She took in a deep breath and returned to view the specimen. *This is cancer*, she thought. With the glasses on, she was consumed by the material. Her only saving thought was that this was all simulated. She could remove the glasses at any time, or so she hoped. For the moment, instead of turning away, she leaned in to the experience.

"Come on, Sky," Argan said, tugging at her clothes. "We don't have time for this."

She didn't look up. "This shit has affected my life for years and I'm not moving."

"I can't wait for you," he said and left for the Sanctuary.

She hardly noticed he'd left. Everything in her view was caked with corroded, black-and-brown-marbled globs of fat. She reached out with her hand to touch it, clairsentiently. *Greasy.* And the stench was intolerable; she had to breathe through her mouth. "What are you?" she asked.

In her mind, she heard the answer: "*I am the result of a long history of hatred. As long as man has walked the planet, there has been hate toward one another, there has been hatred toward the self. When hate perpetuates, I am allowed to grow. My darkness overtakes the light, and when enough light has been extinguished from the cells, the body dies.*"

"Why are you facilitating this monster?" she asked the technician.

"Oh, we're not," he said. "Mankind is doing that on its own on all the timelines. There has only been one time period of peace and that was even before us. We're just refining what humanity has created." He grinned. "The Archer is the Lord of Karma. You know this."

"I do now," she said.

"Cancer is very patient. It can wait for centuries, across time-lines, but it is the seed of hate, waiting. When the karma of a soul comes due, it sprouts. We're just looking to use it at will—on our timeline, not its timeline."

Skylar thought of Cassie and ran out of the lab toward the Sanctuary.

Argan was waiting when Skylar stepped into the room. She approached the mirror.

Magda wasted no time with greetings. "You won't have this mirror to run to much longer," she said back to Skylar's reflection.

"This is important and I need an accurate answer," Skylar said.

"You know the answer," Magda said. "Just like Cassandra knew. She knew her whole life that she would have to pay the karmic debt of unknown lifetimes of hate. The Great Mothers and their kin are not above emotion. They like to think so, but they are the most volatile of beings."

"I always thought she could have been saved," Skylar said. "Modern medicine, what they're keeping from us . . ."

"That is one point of view I won't deny, but remember one vital key: the darkness is always serving the light. Cancer is no different. It runs much deeper than what technology can fix, as it is the reaping of the history of man's hatred of others and of self. Love's healing, on the other hand, occurs on an individual and a global level. It is absolute. If a person can truly eradicate cancer from their cells, they have helped heal the wound of the collective by opening to the flow of love. But here's the other side of it"—she smiled at her secret—"if they don't extinguish the cancer, and they die, they still fulfill that healing. They still help the light. For then the karma is cleared and the collective heals just the same. Those left behind mourn and feel despair, yes, but please know in your true heart, Divine Skylar, that your loved one made the ultimate sacrifice for you. She died so you could live free. Through your pain, you were broken open to love's light. You didn't see it that way at first, but you feel the stirrings of understanding now about what cancer truly is. It is the ultimate price but also the ultimate redeemer. Either way, perceived win or loss, those who carry cancer are your true angels, transmuting the hate most are too blind, or too afraid, to see."

Given the gift of higher understanding of the disease that had tormented her for years, Skylar wept and touched the mirror, trying to touch Magda's face. Through her tears, she smiled. "I can't believe I'm saying this." She crossed her arms and hugged herself, suddenly chilled. "But I don't think there is anything you can teach me that would be greater than this."

"Then this is where I leave you, Divine Skylar. I was only waiting for your say so," Magda said. "You don't need me anymore. Call on your own abilities. They are stronger than mine.

You carry the magic of the human heart." She smiled and faded from the mirror.

Skylar touched the cold glass on the wall again, knowing it would be the last time she saw Magda.

Argan put his arms around Skylar. "I'm sorry, Sky. That was . . . I don't know what that was."

"I know, but good, it was good. A revelation." She didn't have the words to describe the indescribable that was in her heart. "Let's get back to work." She squeezed his hand and started looking through the books along the wall. "I need to know what a lodestone is. Sophia mentioned that's the technical name for my heart light."

Argan joined her in scanning the books. "How about geology?" he asked. He pulled out a textbook and handed it to her.

"Great. I'll go with that," she said. She flipped through. Rocks and crystals dotted the pages. She scanned the glossary for *lodestone* and turned to its page.

Lodestone: Naturally magnetized rock.

"Hmm," she said. She had expected more magic than magnets. Before she closed the book, the gem pictured below the definition caught her eye. It was her heart light, whole and perfect, sitting in the center of a golden crown.

"Wow, Lucifer's crown, just like Ocean said! I almost thought she was making that up." The picture was drawn very primitively. It didn't make her heart leap or give her any sense of direction. "It's hard to believe we're doing all this to get a piece of jewelry back to its rightful owner."

"We're doing more than that," Argan said. He opened the drawer of the desk to get the stone and got a funny look on his face. "What's this, Sky?" he asked, holding up a tourist map.

Skylar gaped. Argan was holding the Porta Alchemica game

Tamsyn had given her at the Salem Witch Museum. Its plastic appearance was an eyesore among the magical items in the room.

"You've got to be kidding me," she said, turning back to the empty mirror. She didn't even see her own reflection in it, only Argan's, off to the side.

She picked up the map and shook it in the air. "Thanks a lot," she said into the ethers.

"What's up?" Argan asked. He peered out the window, then looked back at her. "I don't know how much more time we have, Sky. Can this map help us?"

"This isn't a map," she said. "It's a toy. I got a bunch of them at the Salem Witch Museum last year."

"Have you ever looked at this thing?" he asked.

"Nope," was her one-word answer before she rambled on about having to do everything on her own.

He took the map in his hands and began to pace in the sunlight. Five minutes into her tirade about self-sacrifice, he cut her off. "Yes, Sky, you're the hero. Now look at this." He showed her the map. "This is a map of your journey. Your quest, your purpose, whatever you want to call it, look . . ."

"Give it to me." She held out her hand and he placed the map in her outstretched palm. "Okay, well. I never paid any attention to this thing. I have a half dozen of them back home."

"Something tells me this one's different," he said.

She looked at the colorful drawings. It was a map of all of her travels in the last three years, rendered in glorious detail. It showed Rosen and Ocean's crazy mansion, the black tree prominent in the backyard. Joel's farm, Cassie's tiny tree house. Beatrice's house, flanked by her magical maple. She couldn't help but smile at the places she'd been. Not all of them held fond memories, but here, laid out as a whole picture, it all fit together perfectly, and she appreciated all of it.

Farther north, among dark green triangles, the map showed the details of the long road leading to Silverwood. The camp was intricately detailed, with the Mess, the Greenhouse, and the Pavilion, and even Cabin 3A and Argan's cabin, where they had finally made love after two years of failed starts. Off in the distance, the alchemist's cabin was decorated post-equinox with lush greenery and flowers.

She looked up at Argan. He had been by her side through all of it. And so had Suki. She scoured the East Coast, hoping for a clue as to what her best friend was up to. Her eyes traveled to Washington, DC. She was probably formulating a rescue.

She looked across the page, effectively across the Atlantic, to Italy and Greece. One beautiful woman stood on the shore of a Greek island. It was Leonora. Her long, jet-black hair blew in the breeze. She remembered the dream she'd had of Leonora, and how she had a promise to fulfill—to help Leonora's son as much as he'd helped her.

The picture of Italy pulsed with ancient and future energy. Skylar sensed Milicent was there, or maybe had been, she couldn't tell which. Vivienne's tree glowed fluorescent under the water. Skylar's eyes followed its roots down into the earth's core and over toward the landmass marked Atlantis. Argan pointed to the island. "This is where we are now."

"Yes." She humored the exercise.

"Now look," he said, holding the map up to the sunlight streaming through the window. The sunbeam revealed more under the sea. The mountain of Atlantis was actually one of two pieces of land that were connected under the Atlantic.

Skylar gasped. "Oh my god, it's the Underworld. The land Magus is looking for is so close, literally next door."

"And look in the middle," he said.

Skylar squinted and made out a very small, primitive drawing of Sophia's temple. "The Underworld is on the other side of Sophia's temple," she said. "We have to go past her to get there. Heather told me Magus said it was Hell and to never go there. He's been looking for the citrine wall all this time, but it's beyond the land he dare not go, the land of the heart." She bubbled with excitement.

"One thing I don't understand," he said.

"One?"

"Why is Lucifer in the Underworld, why not here?" he asked.

"Ocean said he's been trapped in earth, in carbon form, since the *Fall*, and as punishment he has shrouded the hearts of man with evil. The Underworld is earthy as it gets. And the citrine wall is the storehouse for all human potential. Magus has tried his best to re-create the heart of Sophia, but it's synthetic. Look at this place: It's a fantasyland. All the crystal technology has an emptiness without Sophia's heart. This place, this world of *Atlantis*, is the left path, the mind. The right path is Sophia's, the way of the heart." She studied the map again. "We have what we need now, both halves of the stone. We can return it to his crown and set him free."

"Can we?" he asked. "You don't have a clue how to get that out of your chest."

"It floated effortlessly out of Rhia because it was time. We have to believe that when it's time, it will release itself from me too."

"Say that happens—then what? I saw Lucifer with Vivienne and he said he doesn't care about the stone. That it's not as valuable as it once was."

"I'm skeptical that his words were true," she said. "The Underworld is our next stop."

They made their way back down the hill to the beach.

"Where has Magus been?" Argan asked.

"I don't know," Skylar said.

"I mean, you could just leave and this would be over," he said.

"Would it?" she asked.

He shook his head. "No, I guess it wouldn't."

They got to the shoreline. "It would be so much easier if we could use that alchemical door," she said. "Of all the things I can't do . . ." She put two fingers in her mouth and blew, as if whistling for a taxi.

The kelpie returned to give them a ride.

"I don't know," Argan said. "I like this way better."

"Hop on," Skylar said.

Together, they rode toward the *right* city.

They passed Sophia's temple and the dwellers muttering to themselves. The kelpie splashed, diving up into the air and then back down into the water, and seemed to enjoy the journey as much as his passengers. It was joyous despite the uncertainty of the destination.

The familiar shore of the Underworld appeared in view. When they got to the shallows, Skylar and Argan hopped off of the kelpie, expecting him to swim away, but he stayed close to shore.

"Do you think we'll see Diana?" Skylar asked.

"I saw her briefly a few days ago when I was practicing Porta travel with Vivienne," he said.

"Hopefully she'll be happy to see us," she said.

"I'm not convinced she's ever happy," he said.

They entered the familiar cathedral, and the throne room was empty.

"Hello?" Skylar called out. "She should be here. I don't think she ever gets to leave."

The regal panther all too familiar to Argan sauntered in. Skylar froze, but Argan seemed relaxed. The big cat circled him. He bent to pet her and she nuzzled his hand with her snout. A loud, affectionate huff came out of her nose.

"This is nauseating," Lucifer said behind them. The cat regained her aloof composure and returned to his side.

"Hello, Lucifer," Skylar said, almost bowing but not quite. "Is Diana here?"

"She's always here," he said dryly.

"I mean, will we be seeing her today?" she asked.

"Probably not, you won't be staying long," he said.

"We've figured it out, Argan and me," she said, pulling Argan close to her side. "We know you're trapped here, and we have a way of setting you free."

"Is that so?" he asked. "I happen to like it here."

"You're fooling no one," she said. "This whole time—meaning all of eternity—you showed humanity the darkness by being its shadow. Now you must bring the light back."

"I thought that was your job," he said.

"The time of savior worship is over. And the church has used the diversion of the devil for long enough. You are not responsible for humanity's downfall. The bad guys, the good guys—we walk a fine line. It's easy to forget, but the shadow is always serving the light, and now we command *you* to serve the light."

Lucifer burst into a fit of laughter. "You command me? Why would I follow your command?"

"Because we have this," Argan said, his hand outstretched. His half of the stone shone brightly from his palm.

Lucifer peered into Argan's palm like a child mesmerized by a new toy. He quickly regained his look of indifference, however, and turned his head away. "As I said before, I have no interest in the gem. It is a fraction of what it once was, what it once meant," he said. "The world has moved on from the beliefs of the ancients. A silly stone, whole or not, will never matter now."

Skylar faltered. "So why am I here?" she asked. "I was dragged into this world against my will, after being told that I had to heal this stone to get you the hell off our planet. And now I'm more in the dark than ever."

"No one is dragged into anything. You can step out of victim mentality any time you're ready. But I am aware that Magus has his own agenda and his own beliefs," he said. "He's been chasing that stone for an epoch, all the while trying to get somewhere that is so close to him, yet he is blind to it. The whole thing is quite amusing, actually."

"Doesn't Magus work for you?" Skylar asked.

"He did at one time. It was a case of reaping what I sowed. Even I can't escape it. As I did to the creator, Magus did to me. He wanted the power for himself. He wants what the stone will never give him—*the power of the human heart.*"

Lucifer's words rang in Skylar's mind. An image of him as holy as God himself came to her awareness. He was the light, a shining angel as bright as an angel could shine. But he wanted to be like man, like humans. The humans had the spark of divine within them. They held the God particle in the human heart. Angels do not have that. They were magnificent in other ways but did not have the God particle within them. He felt a pang of jealousy for what the humans had, and he wanted to come to earth and experience what it was like to be a man. He wanted to be God in form. But it was a mistake. He was missing the crucial component, that which lies in the human heart: love.

Lucifer clearly did not enjoy having Skylar in his head; he changed the subject. "Magus will return to the US. He's clinging to control there, but it is futile. Systems have been broken, karma must be balanced. That country was destined to be the new Atlantis, but corruption by its leaders has put it on an obsolete timeline. The US is due for a reckoning of its history. But that's not your concern." He walked to the scales of truth. With a feather on one pan, the other empty, they were balanced, ready and waiting to judge another soul.

"I will let you in on a secret, Skylar. The whole reason why you're here. And not just here"—he gestured to the cathedral—"but the greater here, this long and arduous journey."

Skylar's eyes widened.

"You are here to do what Vivienne couldn't. You are her kin and this is the end of one era and the beginning of another. Consider it a window, an opportunity. She could not stop Magus the first time. She can't do it now. That is why you are here: to create a different outcome. But it will have a cost. Vivienne is immortal. You are not. A sacrifice must be made. That is true of all hero's quests." Skylar assumed he was talking about death. "But before then, find the child."

A feeling of certainty swept through Skylar. "I have to find the nursery, Argan."

"What nursery?" he asked.

"The nursery of souls."

19

Skylar's mind raced as she bolted down the corridor of the fourth floor.

"I know it's here, Argan," she called over her shoulder. "I saw it in so many of my dreams. The children! We have to help the children. It's an opportunity to choose again. It's our baby, Argan, I know it!"

"Our baby?" Argan asked in a confused tone.

"The girl, the baby Sophia showed us. She is the child Lucifer meant." Skylar was confident.

Argan looked skeptical but kept following her. She grabbed at each knob she passed. They were all locked, as before.

"Which door?" Argan asked.

"This one," she said, stopping at the familiar door. Again it was locked. She shook it profusely.

He exhaled, as if to keep calm. "Sky, you are going on really sketchy information. Stop and think for a moment." He grabbed her arm and she stopped shaking the doorknob. "Who has the keys?"

"I have no idea, Argan." The voices in her head rushed back, and she squeezed her temples with the palms of her hands.

"Kyle," he said. "Kyle has the keys."

Argan was hardly gone before he came back with a key ring with one old-fashioned key on it.

"That was fast," Skylar said.

"I found him asleep in a chair near the tanks," he said.

"I'd love to know Magus's reason for having him here."

"I get the sense Magus thought he'd have inside information on us," Argan said. "Guess he's not so brilliant after all."

She looked at the key ring in Argan's hand. "There's only one key."

"Yeah, I don't know, we'll see," he said, trying it on an adjacent door. It worked. It was a supply closet. He tried another door. It was deceptively large, and full of animals in cages. "More things to set free." He shook his head. They closed the door and tried the next. The key worked for all of them.

When they opened the door to the nursery, Skylar was slow to recognize it. She almost shut the door without going in. It looked nothing like she remembered. Many adolescent-aged children sat hunched in folding chairs, half-asleep. The walls were dingy white, nothing on any of them but for one "Hang in There" poster taped crookedly to one wall.

Each of the kids had a bib number attached to their pajamas. A line a dozen long led into what appeared to be a doctor's office.

"What is going on?" Skylar asked Pamela. "This is very wrong."

"Oh, this is right," Pamela said with a creepy smile. "These children are about to hit puberty. We're shrinking their thymus." She acted like she was talking about a haircut.

"What?" Argan asked.

"Oh, it's standard procedure." Pamela waved off his concern. "Everyone has it done. Right about the time true self-awareness starts to solidify in a human, we shrink the thymus. It helps ease them into adulthood."

"This is the most screwed up thing I've seen yet," Skylar said.

"They don't know it's happening. You didn't know it

happened to you. It happens during the dream state," Pamela said. "They'll wake up tomorrow none the wiser."

"They're children!" Skylar snapped.

"Not really," Pamela said. "They're adolescents. Their childhood is all about gone. They won't miss their thymus." She chuckled.

Skylar had no idea how to help the children there. She didn't know how to help anyone here.

"Fifty-three?" Pamela called out to the group, and a thin girl with pin-straight hair stood up.

Skylar didn't fully understand what shrinking the thymus meant, but she knew in her gut that any manipulation of the human body like this was unnatural. "Don't go in there!" she shouted to the girl.

The girl just looked through Skylar and entered the exam room door.

"No use," Pamela said. "They don't see you."

"They have to see me, my son saw me before," Skylar said.

"Again, this is the dream state. But you have to ask yourself: Was it your son's dream, or yours?"

Skylar started to panic. "He was real! As real as right now, as real as you . . ." she gasped. *Is Pamela real?* She was another woman, here in Atlantis, saved from being thrown in those tanks. *Is any of this real?* She was losing her grip on reality; she looked at Argan for grounding.

"Your son?" Argan asked.

Skylar winced. "Oh, Argan." She ran her hands through her hair. "I never told you . . . we were apart last year and then when we weren't, there was never a good time . . ."

"To tell me you had a son?" Argan asked calmly.

"Well, yes and no." She paused, now unsure of any of her past. It was all blurring with the experiences she was having now, and she couldn't differentiate any of it. "I had a pregnancy. And then I came here, I thought in a dream, but now I'm confused. And I met him." Her eyes lit up with love. "I met a sweet mophead of a toddler, and he was an angel. But then the pregnancy ended."

Argan's face saddened.

"It all happened at the insane beginning of this whole ordeal. Rhia died soon after and we were apart, and . . ." She stopped and looked at him. "It really doesn't matter. I am sorry to not have told you."

"Joshua?"

"Yes."

"Wow. Okay." His face wore confusion. He shook his head as if to try to shake it from his mind—and quickly, the darkness Magus had infused in him started to show. Skylar could see it in the veins on his arms, running through them like black ink.

"Argan, what is happening?" she asked as the ink traveled up his neck.

He backed away from her. "Something's wrong. I need a minute."

"Argan, wait!" She stepped toward him. "I want to help you."

"Don't, Sky." He ran toward the door. "I don't know how you could."

Skylar knew he had to process this information, but she had no idea what Magus had done to him. A part of her wanted to iron things out right then, but she knew that wasn't possible. She had to let him go.

"Okay," she said to an empty doorway.

He bolted down the long corridor that seemed endless. He passed Kyle, who was now awake and diligently cleaning the massive tank. Argan looked into the tank. Deep in the middle, a large, dark object caught his eye. It was a cage of sorts with thick bars of coral and kelp. Pod shaped, it looked like a clam on its side.

"Don't tell me the mermaids get put in that thing," he said to Kyle.

"I'm not sure," Kyle said.

"It's a soul cage," Heather said, walking up behind them. "It's an underwater keep, a place between worlds. The prisoner is neither here nor there but suspended out of time. If one survives the soul cage, they are forever changed. They say it's infused with the magic and wisdom from beyond time."

Argan turned to face her and she saw the black veins across his arms and face. "You aren't well. Let me examine you."

"Hell no." He shook his head and his pupils dilated quickly. He looked back at the water. "Has anyone ever survived it?" he asked. "This soul cage?"

"No," she said. "But the Archer hasn't used it in a very long time. He keeps it in there as a reminder to the mermaids of the men they lost. Those who tried to help them."

Argan looked up through the glass ceiling. The brilliant sunlight had dimmed considerably. "Something's different," he said. "The sun's lower for the first time since I've been here." He looked toward the north; the moon was rising. The sound of the running water from the fountain below drew his attention.

"The fountain." He pointed out the window. "It's running."

Heather looked down and gasped. "I've never seen that," she said worriedly. She looked in the sky. "The moon . . . I don't know what's happening."

"Something's shifting. Can I count on you to help us?" Argan asked, glancing at Kyle. But Kyle quickly picked up the hose to his pool vacuum and skulked away.

She shook her head. "I'm so sorry, but I can't. He's . . . I owe him a debt, my life, everything. I just can't."

Argan's eyes flashed a look of compassion. The darkness brewing within him seemed to subside. "I understand. He's your father. But I have to go, and please don't stop me."

She nodded. "I won't."

Argan ran to the Sanctuary, intent on hiding the stone. He passed the jeweled mirror and stopped. He was curious as to what truths he'd see. He inhaled deeply and looked—and saw his father, Giannes.

His brow wrinkled. All thoughts of the chaos outside the Sanctuary door disappeared. He was focused on the image of his father.

"You've had an extraordinary influence from your mother," his own voice said from inside his head. "She has shaped the destiny of your life. But your soul's karma is attached to your father. He is the strongest link between you and manhood. He has or has not shown you the way, how to be a man."

An image of his dad asleep in his easy chair came to mind.

"Yes, he is tired, but from a lifetime of honest work. This is who he is."

Argan always thought their lives should have been more. His mother wanted more for him than physical work and exhaustion.

"Do you not think your father had a happy life?" his own voice continued.

Argan didn't answer. He honestly didn't know.

"His happiness came from the belief that he was caring for his family. You were taken care of, so he was happy."

"Was he, though?" he said aloud. He remembered Giannes as the man who cared for other people's properties, never his own. His father had always seemed to feel he had something to prove.

"Or was that you?" his voice asked him. "You've trained for this quest like it's your life's purpose, and maybe it is. Saving the world is a hero's journey. But maybe your life's quest is to simply be proud of your heritage and know your father is worthy of ten kingdoms of gold."

Argan grew angry. "What does any of this have to do with where we are now?" he demanded of his own reflection.

"This is the end of things. Timelines are collapsing and the physical world is moving forward into the Golden Age. This is the last chance for individuals to release the burdens they carry. Whether you know it or not, you carry this burden."

He shook his head.

"I will leave you to your thoughts, but I'll ask you, why would I ever tell you something that wasn't true?" He stared into his own eyes. They were his mother's. He always saw his mother in his reflection. She'd been the light of his life for so long. Until Skylar.

He looked away, annoyed that he was confronted with this right now. When he looked back, he took a step closer to the mirror. The slight lines on his face did transform him into a young Giannes.

"If you can release this, you will help release the collective pain of fathers and sons."

"There is nothing to release," he barked, surprised by his own anger. He stared a bit longer and tears filled his eyes. He shook his head in denial. "No." He turned away from the mirror and walked to the window.

The men below were marveling at the water flowing from the fountain. The moon was now high in the sky. It was time to end this. Argan tucked the velvet pouch in the desk drawer. Before he left, he glanced at the map on the desk. It showed him a secret everyone else had overlooked. But there it stood, in plain sight.

He ran out of the Sanctuary so quickly, he forgot to close the door.

20

The voices of the past came roaring back into Skylar's head, and she was too overwhelmed to stop them. All she could do was rub the pulsing pain in her temples with the palms of her hands.

The door swung open and Magus walked through. "Pamela, round up all of these juveniles and take them in the back. This process is taking too long."

"Yes, sir." Pamela made a quick announcement and the room of teens followed her through the back door like zombies.

Magus stood in front of Skylar. He tapped her on the forehead and her mind quieted. She wasn't about to thank him.

"You're welcome anyway. I need you to be clearheaded," Magus said. With a flip of his hand, he changed their surroundings. Skylar was left standing in the row of bassinets that had been there in her dream. All of the children were sleeping peacefully. She scanned the rows; one little soul shone brighter than the rest. She ran to her son. He slept on his belly, his arms and legs tucked under him, his bottom high in the air. She smiled and rested her hand on his back. She wasn't crazy. This was real. She could feel his soul. She could feel his dreams. She could feel his connection to God. She was also acutely aware that even though she hadn't carried him in her world, he lived on in another. She was instantly filled with panic. What would Magus do to him? And the rest of the children?

Sophia had warned her to keep the children out of her head. Magus was manipulating her with her own mind.

"Follow me," Magus said.

Skylar tried to resist but found she didn't have a choice. He overpowered her with his forceful energy. He led her out of the room and down the hall, back to the aquatic tank. She looked up at the sky through the glass ceiling. The moon was bright. Its presence clearly aggravated Magus.

As Skylar approached the tank, she saw a dark figure submerged in the water. It was not a mermaid. The soul cage was now closer to the edge, in prime view. Argan was within it. He was floating, but not lifeless. The rays of the moonlight streamed down, illuminating him, godlike.

"The soul cage is a perfect place for him," Magus said. "Out of harm's way."

"Is he . . ." Skylar hated to ask.

"Dead? No. More like suspended between worlds. His heart isn't beating, but it doesn't have to be in the soul cage."

Skylar seethed at Magus for trapping Argan.

"Oh, I didn't put him there," Magus said. "It would seem he is there of his own accord. But I did come across this." He held up the velvet bag by its string. "How odd it was to see an entrance to that quaint room. I always thought it was a supply closet. I guess even I still have things to learn." He chuckled dryly.

Skylar scowled. *What did he do to the Sanctuary?* The answer would have to wait. "You want the stone for Argan's life," she said. *Sacrifice.* She was being called to sacrifice her life for Argan's. That's what this came to. This whole crazy story she wasn't convinced was a dream.

Argan had come to her rescue many times. And now she would come to his.

"Don't blame yourself for this ending," Magus said. "Blame Ocean. Your life would be so different if it weren't for her. She had ancient wrongs to right and you were a pawn in the game.

Release the stone because it was never yours in the first place. You should want to be rid of it and take your life back."

"I haven't found a way to do that!" Anger welled within her. She couldn't release the stone.

"You've never tried," Magus said. "You've held on to your beliefs about it and about yourself. You've kept yourself small on purpose somewhere deep within you, thinking that stone makes you special and without it you're nothing. And you're right."

"A stone, no matter its greatness, will never give you the power you seek," she said. "Yours is an insatiable lust, never to be fulfilled. Love is the only thing that can fill that void."

"That's what I'm counting on," he said. "Love will release the half within your chest."

Magus turned and walked down the corridor. Heather ran toward them and he handed the velvet bag to her. She took a step toward Skylar, but stopped and shook her head.

The mermaids were spinning feverishly around Argan. Skylar climbed the metal staircase to the top of the tank. She saw the mermaids trying to pry the coral bars open to release him, but they couldn't. She glanced down at Heather, and saw sympathy show briefly on her face.

Skylar dove into the water. She swam to Argan, and the mermaids gave her room to try to free him. She pulled at the bars, but they were as strong as iron. She tried her hand at conjuring energy. She managed a small ball of blue light, but it did nothing but dissipate into the water. She squeezed an arm through the bars and touched Argan's shoulder. He was so peaceful, floating, perfectly preserved. A mermaid swam closer. Skylar froze. It was the one she had seen her very first day. This close to her, Skylar could see the defiance in her eyes.

"Our bodies may be imprisoned, but our hearts are free," Skylar heard in her head. *"Your body is free, but your heart is imprisoned."*

The mermaid placed her hand over Skylar's chest and she felt a jolt. She dared think it was a dislodging.

"*Can you take the stone out of me?*" she asked with her thoughts.

The mermaid smiled. "*It isn't as hard as you think. When you set your heart free, the stone will be free as well.*"

Skylar nodded.

The mermaid circled Argan and stopped in front of him. "*Even in his stillness, I see his confusion. He questions who he is supposed to be. He's done everything right, done everything asked of him—by the Goddess, by his mother, by you. He is the prince yet he struggles, feeling short of the goal. He feels slighted, wronged somehow, and doesn't know how to express it.*" She looked at Skylar. "*This is not the Archer's doing. Your lover locked himself in this cage. He waits in the space between worlds. He will find what he seeks there.*"

"I understand," Skylar said. She touched the bars restraining Argan and swam to the top of the water. Heather reached one hand down and helped her out.

"Thanks." Skylar locked eyes with Heather for just a moment. Then she darted down the stairs and past Magus, headed toward the Sanctuary.

21

A faint knock sounded on Vivienne's front door at 10:00 p.m. "Leonora, you are ahead of schedule," Vivienne said, greeting her. "I wasn't expecting you until tomorrow."

Leonora rushed by Vivienne into the apartment. Her cloak was soaked through from the heavy rain. "I'm sorry to ring at this late hour but something is wrong," she said. "Argan has vanished from my sight. I know he's not dead. I would feel that. But he is not living either. He is between worlds, and Skylar is not strong enough to help him."

Vivienne smiled quietly and offered Leonora a seat in the parlor. "Let me fix you some tea."

"I am not interested in tea, Vivienne. I know we made this happen, but this is my son!" Her voice rose uncharacteristically. She caught her breath and started again. "I have raised him as the Goddess asked. Now I am to throw him to the wolves?" She lowered her head. "I cannot."

"Argan wanted to do this," Vivienne said.

"Because I made it so!" She got up and walked to the open balcony. The wind whipped the rain wildly just beyond the doors, but no rain came into the room. "I bred him for this task and he accepts it as his destiny."

"It *is* his destiny," Vivienne said.

"Because I made it so," Leonora repeated in a quieter tone, ashamed of having manipulated her son his whole life to bend to the path she thought she wanted for him. Now, she was changing her mind.

"Leonora, the most important part of this is that he believes in himself and his ability to accomplish this enormous, lion-hearted task."

Leonora returned to where Vivienne was sitting and looked at her with angry eyes. "We have all done our part, Vivienne," she said. "Now it's time to do yours."

Vivienne paused, knowing there was only one answer Leonora would accept.

"You're right," she said. "I will go."

A t dawn, Suki met Milicent in the Quine library. The irony
of the situation wasn't lost on her, but sleep was. She hadn't
gotten any the night before. She was dressed normally but Milicent
was decked out in a silhouette-hugging, dark purple leather suit.
Her white hair was piled high, similar to how Vivienne wore her
hair, all wisps held back with a thin purple headband.

"It's hot where we're going," Suki said.

"I'll be fine," Milicent said.

"I assume we're only going there as a day trip?" Suki asked. "I
didn't pack anything."

"Of course," Milicent said. "I can't imagine there are any
accommodations suitable for an overnight stay."

Suki moved the bookcase aside and opened the door, as she
had done many times before. She took in a few deep breaths.
"Ready?"

Milicent's eyes widened. "No preparation?"

"I've done it already. Just take a deep breath and hold my
hand. I'll get us where we need to go." She reached out her hand
and Milicent stared at it. "It won't work unless we are connected."

"I got that," Milicent said. She took in a breath but didn't
exhale and grabbed Suki's hand.

"Sorry I'm late," Noah said from the library door. "It's just
sooo early." He stood there decked out in his finest Italian clothes,
including a silk tie.

Milicent pulled her hand from Suki's. "Noah, you aren't coming! There are too many variables and you will weigh everything down."

Noah folded his arms. "I knew you would say that. I'll just man the door while you're gone," he said.

"Fine," Milicent said. She grabbed Suki's hand abruptly. "Let's go."

"Okay, well, these moments are never calm," Suki said.

They both stepped into the blackness of a bent reality. As they stepped over the threshold, Milicent dug her talon-tipped nails into Suki's palm. Suki was unsure if it was out of spite or fear or both, but she kept her focus on the task at hand.

It wasn't long before they came out to the entrance of the cathedral, as Suki had done before. She looked at Milicent, who was trying to dust off the lucina.

"It won't come off," Suki said. "And that's a good thing. It's a protective coating."

"Oh, all right." Milicent tried to appear in control of the situation, but Suki saw through it. Milicent smoothed the wrinkles out of her leather as they walked toward the cathedral entrance. "I've been to quite a few otherworldly places," she said. "This looks about right."

They walked through a courtyard full of people going about daily tasks. When Suki reached for the door of the cathedral, Milicent took in a deep breath.

"This is a big moment," Suki said, pausing.

Milicent remained quiet.

Suki opened the door and they walked into the throne room. Diana was seated in her chair; it appeared she was in meditation.

Milicent opened her mouth to speak but no words came out. She let Suki lead, almost as if she were hiding behind her.

"Hello, Diana," Suki said softly.

Diana opened her eyes. "We have been chock full of visitors lately," she said, not getting up from her chair. "The end of the world must be near."

"Visitors?" Suki asked. "Was Skylar here?"

"I heard she was, yes," Diana said. "With that beau of hers."

"Argan!" Suki was excited, and relieved to hear he had found her. "That's the best news!" She had completely forgotten Milicent was standing there.

"Ahem." Milicent cleared her throat.

"Oh, Diana," Suki said, returning to the task at hand. "I've brought your sister this time." She stepped aside to give Milicent the floor.

"Hello, Diana. You're looking well." Milicent was reserved and cool.

Diana got up and walked to meet Milicent. Milicent stared at her as if she weren't real. "You've been getting more sleep," Diana said. "I'm glad."

"Are you kidding me?" Suki exploded. "You've been obsessed with seeing your sister for twenty years and you're talking about sleep? For God's sake, show some emotion! She's the one person you care about most in the world. Let her know that. God!" She threw her hands up and sat on a marble bench behind her.

Milicent gave Diana an awkward hug. "I'm sorry I lived."

"I'm sorry I died," Diana said. "But it was my time. I know I left you alone and the family unraveled and you had no one. I am so sorry. You must have been very angry."

Milicent tried to shake it off but it showed on her face. Diana grabbed her hand and squeezed. "Thank you for never giving up on me. All these years, you knew I was still here—that I wasn't gone forever. Persistence paid off, I guess."

"I wasn't giving up," Milicent said.

"Well, I'm glad," Diana said. "This is a gift, to be able to say what was left unsaid in the living world."

Milicent relaxed slightly and walked around the room. "I'll agree that life was a mess after you died. And I've spent the greater part of my life with a weight on my back. I want to be free like you."

Diana glanced at Suki. "I'm hardly free."

Milicent got distracted by the glowing citrine wall. "This is truly magnificent. You know all citrine was once amethyst? This wall would be better if it were purple."

Diana laughed. "I guess some things don't change."

"I know you stay neutral down here, but it's time to pick a side, Diana," Milicent said. "You know Magus is looking for the citrine wall, and you don't want him to find it any more than the rest of us. We have to figure out a way to help Skylar."

Diana looked at the wall. It had been restored to its natural brilliance thanks to Skylar. She couldn't ignore that. "Sides have been blurred throughout this story. It's merely a lesson in how malleable life is, and in not getting too attached to one's beliefs. They can change. It's better to live in the curiosity."

"No, no it isn't. That's just like you to say that, Diana, and all your lofty ideals *sound* great—but in the real world, you have to pick a side!" Milicent's switch had flipped and the magic of her surroundings dissipated.

"Mil?"

The women turned toward a familiar voice to see Noah standing at the door of the cathedral. He was full of fear, his eyes squeezed shut. "Mil, where are you?" he cried blindly, like a desperate child.

"Good god, Noah," Milicent said. "I told you not to follow us." She glared at Suki, her anger visible. "How did he get through the door?"

Suki was surprised too. "I have no idea. Maybe we didn't need to be holding hands. I'm still learning this stuff."

"It is possible he rode the energy wave still lingering in the ethers," Diana said. "He would only be able to get to wherever you went, nowhere else."

Noah opened his eyes and ran over to her side. "Thank you, sweet goddess of the Underworld, for not keeping me here in darkness," he babbled.

"All you did was open your eyes!" Milicent chided. "Diana, this is Noah."

"Great goddess of the Underworld, I am humbled to make your acquaintance." He bowed.

"Get up!" Milicent smacked him to stand upright. "She doesn't need your worship."

Diana laughed a belly laugh. "You are sweet," she said to Noah. "Be kinder to him, Milicent. He's fragile." She walked back toward the courtyard. "Since you all have made the trip, let's have some food. I'm sure the traveling took its toll on your system."

"I'd actually rather head back," Suki said. "I don't really see a reason for me to stick around. They can go back through the door without me, can't they?"

"As Noah followed once, he can follow back," Diana said. "The energy signature should carry them through."

"Should?" Noah asked. "I don't want to be stuck here. No offense, Your Queenship."

"It sounds fine," Milicent said. "Suki, you can go."

No thanks were given, sealing Suki's decision to go back.

"See you on the flip side," she said to them all and headed back toward the door.

"Suki," Milicent called after her. "Thank you."

Suki smiled, raised her hand to wave good-bye, and ran out of the courtyard.

23

"I'm not sorry," Heather said quietly, staring at the hologram of Skylar suspended lifeless in the lab. She had taken part in heinous acts, dismantling layers of this young girl's body, and *for what?* To find a way to extract the stone from her chest.

She had only come up with one way the plan worked, and it didn't end well for any of them.

She looked at all of the technology in the room. *What has it all been for?* All of this had been created so the Archer would get what he wanted. *Why is that the most important thing? What about what I want?* She'd been raised by a warrior and scientist. She'd been taught how to disconnect from her conscience and create masterpieces in the laboratory. Nothing was beyond their reach—cloning, cancer, any weapon was possible. She looked at her latest creation: the dagger with the emerald tip. This was the answer. This half of the stone, now attached to an orichalcum blade, was powerful enough to pierce the protection of the three doves and remove the stone from Skylar's chest. She loathed the three doves, how that image remained an open wound in her life. Revenge and sorrow teetered back and forth in her heart. One tear escaped her eye and she wiped it away, angrily. But Argan was a prisoner in the soul cage. She felt compassion for him, and anger. He loved Skylar too. Everyone loved Skylar. It made Heather more infuriated as she thought about it. That anger fueled her to finish the dagger.

"Hello," an unfamiliar voice said from behind her.

Heather whirled around to see an ethereal presence. Like the primordial ocean mother herself, this woman embodied the dark sea. Her long dress, rich and luxurious, was black as night. A black so dark it didn't exist in the material world. A slight shimmer of stardust undulated like waves as she walked. Her tendrils, piled high, were entwined with a thin, black-and-silver roping.

"Hello," Heather said, mesmerized.

"My, you've grown into such a beautiful young woman," the woman said. She walked toward Heather; behind her followed a train of shadows. "I could not have foretold your impeccable beauty."

Heather blushed and touched the scar on her face self-consciously. The other woman looked down at the dagger on the table in front of her. Heather quickly covered it with a cloth.

The woman glanced around the room. "I am looking for Cyril. Where can I find him?"

He stood in the doorway as if beckoned by her. "Leave us," he commanded Heather. She stood where she was, confused. The woman gave her a kind smile and Heather left the room, her head down.

"Don't pretend to be kind to her," Magus said harshly.

"I wasn't pretending," Vivienne said. "She's beautiful."

"Yes," he said curtly. The slightest hint of pride escaped in his voice.

Vivienne walked across the laboratory toward the window. The trail of shadows followed her. Magus glanced down at the spirals of dark energy behind her, then out the window. The moon was high.

"It would seem a new era has arrived," he said calmly.

"The thirteenth moon. The reign of night has come," Vivienne said. "It is the realm of the feminine. You must be so pleased."

"Water hasn't flowed in that fountain for thirteen thousand years," Magus said, staring at the fountain below.

She nodded and turned away from the window. She returned to the worktable and looked at the cloth covering the dagger. "Still clinging to worn-out plans, I see. Still shrouded in ignorance and revenge."

"Revenge was your domain," he said. "I simply want power. It's what runs the world."

"Your world, maybe," she said.

"It was your world once," he said.

"No," she said. "This was never my world, this synthetic shell. You could never replicate Sophia's world without love."

He laughed. "You don't know love any more than I do. You think you do. I don't make such pretenses."

Vivienne winced. "Your words hurt, even now, after all this time. It would seem some wounds wait unhealed, only to be ripped open again by the one still holding the knife. The life between us remained frozen, just waiting for this moment. The Dissolution is upon the world. And that includes us. We are not above it. I must face you, face our past and forgive it. I am not above the wheel of Karma."

"Karma is for the ignorant," Magus said.

"Yet here we stand, back in our same bodies, our same feelings. Thirteen millennia later, we are exactly where we were then," Vivienne said. "That sounds like karma to me. I've spent a great deal of time thinking about our relationship, Cyril. We attracted each other for different reasons. I wanted your attention. You wanted my expression, the life force that ran within me that no other could possess. Did you really believe you could own the power of the sea?"

He looked at her with intensity in his eyes, and the corner of his lip turned up slightly.

She shook her head. "I fell for that look once. I was so stupid to be so naïve, mistaking what you had to offer as love. So you're right, I do not know what love is. But you still covet the light. You've been chasing the light you wanted from me for an epoch. And you've attached its worth to that silly stone."

"Don't pretend that stone means nothing. Its energy has the ability to control the planet. It will be whole again."

Vivienne picked up the dagger within the cloth. Magus made no move to stop her. She removed the cloth and a rose-golden orichalcum blade shone brightly, its tip encrusted with one half of the emerald. She took in a deep breath. "You cling to the notion that you can erase all of the responsibility of the past with violence."

"Knowledge!" he snarled. "If arrived at through violent means, so be it. You have your own trail of casualties."

Magus stepped closer to Vivienne and she appeared to grow in size. Her blue-black aura shone off her skin, transforming her appearance into the goddess Kali.

"You never were the goddess of death," Magus said. "You embody life, and that's why I loved you."

He reached out to touch her face and she pulled away. "Where is Argan?"

Magus smiled. "He is taking a break from his duties. I think it became too much for him."

"I'm sorry this is what you've become." She spun around and strode out of the laboratory, her dark trail following.

As she walked down the hall, all the men bowed at her feet. She paid them no mind. When she reached the aquatic tank, the mermaids were already lined up, waiting for her arrival. She climbed the metal staircase and stared at the soul cage trapping Argan. She looked back at Magus, who stood at the bottom of the stairs. He was clouded in a fine, dark mist that filled the room.

She descended the stairs slowly. "I cannot help him. He is there by his own accord."

"You didn't believe me," Magus said. "This is the realm of the gods, not a playground for children. It all became too much for him. You see, Vivienne, we are shown time and time again that love does not conquer all. It is not enough to heal the betrayals of the heart."

She had heard enough. Turning on her heels, she left Magus standing alone in the great room.

S kylar stood in the Sanctuary doorway, disheartened. Magus and his goons had torn it apart. The one shred of love in this whole place was ruined. She looked on the desk. The map was gone. He knew how to get to the Underworld now. He had Argan's stone. All that stood in his way of completing all of it was the stone in her own chest.

She looked at the wall for the jeweled mirror. It had been smashed; pieces of glass lay on the floor. She knelt down and held it in her hands. She was startled by her reflection in the shattered glass: she saw her face cut in pieces—not just by the glass but by life. How similar she was to Heather, the wounds of loss sliced across her face. She touched the glass and for the first time, she had compassion for the girl staring back at her. Seeing what she carried on the inside, so emblazoned on the outside, she couldn't help but love this girl. She was able to appreciate her strength and all she'd endured.

"Life isn't meant to be endured, child," Vivienne said in the doorway. She shut the door behind her as a trail of shadows followed her into the Sanctuary. "It's meant to be embraced."

"Grandmother." Skylar stood. "How wonderful to see you. I had half expected Ocean."

"She won't set foot in this realm," Vivienne said.

Skylar saw the trail behind her. Vivienne tracked her gaze.

"As this mirror shows you the pain you carry, here in Atlantis,

I can't hide mine either." She looked around the torn-up room. "Things appear to be quite a mess, don't they?"

Skylar nodded. "But I've been in these situations before," she said.

"I've been far away but closer than you may believe," Vivienne said. "I've seen the last few years of your life unfold. You started your journey as all young women do: giving away your power to men, to misplaced desire, on the quest for wholeness. We simply don't know any other way. Only through experience is wisdom gained."

Skylar questioned if Vivienne was talking about her or herself.

"Cherish your experiences, they have made you who you are. And they have given you perspective to choose differently in the future. You have grown so much yet are still so young. Think of all that you can accomplish with this new awareness."

"Thank you, but Magus has everything," Skylar said. "All that's left is my heart light. I have to surrender it to him to get Argan back. Even if it means I die."

"That's very noble of you, child. But the Goddess doesn't require your death to fulfill your mission. She's never been fond of martyrs."

"I know Argan put himself there to escape the shit—excuse me, *trials*—I've put him through. He's tired of my immaturity."

"One may view it as immaturity, another may see it as innocence. They are vastly different perspectives of the same coin. Who gets to decide what maturity is? And then, any label of deviation is judgment. Argan didn't consciously escape to the soul cage. He didn't voluntarily imprison himself. But this land of water magnifies intention. And manifestation is almost instantaneous here. Most likely he had a passing thought and the water's answer was the soul cage." Vivienne walked to the small fountain in the room. It was broken in half. She picked up the pieces and sat them side by side. She continued to talk as she got to work repairing the statue.

"You've put your faith in your mentors, and I'm sorry we've let you down. We've done our best, but we have our limitations too. Now you have the opportunity to step into a new world, with your innate innocence in one hand and your wisdom in the other." She held the two pieces of the fountain together. "That is the path all women take. You feel sullied by your life choices. Despite your accomplishments, you only focus on your mistakes. Why is that? You yearn for a life unblemished, but no one escapes your world that way unless they never enter it."

She stopped her work and looked intently into Skylar's eyes. Skylar knew she was referring to her son.

"Souls have different journeys. Do not judge what you do not understand."

Skylar nodded.

"And do not judge Ocean. The karma you would have created with a union with Joshua could not have been undone. Your time to be a mother is ahead of you."

"Thank you for coming to help me," Skylar said.

"Oh, I'm not here for you," Vivienne said. "You've proven you're just fine on your own. I'm here to right a few of my own wrongs." She stepped back from the fountain. The goddess figure was whole again, but for a line of silver sand packed down the middle. She touched the spout and water resumed its trickle. Her shadowy trail shimmered slightly, and for a moment it resembled a tail. Skylar thought Vivienne might have been a mermaid once.

"I know about Heather," Skylar said.

"You see? No one can walk the earth unscathed by wrong deeds. Not even me."

"She's . . . interesting. I want to help her but I'm not sure how."

"You can't save everyone, Skylar. Like I said, each soul is on its own journey."

It was as if Vivienne had given her permission to exhale.

She didn't have to save everyone. Just Argan.

Skylar and Vivienne walked out of the Sanctuary.

"Don't linger, child," Vivienne said. "I'm afraid Cyril is mobilizing faster now." She walked in the direction of the lab, while Skylar headed to the aquatic tank.

The mermaids were still keeping guard over Argan.

"I appreciate you standing watch," Skylar said to them. It wasn't even odd that this interaction had become commonplace, although Skylar never wanted to lose sight of the magic inherent in these creatures. "We're going to get him out and then we'll get you out too."

"*There is no world where we exist outside of these tanks,*" one said.

"That can't be true," Skylar said. "Aren't there others like you, free in the ocean?"

"*Yes, but they are just as captive as we are, forever marred by the origin of their creation.*"

"I understand carrying the scars of the past," Skylar said. "But your beauty and the beauty of your kind deserves to be as free as possible, even if not completely. You should live with all the sovereignty the constraints of this world allow."

The mermaid gave Skylar a placating smile. She smiled too, removed her shoes, and took a knife she'd found in the lab from her pocket. She climbed the metal stairs once more and dove in, the knife gripped securely in one hand, then swam to the soul cage and sliced her forearm. She had hoped the shock of it would jar Argan, but he remained still. As the dark red fluid mixed with the seawater, it turned a bright copper bronze. As she had hoped, it attached itself to the coral and kelp bars. But it created a different outcome than she had intended. It appeared as if the coral was feeding on Skylar's blood, swelling with life, the bars growing thicker. She waited, but it didn't break the coral—it only made it stronger.

She stared at Argan as the moonlight shone down into the water. She could see him being fortified with the energy. His aura expanded to the most brilliant green.

The mermaids could see it too. They floated back to give it room to grow. It glowed in the water as Skylar imagined her stone would glow if she ever saw it whole. She could sense a transformation within him that couldn't be seen with the eyes.

"*Is he coming to?*" she asked.

"*I don't know,*" the mermaid said. "*I've never seen this before.*"

The mermaids were right and so was Skylar. He'd had a reason to put himself there. He was claiming his sovereignty amidst the constraints of this world. *He heard me.*

Kyle came running down the corridor and banged on the glass, shattering the beauty of the moment. "Skylar, you're needed. Miss Vivienne asked for you," he shouted through the glass.

She and all the mermaids covered their ears from the noise, and she looked back at Argan. "I love you," she said. She got out of the tank and followed Kyle back toward the lab.

25

S uki closed up the tiny house the best she could with a couple day's notice. She'd never been one for attachments, so she only had a couple of duffel bags in the car for her move to Washington. Ocean had promised she'd have an apartment waiting. She assumed it had furniture. With everything else going on, furniture shopping wasn't on her radar. But clothes shopping would have to be. DC was a long way from what she wore at the barn.

"Welcome," Mica said as Wren showed Suki into the Oval Office. "I'm pleased to meet you, Suki. Ocean tells me you're the one I need."

"It's an honor, Madam President," Suki said.

"Please call me Mica. I've never been one for formalities."

"I'm not sure I can do that, ma'am."

"All right, how about Judge?" Mica asked. "That's what they called me back in New Orleans."

Suki nodded. "I like that, thank you."

"Ocean has debriefed me about your pedigree. Very impressive," Mica said. "I'll get right to it. Things are happening fast now, and I'm trying to balance more than one world on my shoulders. I'm in charge of the Dissolution, but I also have ideas about how we can rebuild when it's over. I'm putting out fires, literally. I'm sure you've seen the news. There is so much devastation, and not enough aid. And that's the whole idea. This world we've built on lies has to fall for the original intent of the country to emerge. With all of the karma balancing, the wheel has come around again for the country as well. Individuals are finding patterns repeating in their lives and old opportunities coming back, allowing them to choose again. The same is true for the country. We are being offered the opportunity to choose the path originally intended by the founding fathers."

"That makes sense," Suki said. "So, how can I help?"

"Ocean gave you no explanation?"

"I figured it was part of helping Skylar," Suki said. "That's all the explanation I needed."

"You are a true friend." Mica smiled. "We are all called to be brave now, Suki. Time's run out on holding back. People are hurting. Your loved ones are hurting. You can help. Think of Skylar and all she's risked to do what she believes is right."

Anguished pierced Suki's heart. "I don't know how I add value."

"Speaking up for what you believe in your heart but can't prove is the ultimate act of bravery. Certainty will never come. You have to do it before you're ready. That's the secret. Taking the leap, knowing the universe will catch you."

Proof was a concept Suki clung to. Research defined her. But now she was being asked to move forward and do this without clarity. She needed to connect to her internal knowing—to step into her role as alchemist.

"We need the magic of the original blueprint of America," Mica said. "You've seen it."

Suki froze. Had she been bugged?

"*No bugging,*" Mica said in her mind.

Suki smacked her own forehead with the palm of her hand. "I give up. I can't handle having people in my head."

"You can give up or find a way to use it to your advantage." Mica shrugged. "Telepathy is a tool coming online for the new earth. You will have to master it eventually. Now, about the blueprint. I need you to recall it and re-create it. And not the dysfunctional one in Devlin's book. I'm talking about the original plan."

She led Suki out of the Oval and into the adjacent room. It had always been the waiting area for the chief of staff's office, but seeing how Mica had no chief of staff, the rooms were available.

Suki gasped. It looked like an alchemical command center. Each of the walls was a different color—one white, one black, one red, one yellow. Ancient-looking maps hung on every wall. Symbols and intricate pictures of various sizes covered the windows and papered the tables, and some lay strewn on the floor. They overlapped with many newer pictures of conspiracy theories and printouts of recent internet articles on the fleecing of America.

"Welcome to Operation Liberty Tree," Mica said. "We will be a part of the re-creation of actual and true history."

Suki walked around the large room with wide eyes. It was even more thrilling than Milicent's library. In the library, she felt the energy of the past. In this room, she could see the possibility of the future. And she could help design it.

Mica didn't have to tell her how to read any of it; she knew what everything meant. On the four colored walls, she saw the four stages of alchemy come to life as she had read in the words of Mary the Jewess, one of the original female alchemists. The colors also represented the four races and the four directions of Native American prophecy.

On the table lay a picture of the great seal and eagle holding arrows. She had conflicting information running through her head about what the arrows truly represented.

"There are nuggets of truth in all of this shit," Mica said. "I don't have time to uncover them. That's why I need you. The Freemasons were the original alchemists, using magic to create and set the lines and path for the country. Think Ben Franklin and Thomas Jefferson. But then it became corrupted about a hundred years ago. And now we are here to get back on course. We need a new plan based on those original ideals—sovereignty, freedom, individual expression. This Dissolution is zero point. We've reached it. Just look outside. I have to ride this out. I don't know how long it's going to go on. The future isn't going to be created by those that have been here this last twenty years. It will be created by you, and those like you. Smart people who have a connection to their heart. This country will not succeed without compassion."

"I understand," Suki said. It was the first time in her life she'd felt patriotic, like it was her duty to serve for the betterment of the country. And she was excited. "It would be my honor to serve."

26

Vivienne and Heather stood staring at the magical Mother Earth globe. Various points on the orb were lit up like twinkling stars, and as Skylar approached, more lights popped up. Lines of gold light snaked like rivers around the sphere. As Skylar watched with wonder, the rivers began to find each other, connecting like a giant grid around the earth. The sight triggered her memory of a passage from Sophia's book: *The dragon lines are igniting.* She wanted to touch them but dared not. The dragon lines—or ley lines, as they were sometimes called—used the magnetic field around the earth to communicate across the world.

"Magnetics," Skylar whispered. *My lodestone.*

"Yes," Vivienne said.

Skylar looked at Vivienne and they locked eyes. When she looked back at the globe, she could see the dragons themselves in the water. Her imagination lit up with the earth and became a reality. The water dragons, beautiful blue and green creatures of the sea, traced the lines of energy above the sea floor. Their colors mixed iridescently and glowed, creating a light that shone outward from the earth's crust.

Skylar felt heat running through her body. She looked down at her arms. Her veins lit up, just as they had to match the leaf at the barn over a year ago. Yet again she felt the pull from Mother Earth. She felt the connection, the love of nature. She thought of the trees and instantly made the connection between them and the ocean. Humanity's protectors both created oxygen and were both being depleted—one by deforestation and one by pollution.

"Antarctica is melting." She pointed to the caps that were shrinking before their eyes. "Is that happening back home?"

"Yes," Vivienne said. "But the melting is not just from the hand of man. It's also from the heart of man. Human emotion creates many of the 'natural' happenings in the physical world. It has been that way since the First Age."

Skylar saw the image of Vivienne's tear falling into the sea.

"Yes," Vivienne said. "I am not above the law of cause and effect." She looked back at her tail of shadows. "But now we have the possibility of a new beginning. My time, and that of my sisters, is over. We were at the mercy of the era of Aries. But you have help, Divine Skylar, from the Feminine that has returned to the sky." She gestured to the moon, shining brightly above. "The planet and her sisters are in a new place in the solar system, raining new energies upon you. Eris, the Divine Feminine warrior planet, has returned to assist. Mars is a great combatant but is no match for the woman warrior. Think of the mother who would kill for her child—that is Eris. She will wait for eternity until the right time to strike. And then the ignorant can only pray for mercy."

Images of constellations flooded Skylar's mind. "I was just getting the hang of earth magic, and now you're throwing the stars at me." She watched the melting ice on the ends of the globe. "There are secrets there. Magic and wisdom thawing that will amaze humanity."

"Yes," Vivienne said. "This magic is trickling into the world of form through the fresh, pure water. Today is the summer solstice, coinciding with the arrival of the thirteenth moon—my moon. I knew coming here was a risk. Everything is *coming online*, as it were. Time portals are now open, timelines are malleable. This is Cyril's window to act. If he finds the citrine wall or takes your stone now, before all the ley lines are connected, he will have the power to take hold of all human potential for the next thirteen thousand years."

Skylar's eyes traveled away from the globe and around the room. She looked at all the empty workstations. The countless hours spent on the experiments to conquer, missing the heart carried by humanity. They knew it sat in the citrine wall. They were looking to take that imagination by impure means when the magic of water flowed all around them on this island. They were too blind to see its secret waiting to be unleashed, given freely to all who asked. This was Vivienne's secret. She was water. Magus could have had her love, but he'd only wanted power he could control. He could control fire, but could never control the sea.

"The Dissolution has started, the release of energy is happening all over the planet. Look at the area of the US over Hollow Earth." Vivienne pointed to the middle of the US on the globe. The Mississippi River glowed red. Its fire was burning the country into two pieces.

"Oh my god." Skylar's jaw hung open. "Is that our country? Does it actually look like that right now?"

"I'm afraid so," Vivienne said. "And it's only the beginning."

Skylar felt a rush of energy surge through her. For the first time, the heart light moved on its own.

"This tumultuous time has intensified your abilities, has it not?" Vivienne said. "I ask you, have the earth changes increased your powers, or have your powers increased the earth changes?"

Skylar's eyes pleaded with Vivienne. "The Dissolution. A great flood, Grandmother. It's coming."

"Yes, it is," Vivienne said. The globe glowed with energy. Vortex points were igniting fires and causing craters all over the world.

"What will happen to this world?" Heather asked. "We exist outside of the timeline of earth."

"So you've been led to believe," Vivienne said. "That was only the case until the return of the Divine Feminine. If Cyril's plan fails, this world will end."

"We must stop it!" Heather blurted. "It's not supposed to happen like this."

"How is it supposed to happen?" Skylar asked.

"Change is never easy. There must be a balancing," Vivienne said. "Water is emotion. The water in your blood, the salt in your tears. Every one of you is connected to the other through your veins. Your blood is made of the same substance as the ocean water. You are the conduit for Gaia to rise and restore herself to wholeness. She can never be whole until you are. There is much to do, but not as much as you'd think. As simple as making a decision, everything changes. Simple and hard at the same time." She took Heather's hand. "It takes great strength to let go of what you've created, but the separation is necessary for something new to emerge."

Heather quickly withdrew her hand.

Skylar looked back at the globe. It continued to morph and illuminate with light—some from the lines, some from the fires.

Skylar looked down again at her veins. She knew she had the power to help. "I can fix this."

"Yes, you can," Vivienne said. "But you won't. I told you, you don't have to save the world. And many of these souls are playing out lifetimes of karma. They need this experience, even if it ends in death, to balance their soul on the scales of truth. Gaia's in charge now. She is the bearer of illumination this world has not known before. The Great Mothers have tried their best over the timelines, but at the end of all things, there is no one that can compare to the power of Mother Earth. She has allowed us to live on her back and she tells us when the ride is over. If our time has come, so be it."

Skylar looked at the globe in front of her. She closed her eyes, as she had done in Sophia's temple, and the globe replicated, becoming a row of infinite globes stretched in every possible direction, representing the pure potential of the moment and its limitless outcome. She opened her eyes and looked at Vivienne. "We are just conscious of this one reality, manifesting this one outcome," she said. "There are more to choose from. You may be quick to accept this one, but I'm not."

A piercing sound exploded in their ears. Heather covered hers with her hands.

"What is that?" she shouted.

"Whale song," Vivienne said calmly. "But it's strained. Something is grave."

"You're not kidding," Skylar said, trying to shake the sound out of her head. She and Vivienne left the lab to head to the shore. Heather followed behind.

The moon was bright and calming. In different circumstances, the reflection off the water would be wistful and romantic. But with the sounds the whale was making, it was ominous.

They followed the sound to the water's edge. The whale had beached itself on shore. Vivienne stepped into the water, and the line between where the water stopped and the shore began faded.

"She's confused with the shift in the grid lines," she said. "Her sense of direction is all off." She looked at the horizon. "There will be more of them." She kneeled and placed her hand on the giant creature. The whale's eyes were open, yet she remained unmoving. "We don't have a lot of time. The weight of the air will crush her organs without the buoyancy of the sea."

Skylar looked more closely at the whale, and recognized

her markings. It was the whale that had given her the ride with Argan. "I know this whale!" she shouted. She tried to push her toward the water but was no match for her weight.

"Sound," Heather said from behind them. "Sound frequency can displace her weight and we can move her. We have the technology here."

Without waiting for a response, she ran for the lab.

Heather came back quickly, this time carrying a bright silver box resembling a cross between an intergalactic crystal radio and a toaster oven. It had various dials made out of geodes, and she knew exactly how to operate it. She switched it on and turned a few dials, and they all waited.

The box caused a ringing in Skylar's left ear, but nothing else seemed to happen. Heather repositioned the box closer toward the whale—and, finally, the body of the great creature started to shake and visibly lift from the sand.

"Okay, let's guide her back in," Heather said.

"Allow me," Vivienne said. When the whale hovered just above the sand, Vivienne touched her lightly, and the energy from her hand guided the creature back into the water.

Once in the water, the whale's body continued to float down until it was submerged. It took a few minutes for her to move, but she soon swam toward deeper water.

"How did you know to do that?" Skylar asked Heather.

"We used the same technology to build the pyramids," she said. "How else did you think those stones got in the air?"

Skylar smiled. "What about the others? How can we stop this from happening again?"

"I can set up some crystal transmitters around the water," Heather said. "Three should do it. But that's just here. This is going to happen around the globe."

Skylar felt a wave of panic. This was happening and affecting real animals, and real people. This wasn't just some cockamamie story, or a dream she'd wake up from. There were real casualties in her face right now. And there would be more.

She sat in the sand and stared at the sea. It continued to pulse and breathe and sway to its own rhythm, receptive to all outcomes. She felt a moment of desperation.

"Faith in the face of disappointment, Skylar," Vivienne said. "Look."

Skylar turned her head and looked back up the hill toward the laboratory.

A figure walked toward her, the moon bright behind him. He was a massive, godlike man. Skylar's breath caught in her throat. She choked in as much air as her lungs would allow, sputtering at the end. It was Argan. But he was not the same. This Argan had a saunter.

She rose to her feet and stood waiting on shore, unable to move at the sight of him. This man she had loved since the beginning of time had returned, transformed—his black hair longer, his face darker from a thick smattering of a beard. Gone were any hints of the boy he'd still carried before. His gray shirt, ripped and bloody, exposed a body she hardly remembered. He had always been perfect, but now his perfection had exploded into something greater.

He stopped inches away from Skylar, and she was unsure if it was another dream. As she touched his face to see if he were real, he stared into her eyes. Yes, this was her Argan—the man that forced her to tell him with her eyes what her words could never say. He kissed her hard on the mouth, and she felt his desire for her roll off his body.

"You're free," she said when he released her.

"Likewise," he said, his stare so intense that she had to look away. For all the power and confidence she had gained in recent months, his new intensity made her blush.

"Argan, what happened to you?" she asked, still processing the sight of him. "You look beastly."

He chuckled. "Legend is, no one is the same after the soul cage."

"So you're different on the inside too?"

"Let's just say such prolonged silent introspection is enlightening," he said. "Especially when you don't take a breath."

"You mean like the Buddha?" she asked in all seriousness.

He shrugged but didn't answer.

"No one had ever survived it," Skylar said.

"Until now," he said. He greeted Vivienne, and then Heather, whom he caught gaping at him in his new form. He smiled at her. "You look different too," he said.

Her hand flew up to her cheek.

"We don't have much time," he said. "Magus is rallying his men. Something's been switched on."

"Mother Earth," Skylar said. She looked at Heather.

"I can't stay here," Heather said.

Argan closed the distance between them. "Won't you help us?" he asked. "You know you want to." He winked and flashed a fatal smile.

A squeak escaped Heather's mouth, and she ran toward the laboratory without a word.

"She'll come around," Argan said.

"Argan, what the hell are we doing here?" Skylar said. "Going to battle? Seriously? You and me against Magus and his goons?"

"Yes. We are going to battle. All this time, we've been changing ourselves and honing our skills and fighting to get to the light, but all along we didn't need to change into something, Sky—we just had to uncover something. The light is inside but so is the dark. That's what Magus is afraid of. That's why he can't see the Underworld. He denies his own darkness and will never attain ultimate power until he embraces that. He can't win."

"That's hot, babe," she said. "And it makes me want to take you right here on the beach. But your words don't stop the fact that he's coming down here with a hundred men." She pointed up at the hill. Magus was riding down it on horseback. Behind him, a wall of men walked like an army. "Man, that's overkill," she said.

"Not necessarily," Vivienne said. "He knows what he's up against."

They both looked at her.

"Me." She closed her eyes and the waves parted as she stepped into the water, submerging both her feet. A path emerged down a lighted line. It ended far off in the distance, exposing the cave that contained her luminescent tree. The light shining upward was so bright that it overpowered the moon and lit up the sky.

A swirl of wind kicked up on the horizon. Skylar thought Beatrice might have come to help.

Vivienne mouthed an incantation quietly as the swirl of air got closer. As it approached, Skylar could see the squall was made up of beings. She could make out faces in the mist.

"Ten thousand celestials," Vivienne said. She had summoned the mass of souls from the Underworld, and they were ready to take orders. "Well, maybe not ten thousand, but it's important to remember the help from the unseen realms, dear ones." She winked and raised her arms high in the air. The tempest of souls flew toward Magus's army. They acted as one, diving down and leaving a wake of bodies behind them. Magus's men were shells of humanity—no match for the souls of the Underworld.

"Cyril's world is just an illusion, remember that," Vivienne said. "Anything is possible now."

Magus reached the shore as the last of his men fell behind

him. The souls dissipated after their task was complete. Skylar thought again of Beatrice, and hoped she was on the other side to receive them.

Magus dismounted his horse and Argan stepped in front of Skylar.

"How right you are, my beloved," Magus said to Vivienne. "All of the magic of the ages is right here, before our very eyes." He leered at Skylar, and Argan grew even bigger in stature. "The magic in your blood has fortified the stone within you. You carry the heart of the world, goddess of water. I know you were hoping to return that heart to Gaia, but worlds are in motion and there is one more step to take."

He took a dagger from his jacket pocket and Argan's eyes grew wide. Skylar recognized the design too. Milicent's secrets stretched back to Atlantian times.

The light from the emerald rivaled that of Vivienne's tree. Argan didn't hesitate; he lunged forward to take it from Magus. As they struggled, Skylar saw more men pouring out of the laboratory and running toward the shore.

Magus fired a blow of electric energy at Argan. He fell to his knees but regained his strength quickly. A shine reminiscent of the black jaguar glowed from Argan's eyes. It was as if the blow had fueled him from within.

The new round of men had reached the shore and went after Argan. The newly enriched dark power within him gave him the ability to fight off each one.

With Argan distracted, Magus went after Skylar. The movement of the dagger created a ray of light that blinded the men on the shore, but Skylar's vision remained clear. She raised her hand to reflect the light back at Magus, hoping that was enough to buy some time—and it was. All motion sped up, but she was still able to catch what others would have missed.

It happened so quickly, all she could see was a flash of white hair, but she knew it was Heather, and she caught the girl in her arms when she fell.

Argan felled the last two of Magus's men. He rushed toward the girls but Vivienne put out a hand, stopping him.

"Wait," she said.

Magus stood before them, frozen. "That was not the plan," he said, confused. "We practiced this many times. This was the moment. I don't understand. There was a plan."

"She changed the plan," Argan said.

Skylar held Heather in her arms, staring at the dagger in her chest. With a motivating growl, she forced herself to pull it out. She dropped the dagger to the ground. The jewel on the tip was gone. Nothing but the orichalcum blade remained.

She put her hand over the hole in Heather's chest. Blood poured out, too much to repair. Skylar closed her eyes and channeled all her energy and all her light into the girl. In her mind's eye, the scene in front of her wasn't a gruesome one. Instead, she saw a web of luminous threads weaving its way from her hand to Heather's heart. She was able to see the filaments of energy connecting them. Everything stood still and quiet. And then Skylar saw a different girl's face . . . *Rhia*.

The bright, golden web spread over Heather's body and crawled up Skylar's legs and torso. She felt the tingle of the divine pulse in her head as the web engulfed her body and she and Heather became one.

She was so consumed by the moment, yet she could feel a burning sensation growing in her chest. The two halves of the stone sought to merge, to be together as they had been in the First Age; each yearned for wholeness. *Sacrifice*, Skylar thought. Heather had made the ultimate sacrifice for someone she hardly knew, had even gone against the wishes of her father, to do what she felt was right.

Being so close to Heather, so intimately connected, Skylar could feel her aligning herself with God's grace, surrendering to the perfection of death. In a moment as quiet as the flutter of dove wings, Skylar felt the emerald release from her own chest. With her eyes closed, she watched as the stone floated effortlessly toward its other half, completing a thirteen-thousand-year cycle.

Heather's face turned pale, and Skylar saw her life force drain out of her body like a cyclone in the middle of her chest. Her life was pouring into the stone. Skylar held Heather's head in her lap.

"She's dying," Skylar said, confused. "She has the stone now, how can that be?"

"The stone was never the key to immortality, Skylar," Vivienne said. "You have your journey, she has hers."

Skylar stroked Heather's blond hair and watched the scar on her cheek fade into the mark of the three doves. Her appearance changed slightly and Argan dropped to his knees to hold her hand.

"You knew she was Rhia," Skylar said.

"Yes," he said. "I figured out a lot in that cage."

"I'm going to marry you someday," Heather whispered to him.

He kissed her gently on the mouth. "It will be my honor," he said with a smile full of love for the girl.

"The stone is now healed within Heather," Vivienne said. "Her heart is whole, and when she returns to the earth plane as Rhia, she will carry the compassion of the mother within her, no longer fractured. She will no longer need to die in order for future generations to flourish in the Golden Age." She placed her hand over Heather's chest and said a quiet prayer.

Magus fell to his knees and picked up the dagger lying beside Heather. No stone was attached to its tip; its only decoration was the blood he'd soaked it with. He had killed his only heir. By doing so, he'd lost the immortality one creates through their children. The continuation of his bloodline had been severed. He looked at Vivienne with pained eyes and she reached for him, ready to console the only man she'd ever let into her heart.

For a brief moment, she held his hand as it began to age before everyone's eyes, and Skylar knew the effects would soon overtake his body. He was returning to his seventy-five-year-old self. He pulled away from Vivienne.

As they stood at the shoreline, the cyclone that had been created in Heather's chest was mirrored by a whirlwind that rose up around Vivienne's tree. A torrent of water poured into the crevasse around it. As it cycled back, it headed toward them, and another cylinder of water swirled up around the tree. As the water filled in, it covered the tree back up, extinguishing its light. Soon, only the moonlight lit up the night.

"This land will be submerged soon," Vivienne said. As the water continued to loom near them, the top of a cathedral began to surface in the distance. The mist shrouding the Underworld was disappearing.

"Diana," Skylar whispered to Argan. She held her breath, waiting to see Sophia's temple, but it never emerged. *Only certain eyes can see*, she thought. It was there. She had faith.

Magus took a last look at Heather and then untethered a small boat. It was something Skylar had only seen in movies, more like a hovercraft than a normal watercraft. He stumbled briefly, then hopped in and left shore, headed in the direction of the cathedral.

Vivienne watched him go.

"Grandmother, stop this!" Skylar cried out. "Magus will have a clear line to Diana now."

"It's all right, Skylar," Vivienne said. "It's time for all of this to be over." With a flip of her wrist, she molded a thin wave at the shoreline to raise Heather up and carry her closer to shore. "I will take care of the girl."

Before she left, she grasped one of Argan's hands, and then one of Skylar's. They joined in a triangle on the sand.

"I stood in this very spot with my sisters in the First Age," Vivienne said. "Life looked eerily similar then. Time was ending. The same as now. I am so fortunate to have you both here. You will do what we could not. You are pure of heart, Skylar. When you can see the perfection in yourself, you claim your mastery. And you are pure of mind, Argan. You are able to uncover the secrets hidden in plain sight. Together, you will rule the Golden Age." A silver thread of moonlight could be seen connecting them. Skylar felt the pure power surging through her. "This is where I leave you. Be well." She dropped their hands.

As the water continued to rise around them, Vivienne's shadowy tail combined with a wave and engulfed Heather. Vivienne slowly made her way up the hill toward the laboratory, a funeral precession of one.

"Argan?" Skylar hardly got out his name.

"Let's go," he said. "We won't be far behind him."

They dove in the water together and started to swim down to the bottom of the ocean floor. The water was erratic from the cyclone still whirling around Vivienne's tree, and it was hard to navigate. As they swam, the sand below them began to kick up as if blown by a massive wind. Skylar heard a thunderous roar behind her, and turned to look.

The sand had formed into a team of horses rising up under them. At first Skylar thought it was Vivienne's handiwork, but she soon realized it was Argan's. He commanded them as easily as if they were back at Rosen. She could feel the strong, masculine energy of the sand horses. She felt their desire to accomplish their mission, and the rush of energy was contagious. Despite the danger, she was excited for what was to come.

Vivienne made her way up the hill, the power of the sea propelling her effortlessly, her shadowy tail carrying Heather behind her. When she reached the steps of the building, she turned back and looked at the ocean. It was her home, her very essence. It gave her power and protection. It also gave her a place to hide. Its depths kept her secrets and her wounds in its dark waters. Now back to where it all started, out of the sea, she carried those wounds in the very shadows of her body. But it was time for them to be released, and there was only one way to do it.

She had thought the island had been emptied. The celestials had done their job. Not one of the astral shells remained. But a young man approached her from the top of the steps. He was soaking wet.

"Oh man, what happened?" Kyle asked, looking down at the carnage of Magus's fallen men. He was more bewildered than usual.

"I'm not sure." Vivienne was also perplexed seeing him. "Where were you hiding?"

"Hiding?" he asked. "I wasn't hiding, I was cleaning the tank." He walked down the steps toward her. "I mean, well, I *was* cleaning. Then one of the seamaids jumped into the air and pulled me off of the staircase. That's all I remember. I'm not a strong swimmer, but the next thing I knew, I was lying on the floor next to the tank. No one else was around." He finally noticed Heather. "Is she . . ."

"Yes," she said. "And there is no one here to pay her final respects. So I will do it. But I need your help."

"Of course, ma'am," he said. He picked Heather up out of Vivienne's tail of shadows and followed her inside.

When they arrived at the mermaid enclosure, Kyle's pool vacuum was still draped over the side. Vivienne gave him a scolding look and he bowed his head like a naughty puppy.

"You knew in your heart that keeping these creatures captive was wrong," she said.

"Yes, ma'am." Still holding Heather, he wouldn't look at her.

"But you lived outside of your integrity for money," she said.

"Yes, ma'am."

"Young man, I will give you the best advice you will ever get in your whole life, so listen up," she said.

He lifted his head and met her eyes.

"*Pay attention.*"

He waited.

"That's it, that's all you have to do," she said. "Pay attention to your life, and to the world around you. The one you can see but also, and more importantly, the one you can't. You were obviously given a second chance by the Goddess that I have no explanation for. So lose the absent-minded persona and go create something in this world."

"Yes, ma'am," he said.

"Now step aside," she said.

He obliged and Vivienne took Heather into her arms. She climbed the metal staircase; when she reached the top, her cascade of shadows extended all the way to the floor. She looked back at it and sighed but continued to fulfill her duty. She placed Heather in the water and the girl's body floated peacefully. Vivienne held her hand over the large tank.

"I am sorry," she said. "Through my thoughts, emotions, and behaviors, many have suffered. I take responsibility and fully apologize with my whole heart for the pain I have caused you." Tears came to her eyes and she didn't try to stop them. Instead, she let them flow out like healing water, cupping her hands to capture them. When she'd accumulated a pool of tears in her palms, she flung her hands out over the tank, and her tears fell like crystals into the water.

"Be free, dear ones. Rise out of the sacred waters of the Divine Feminine, the ocean of Mother Earth."

The water turned choppy, as if stirred by a storm. Vivienne continued to pulse her energy over the water, and the walls of the tank began to shake from the pressure. She looked up at the moon, still glowing brightly above. The glass finally gave way to the pressure and burst into a blinding shower of glass and water. She held her right hand up and an energy shield formed over Kyle, protecting him from the deluge.

It took only minutes for the water to drain out of the room and join the rest rising from the sea.

In the moonlight, at the center of the tank, stood six radiant women, all with hair down to their knees. Not one of them took a breath of air.

"The curse is over," Vivienne said from her perch at the top of the stairs. "The stone is healed. You are to take your rightful place among the stars. Thank you, dear ones, for holding the magic of the sea within your hearts until it could return properly to the physical world. I bless you all. Go in peace."

Vivienne and Kyle watched as all six women turned crystalline, their bodies absorbing the moonlight. Kyle's jaw hung open as their forms rose into the sky as twinkling lights.

"Is that how stars are made?" Kyle asked, mesmerized by the sight.

"Pretty much," Vivienne said with a smile.

Heather's etheric body waited where the mermaids had stood. She was whole and happy. Her appearance vacillated between her most recent form and Rhia's. Vivienne watched with Kyle as her spirit crystallized and wed with the moonlight.

Vivienne made her way back down the stairs. "Find your way home, child," she told Kyle. "This place will be gone soon."

28

As the mist continued to fade, Diana's cathedral came into sharper relief, and Magus saw his clear path. As much as Atlantis was the epitome of advancement, Diana's cathedral held a magic unattainable by technology.

He slowed the boat and stopped near a cave. He stepped onto the sand, still overdressed in his maroon suit. Age was gaining on his frame, but he delayed it as best he could with his powers.

The air was different than he was used to, heavy and thick. He was accustomed to keeping his environment thoroughly controlled. He loosened his tie and smoothed his hair.

The cathedral's courtyard was empty yet the tables were abundant with food, as if a gathering had been cut short.

Diana sat on her throne, waiting. She had released all of the souls at Vivienne's request. They had fulfilled their karma and now it was time to fulfill hers.

She sensed him before she heard the knocking—the rumblings of the earth beneath her feet tipped her off. Gaia would implode on herself before letting Magus take the citrine wall. Diana was unsure there was any other solution with him this close. She just had to kick out her houseguests.

"I'm so excited!" Milicent said. "We are going to kick his ass. I'm so glad we didn't leave yet."

Diana shook her head. "Milicent, that's not what this is

about. It's too late for that. Once he breaks through, the mystery of the Underworld is lost. It cannot be repaired."

"Of course it can," Milicent said.

"No . . . it can't." Diana's tone was grave. "The time of the Underworld is over. Gaia is waking up, the dragon lines are lighting." She looked at the citrine wall. The facets of the giant stone looked like a honeycomb filled with illuminated honey. It was perfect and complete. "Humanity is liberated, and there is no more need for the Underworld. This is Magus's last try but he won't succeed. I will make sure of it." She got up from her seat and hugged her sister. Her eyes grew distant and seemed to look past Milicent. "Go now or you won't be able to."

"No. I will help you fight."

Diana shook her head. "There is no more fighting. It's time to surrender to what is. That is what's being asked of me."

"Surrender?" Milicent was appalled. "That is not part of the Cannon vocabulary."

"Sometimes surrender is the bravest thing you can do," Diana said.

"Then leave with me!" Milicent pleaded, trembling. She grabbed her arm and pulled her toward the door, but Diana didn't budge.

Noah, who had been pacing in the background for hours, stopped moving and watched the two sisters.

"Milicent, I died on the physical plane," Diana said. "There is no going back for me. I am entrusted with the care of this place." She was serene. "There is no living again. If the Underworld dies, I die again with it." She turned her back on Milicent and slowly walked to her jeweled throne.

"You were everything to me, I can't lose you again. I . . ." Milicent started toward Diana.

Diana put her hand up. "I love you too, Millie," she whispered.

Her soft words carried over the waves in the air and reached her sister. She motioned to Noah.

He took Milicent by the arm. "Mil, we need to go," he said.

Pieces of the wall crashed beside them.

"Now."

Milicent's shoulders slumped and she allowed Noah to lead her away from the throne room and out into the courtyard.

Milicent and Noah were almost to the alchemical door when she saw him. Magus was younger than as she had known him, but she recognized his energy signature.

"Milicent, what a surprise," Magus said. "Getting in here is no easy task. I underestimated you."

"I could say the same, although it took you half an age to find it," Milicent said. "So I won't say the same for you. In fact, you're completely incompetent, Cyril." Noah pulled on her arm but she wrenched it away. She crossed her arms over her chest and stared at Magus. "You clean up well, though, aesthetically speaking. Although something's going on there with your neck." More of Magus's age was showing. "As far as your soul goes, I know there's no hope for you."

He felt his neck with his aged hand. "You talk about souls like you have one."

"In fact I do—got it back a few months ago," she said.

Noah stood watching their exchange, looking confused. "Mil," he whispered. "We've got to get out of here. Why are you talking to him?"

She ignored him.

"I misjudged you, Milicent," Magus said. "You had promise of being on the winning side of things, but in the end, the lure of the light was too strong."

"I straddle both well, I think," she said. She charged toward him. "You son of a bitch! All that time you were controlling Devlin for your own gain. My marriage was a sham because of you."

"It's unlike you to stand in victim mentality. I'm disappointed." Magus grinned.

"If you think you are taking my sister too, you're mistaken," she said. She conjured a purple flash of light; it hit him in the chest, and his black aura shrank.

"What just happened?" Noah asked. Even he seemed to be able to see that the shadow around Magus had diminished.

"You've lost your immortality, Cyril. It's all written on Diana's walls. Once you pierced the heart of your own daughter, it was over. At least the girl died believing you cared for her, instead of learning the truth—that you spared your daughter from being thrown in those torture tanks only because your immortality lived through her. You knew this. Now that she's gone, you've become vulnerable to death. I look forward to a front-row seat for that."

Magus grabbed at the trunk of a tree for support, seemingly depleted, although there were no physical wounds to be seen.

"We really can't stay for that, Mil," Noah said. "I'm hoping that energy signature at the door is still pulsing. We've waited longer than planned." He took her by the arm again.

"Fine." She sighed. "That son of a bitch doesn't have a chance anyway."

They walked back into the blackness of space.

29

Argan slowed the sand horses when they reached Sophia's temple and guided them into the cavern.

"We have to keep going," Skylar said.

"No," Argan said. "This is where we need to be."

"Argan, Magus saw the cathedral. We have to help Diana."

"Sky, I'm sorry to tell you this, but I think you already know. There is no going back for Diana." She knew what he meant. "This is how we help," he said. "Trust me."

"Right." She followed him as he ran around to the back of the temple. All of the dwellers were gone. It seemed they had been summoned as part of the ten thousand celestials who had come to their rescue.

"We don't have much time," Skylar warned as they hopped inside between the broken stones.

"It's actually the perfect time," Argan said.

"What do you mean?" she asked.

"What's today, Sky?"

"I have no idea," she said. "I've lost track of everything."

"It's the solstice—the time when worlds open up, remember?" He pointed to the moon shining brightly above them. "Vivienne's moon. It hasn't shone here in thirteen thousand years. Come with me." He took her hand and they ran to the well of the interior chamber.

"Of course," she said. "I remember the light of the moon

opening the portal to the Underworld during Milicent's big show, and it was the solstice! Argan, you are brilliant!" She kissed him on the lips and squeezed his arm. "What happened in that soul cage?" She ran her hand down his arm.

"Hey, I was always this way," he said.

"Yeah, you were," she agreed. But in her mind, she couldn't be sure. If nothing else, he had an added allure now—something to do with the darkness. He had been seasoned by life, and she loved him more for it.

"Your map showed the green stone here at the well." He took the emerald stone out of his pocket and held it in his palm. Its light was dim from Heather's blood.

Skylar's eyes grew wide. "What?" her words caught. "I don't understand. Heather?"

"Vivienne handed it to me on the beach," Argan said. "We aren't returning the stone to Lucifer's crown, we're returning it to Sophia's." He beamed with excitement.

"What do I do with it?" she asked.

"You'll know," he said. "Follow your heart."

She took the stone from his hand and stared at it. It held a quiet magnificence that seemed veiled in her hand. Here in the interior chamber, surrounded by broken stones and dust, it held back from shining with all its brilliance.

She closed her eyes and everything changed.

The golden threads that had connected her and Heather on the beach returned, this time traveling from her hand to Argan's. It quickly spread over the floor and walls of Sophia's magical temple, expanding out into the sea. Skylar saw the luminous threads light up the ocean floor, and her sight expanded far beyond the scope of human eyes. She could see the pure truth in the water. It opened, allowing her to become one with its magic. She felt every person connected to every other through the blood of earth: the water. She could feel the vibration of the planet rising and the souls on Gaia readying themselves to step into the Golden Age of peace. Her vision expanded to the children she'd seen on the fourth floor. They were the future, the true light bearers of the Golden Age. With this healed stone, they would be allowed to keep their innocence and sovereignty, and never have to relinquish it to those hiding in the shadows.

Skylar held her breath when the thread from her hand reached the heart of the soul that had once been her son. She was flooded with the internal knowing that they were connected beyond time, although they'd never met in the physical world. She knew he was whole and life was perfect despite outer appearances. She stood on the fine line between joy and sadness, knowing it was perfect. It was the closure she hadn't known she needed until now. She saw the truth in the web of light—that everything we think, feel, and do creates the world we live in. Even with its brutality, she cherished that world.

The light began to fade from her view. "Wait!" she said, but it didn't listen.

She had been given a gift. She slowly came back to the world in front of her.

"Thank you," she said softly.

She opened her eyes and looked at Argan. He was her love. She wouldn't fail him. The desire to finish this grew within her belly and her heart. She could see the threads with her eyes open now. They were coming from within her own heart. She didn't need the stone to connect to some outside magic. She only needed to connect to the magic of her own humanness. It was a yearning with purpose. She had a desire to connect with the greater part of herself that could only be expressed through giving her love away to another. And she knew it was that love that would be the catalyst to finish this.

Standing by the well, Skylar felt the love of a good man, the love of her family, the love of a child, the love of her self. She knew this love determined the destiny of the whole human race—that it could change the outcome of the globe in the lab. She connected her own destiny with the divine fire burning in the well, and connected her heart with that indescribable love. It filled every molecule of her being.

The light within the well called to her, and she answered.

30

Diana took in a deep breath and looked at all the treasures in her throne room. They all represented a part of the world she was entrusted to protect. The Petelia tablet, the scales of Maat, and the citrine wall, collecting the memories of humanity. Her reign as the Dark Madonna was over, but for good cause. Humanity was waking up and would soon lay down its old ways and embrace what it was meant to become.

She touched the scale; it was only slightly off-balance. One feather lay on the left pan, almost weightless. She placed her finger on the right one to make the pans even, for just a moment.

"So, what do you think?" she asked Magus. She didn't need to see him to know he was there. "She's breathtaking, no?"

Magus stared at the citrine wall. Its light sparkled like sunshine breaking through white clouds, its beams bounced around the room. It remained intact despite the hard rumbling of the earth beneath it.

The wall behind him cracked, sending a rift up to the ceiling. The one wood beam above their heads cracked in the rafters and fell. Magus moved one step to the right to avoid it, never taking his eyes off the citrine wall. He said nothing to Diana as he approached the yellow rock.

He stood before it as if it was the altar of the most holy place on earth. His eyes were entranced by its energy; he stood as if frozen, completely silent.

Diana stepped forward and retrieved a memory from the wall. She displayed it for him to relive. As he stood motionless, scenes of the First Age rolled out before him. His betrayal of Vivienne, the child that had always felt his rejection, the power he'd gained, his perpetual dissatisfaction with what he had. It all spilled out on display.

To Diana's surprise, instead of using his dark powers to try to harness the crystal, Magus used his failing physical strength to attempt to destroy it. He began slashing the wall with his orichalcum blade. He wanted the world to feel the hurt he could no longer carry.

"Cyril," Vivienne's voice sounded quietly in the hall. Magus refused to stop. Small chunks of the rock began to fall, igniting the floor underneath the wall.

"Cyril," Vivienne said again, louder this time.

He looked behind him. She wasn't in the room.

"What are you doing?" Her voice echoed in the room. "Was your intention to destroy Diana's house today?"

He dropped his blade and covered his ears.

"Cyril," she continued. "We've spent eternity inflicting wounds on each other, and look where we are: thirteen thousand years have gone by and we are in the same place doing the same thing."

He bent in half, as if in pain from the sound. "I forgive you, Cyril."

Magus let out a blood-curdling cry and heaved himself onto the citrine mainframe, resuming his destruction of the great wall. He had gone completely mad, and was ignoring the devastation happening around him. The rumbling grew louder; everything was shaking. Large pieces of the wall were now collapsing. The end of the Underworld was upon them.

"One last act," Diana said, picking up a lit torch that was burning on the floor. She blew an incantation into its flame.

Gold of the masculine sun
Silver of the feminine moon
Once severed, now together in flame and stone,
Bound in blood and bone
Whole within, whole without
Released from chain and curse
Ending in magic of the Crone's purse
Trinity in one
Blessed in fire, air, and water, so it be done

She touched the two rivers with the torch—first the gold, masculine Mnemosyne, and then the silver, feminine Lethe. They both ignited, fire on water. The flame traveled down the length of the room. More embers fell from the ceiling into both rivers, fueling the flame. She held her breath as the two rivers of fire intertwined.

The smoke began to build as the flames spread up the walls and reached the citrine wall. Instead of the explosion of rock Diana expected, the wall of light extinguished, like a thousand candles blown out at once. The room went dark but for the flames around them.

Magus woke from his manic thrashing and let out a cry of anguish. His body completely morphed into the frail, old version of himself he projected in the physical world. Elderly Magus arrived just in time to witness the crumbling of his precious wall. It detached in one piece from the stone behind it and crashed to the floor, crushing him completely.

Diana turned her back on the rubble and was able to sit on her throne just before the fire consumed her.

The rivers snaked out of the throne room and into the courtyard. They traveled like heat-seeking missiles, armed with intention.

As the walls of the Underworld fell into dust, the undulating fires sought Sophia's temple.

Skylar and Argan stood at the well, side by side. Skylar refused to allow fear to enter her heart. She had no idea what would happen, but she'd come this far, and Sophia was there. And so was Argan.

He took Skylar's hand in his and they held the stone together. The strength of the well braced them from behind. A line of sweat started on Skylar's brow and she tried to ignore it. A moment later, Argan released his hand and wiped it on his pants.

"Sorry," he said. "Did the heat crank up in here?"

They both looked behind the well and saw the braid of two glowing fires, one gold, one silver, pulsing toward them. The stones of the well grew hot on their backs.

"We can't leave now," Skylar said. "We've come too far."

"Agreed," he said.

They joined hands again and watched the fires climb the wall of the stout well. When they reached the top, they cascaded down, merging with the flame below.

The heat was barely tolerable but they stayed still, holding hands. Argan turned to her and lowered his forehead to hers. He looked deeply into her eyes and managed a smile. "You are so beautiful, Skylar, and I've loved you for eternity." He kissed her softly on the lips. "If it all ends here, I'm thankful for what we've had."

The light that poured out of the stone engulfed the two of them in a torus field of energy so bright that the fire paled in comparison. She gasped as all of the breath left her body and her chest propelled her forward, making her collide with Argan. Her body wanted to continue forward, but his own force stopped her and they merged as one. The lines of where each individual ended blurred into the light.

✍

Argan held her close and bounded off of the ground into the air. Skylar felt the sensation of flying but couldn't see anything. After clearing away the clouds in her view, Argan landed them in a familiar pasture. It was Joel's farm. She saw two children playing in the field, under the great oak tree.

"I'm going to love you forever, Skylar," eleven-year-old Argan said in the glistening sunshine.

Before their eyes, Argan aged.

"I'm going to love you forever," twenty-one-year-old Argan said.

"I'm going to love you forever," thirty-year-old Argan said.

Skylar's profile was visible and she was holding a baby in her arms. Argan caressed the baby's head.

"I'm going to love you forever," sixty-year-old Argan said. Three children played in the field behind them.

One-hundred-year-old Argan beamed at Skylar. Then he returned to his eleven-year-old self. "We are timeless, you and I."

Skylar looked beyond the field of their future selves to the infinite sky above. She knew Cassie was there. She understood this was all a plan, her plan. Every wrong turn or seemingly bad choice had led her to this magical end that had been waiting for her since time began. Oh, how she wished she hadn't wasted so much energy fighting the things she'd thought were wrong. It was always right. It was all right.

She opened her eyes and they were back at the well. It felt like a long time had passed, though she knew it must have been only minutes, maybe seconds. The fire had extinguished itself and the room was quiet. She and Argan fell to the floor, breathing heavy, one on top of the other.

Skylar rolled off of Argan and sat beside him. She rested her elbows on her knees to catch her breath. "Now what?" she asked.

He looked at the well. All that remained of the cascading fire was a faint glow deep within the well. "Throw it in?"

"I'm not Frodo, Argan," she said, dusting off her bottom. "And that's a one-shot decision. If it's the wrong one, we're done."

He nodded in agreement.

Skylar threw it in.

"What?" He was dumbfounded.

"You're right, so I made a wish," she said. They both peered in. "Besides, if I kept the stone, I'd be just like Magus, believing my power was outside of myself in some trinket. Throwing it in means I control my own destiny."

"Gutsy move." Argan smiled and kissed her.

The light from within the well lit up the room as it rebuilt itself. The embers of the flames burned off the millennia of accumulated debris. Pink, gold, and red coral fanned over the walls and hung like a canopy over the stone well. The shattered throne repaired itself from the floor up. Once it was fully restored, Skylar was surprised to see that it was made of simple packed sand, its only decorations shells and starfish.

They got to their feet and watched the room transform into a life-size sand castle. Skylar looked at Argan; he was grinning widely.

The well transformed itself into a large, multi-tiered marble fountain. Sand dollars fanned the top, and underneath, two staircases made of slipper shells cascaded to the bottom. Fine veins of gold and silver ran through the stone. Instead of fire, a cool stream of healing waters flowed from the top and formed a crystal-clear pool of turquoise water underneath.

In a moment of exuberance, Skylar jumped in. The water made it just to her shins. "This is amazing!" She laughed like a kid.

Argan followed her into the water. She splashed him playfully and he splashed back. They were eleven again, giddy with the moment. He splashed her once more; this time the water reached her head. Blue crystals dripped onto her forehead.

"You look like a sea goddess," he said to her.

She laughed.

"I'm serious." He touched her hair, now glistening with crystals from the water.

She pulled a strand of hair forward in front of her face and giggled. "That's me, just crown me queen of the sea."

"Or the Sky," he said, drawing her to him. He kissed her where they stood in the water. His eyes were intense, and she blushed.

"Argan, this is Sophia's temple," she said, seeing the desire grow in his eyes. "It's sacred. And she's probably here, watching us, right now."

"Then she will be quite pleased," he said. He pulled his gray shirt off over his head, exposing the rest of his brawny physique.

"Really, Argan, I don't know—"

She didn't get out another word. He kissed her again on the mouth and she enjoyed the salty taste.

"You don't know what, Sky?" he asked, pulling her shirt over her head. He kissed her neck and started his way down toward her breasts. As she ran her hands through his long, black hair, she looked up at the moon, shining down into this incredible sand castle, and knew it was perfect. There couldn't be a more sacred act than making love to Argan here in the water. The connection of man and woman, the joining of opposites, the divinity of sex—it was the expression of everything they had worked for.

"I don't know if I'm ever going to want to leave," she said, kissing him.

He shed the rest of their clothes and laid her down in the shallow water. He pulled her legs around his waist. The moonlight reflected off the droplets of water on his skin, looking like thousands of tiny stars all over his body. He was stronger than she had remembered. With each thrust within her, he grew bigger and her moans grew louder. She relished making sounds in the temple. They were sounds of passion, of joy.

The speed of Argan's thrusts increased and he picked her up, still within her, and carried her to the edge of the water. She rested her head in the sand as he circled one nipple with his tongue, the other with his fingers. Her excitement crested and exploded in an orgasm, sending choppy waves through the calm water of the pool.

She rested in the water, fully open and fully satisfied. Argan held her body close to his as he thrust only once more within her. His own orgasm sent the water in the pool over the side and onto the floor of the temple.

She grinned. "Definitely different."

"This was always me," he said. He looked at the pool, which was now almost empty of water. "Well, maybe." A smile crept across his face. They lay there, entwined, as the fountain water refilled the pool.

"This is so perfect," Skylar said. "I was serious when I said I don't know if I want to leave."

He looked up at the sky shining through the open ceiling. "That doesn't sound possible. I mean, what would we do every day?"

"What are we going to do back home?" she asked, stroking his hair.

"You don't have to decide now," he said. "We could go on a vacation."

The thought of travel reminded Skylar that the world was far from perfect back home. But she was curious if she had helped to fix it, even if just a bit. She sat up and started to dress. "Argan, we're not done. The globe back at the lab showed the world falling apart. Fires, melting ice caps, burning rivers—it's quite a mess."

He sat up and dusted sand off of his hands. "Well, I guess the moment's over."

"I'm sorry," she said. "But there's more to do."

Sophia's image burned into the air like a glimpse of an angel, and she slowly became more corporeal. Argan sprang up and grabbed his pants. Skylar had never seen him move so fast; she laughed loudly.

"No need to cover that gorgeous physique, dear one," Sophia said. "It's been a long time since I've had the divine pleasures of the body satisfied in these halls. I miss it."

"All due respect, I will still put on my pants," Argan said, already tying the drawstring.

"You both have done what no one has been able to do since the First Age," Sophia said. "Because of your work, the Golden Age is assured. I thank you, and a celebration is in order."

"Thank you," Skylar said, humbled. "But Sophia, I can't celebrate knowing so much of the world is in pieces. Back home, my country is literally torn in half. The sea is rising from melting ice caps, and even Atlantis will soon sink for the second time. I really don't see much to celebrate."

"Yes," Sophia said serenely, "those are the experiences happening in the fallen world, but this celebration is for a different reason. It is your baptism, as the new queen."

"I'm sorry?" Skylar asked.

"You said yourself, you are the new queen of the sea," Sophia said.

Skylar studied her face, sure it was a joke. "I was kidding! We're standing in a life-size sand castle, for goodness' sake."

"You returned the whole stone to the well, Skylar. The Underworld and the Atlantis representing the past are gone. That world you speak of is also gone." She gestured to the sand chair. "That throne sat broken during the reign of the sun. Now the moon returns, and the Divine Feminine has arrived. You fixed all of this. This castle rebuilt itself for you, not me. You are the rightful heir. You must take my place."

"Here?" Skylar's eyes widened. "Take your place here?" She repeated the words, unsure they were the right ones. "No, that can't be right." She looked at Argan. "Did your mother tell you this would happen? Did you know about this?" Her voice squeaked higher.

"Can't say I did," he said.

"You were asking about your future," Sophia said. "*This* is your future."

31

Noah and Milicent found their way safely through the alchemical door but returned to a blaze in the Quine library. It would seem that despite her connection to the Great Mothers, Milicent's library was fair game. Or perhaps it was because of it.

"My books!" Milicent screamed, stunned at the sight of the burning room. She tried to use what little she knew about sound technology to extinguish the flames, but she didn't have the right materials, or enough time. She switched to an incantation and Noah grabbed her arm.

"Mil." He pulled on her. "Let's go!"

The flames loomed closer but she refused to move. "I can do this." She whirred her hands and only flame came out.

"Mil!" Noah yelled over the noise. "You are literally fighting fire with fire, this isn't going to work." He grabbed her by her clothes and pulled her toward the door.

"Get your hands off of me!" she yelled as she grabbed an armful of manuscripts from the ancient Egyptian section.

"Leave them!" he yelled and pulled harder.

Her energy shifted away from fighting the fire and over to fighting him.

"These cannot be replaced! I am not leaving without them!" The flames grew brighter and all the oxygen in the room was swallowed up. Milicent gave one last effort to create an oxygen bubble, but nothing worked. Nothing in the room was meant to be saved.

As if she'd just snapped out of hysteria, she finally gained full awareness of what was happening. She stopped resisting and collapsed on the floor.

"Let me die here, Noah," she said. "I'm supposed to die here. Like Diana. Like my books. Let me burn." She slumped even farther to the floor.

"You listen to me!" He got in her face. "You get your ass up and we are walking out of here, do you understand? You've never been a wimp in the face of hardship, and you sure as hell aren't starting now. Get up!" In a feat of strength, he hauled her to her feet and took her by the hand. "Let's go!"

She reluctantly followed him out of the library but slumped again in the hall.

He flung his tie over his shoulder and wrapped his arms around her waist. "Mil, you've got to work with me here. I can't drag you up the stairs."

She let him lead her up the stairs and outside. The fire trucks were already on the scene.

"It will be no use," she said. "Those books aren't meant to survive." She broke down and cried.

"Let these boys feel useful, Mil," Noah said as they watched the team fight the blaze that had now completely engulfed the Quine.

Suki and Mica were watching emergency personnel battle a blaze on the White House lawn when the sky opened up and a deluge of water rained down from above. Within ten minutes, the fire was out. And the rain kept coming.

Wren approached. "Madam President, you're not going to believe this."

"If I had a nickel, Wren," Mica said.

"It would seem to be raining," Wren said.

Mica gave her a look that questioned her intellect.

"Everywhere, ma'am. It is raining on every continent of the globe . . . at the same time."

"Even Africa?"

"Yes, ma'am."

"Huh, okay . . . well, if it doesn't stop, we'll have another problem. But for now, let's say this is a good thing."

"Yes, ma'am. You're due back in the press room to comment." Wren ducked her head and left them.

Suki and Mica stood under a canopy and watched the smoke turn to mist.

"She did it," Suki said.

"No," Mica said. "*We* did it. This rain is the realization of all our hard work—the work of the collective. A nation is the reflection of its people. Those fires were its anger. This rain is its peace."

With that, Mica left for the press room, and Suki returned to Operation Liberty Tree to think about next steps. A great part of the country needed rebuilding.

Suki had accomplished much in the short time she'd been in DC. She loved the pace of the city. A year's worth of work was done in a week. At first she had been hesitant and stuck to what she was familiar with, reading and interpreting the antique texts. That, overlapped with the early colonial volumes she remembered from the Quine library, made for a re-creation of the original intent for America. It was fine, but she wanted to make it better. So she researched further.

In the new vision she'd constructed, she'd added back components from the Great Law of Peace that had been left out of the Constitution—one being a woman's council, similar to the Supreme Court, but with more of a spiritual spin. Peace was the ultimate goal of this new plan, and all decisions would have that end result in mind, not the highly profitable war mindset that had ruled the country since its inception.

She picked up an antique parchment with hieroglyphics on it. The cracked globe, the rain, and sea creatures dotted the paper.

"Of course," Suki said. "This has been written for thousands of years." Down on the bottom of the page were drawings of six snakes; as they were drawn from left to right, they ate an Egyptian queen. "Huh."

She fished out her phone buzzing in her pocket. "Oh crap, I completely forgot," she said aloud at the screen.

"It's about time," she said, answering the phone. "Did you find the door?"

"I didn't get that far!" Britt screamed into the phone. "I have an emergency. The house is on fire! It's pouring rain everywhere else on this bloody street except over this house! What the hell is going on? I didn't have anyone else to call. I don't know what to do. There are a bunch of snakes in there and one talked to me the other day and anyone else would think I'm crazy except you. I'm freaking out, what do I do?"

Suki stared at the parchment. "You have to free the snakes," she said calmly.

"Excuse me?" Britt asked.

"They can't die in that fire. They need to be freed."

"I'm just supposed to let them loose? In the streets of Valhalla?"

"No," Suki said. "You're going to have to kill them."

Britt went silent for a moment. "Kill them to free them?"

"Yes."

"I'm to go into a burning building and kill a handful of snakes? That is the most insane thing I've ever heard."

"You are a granddaughter of the Great Mother of Air. You are not standing there in front of that house in this moment by coincidence," Suki said. "You have to do this."

"How do you suggest I kill these snakes?" Britt asked.

Suki saw the scene unfold in her head as she studied the parchment. A new talent had apparently emerged. "Beatrice would have a dagger somewhere in the house. It will look ceremonial, with a crystal tip. The only type of blade that will work for something like this."

"Now I'm supposed to hunt around for a blade as this house burns?" Britt snorted. "No."

"Look, you're eventually going to do this, so you might as well agree now," Suki said. "Take a leaf from Beatrice's tree to cover your mouth. It will help."

Britt shook her head and stared at the house. Events had gone incredibly sour, and she almost wished Al would return home. But he was not the answer. Suki was right: she had this magical lineage coursing through her veins, and for some strange, divine reason, she was being called to do this right now.

"Okay," she said into the receiver. She dropped her phone on the front lawn, moving as if in a daze, and followed Suki's orders.

She grabbed a leaf from the great maple, said a small prayer for help, and ran into the house.

She ran down the smoky hall into the living room. She opened a few windows, hoping to get some of the smoke out. It wouldn't be long before the fire department came.

Nothing in the sparse rooms gave her a clue to the whereabouts of any dagger. All of Beatrice's stuff had been cleared out. "Where would I find a knife?" she asked aloud as she ran into the kitchen. Her heart lurched; large flames engulfed the stove.

She looked quickly for a fire extinguisher but was doubtful it would help. The flames were spreading up the walls; the fire was quickly spiraling out of control.

She ran back down the hall to the front door. A fire extinguisher sat next to the umbrella stand. She dropped the leaf, grabbed the extinguisher, and ran back to the kitchen. Reading the directions on the fly, she pulled the lever and sprayed foam across the room. The pressure was more powerful than she'd anticipated and it shot her backward. She regained her footing and continued to spray until the fire was out. She was shocked at her own capabilities.

She looked out the window; no one was around. The charred kitchen was now all covered in white foam. She grabbed a wet towel and opened drawers with melted handles, looking for the dagger. Coming up empty, she glanced on the counter. A butcher block of knives sat in the corner. One handle was different from all the rest, made of ornately carved white bone.

She pulled it out of the block of wood. It was a tiny paring knife with a quartz crystal tip. She laughed out loud at the small size of the blade.

She ran down the steps to the basement, carrying the fire extinguisher and the knife. She was glad to see there were no fires on this level of the house. She ran into the red room and, after her eyes adjusted, searched for a way to get into the glass enclosure.

"I can't believe I'm doing this," she said aloud. She picked up the fire extinguisher and smashed the wall. Glass shattered and she turned her head away from the flying shards. The snakes quickly scattered about the room; all but one—the great white serpent, the largest of them all.

Britt slammed the door shut to keep them in and switched on the fluorescent light. She needed to see, they didn't.

She locked eyes with the great snake. "I never feared snakes," she said. "I was around a lot of them as a child. I really don't want to hurt you." She looked around the room, and all of the others had coiled themselves in corners, watching curiously. The white serpent undulated as Britt started to back away. *There is no reason to kill this creature,* she thought. *Suki must have been mistaken.*

She lowered the knife and the white snake lunged and sank its fangs into her forearm. Britt yowled and, in a reflex action of self-defense, sank the blade into its neck. She let go and fell backward against the wall. She searched quickly for her phone and remembered dropping it somewhere outside. She barely took a step before she started to feel woozy. The venom was traveling through her veins, turning her skin hot enough to make her break a sweat. She leaned her head back on the wall and held her arm with her other hand. A sense of hyperawareness came over her eyes, and she thought she might be starting to hallucinate.

She watched the mouth of the snake move and instead of a hiss, she heard it speak. *"Like the Kundalini, the serpent is the life force of Mother Earth. She has awakened. We that traverse the ground felt this coming long before humans sensed it. It is now time for us to leave and take our rightful place among the stars with the other creatures out of time. I offer you the forbidden fruit that will set your passions free. After all, you have done that for me."*

The snake's body fell like a costume had been unzipped. A fine pink mist remained in the air, a combination of blood and water vapor. The mist became denser as seconds clicked away.

Britt sank to the floor, sure she was hallucinating, as she watched a woman materialize out of the mist. She seemed out of a storybook. Her black hair was cut bluntly, and a crown of gold and red jewels adorned her head. Britt couldn't make out if she was wearing clothes. A shimmer of gold mist clung to her body, hiding it.

The goddess-like creature moved very slowly. "Thank you, dear one. You did a great deed. I have been in that encasing for a very long time." She lifted her arms in a flowing manner, stretching her body. "It feels so good to be free." She looked at Britt's arm. "I am sorry for that. It won't kill you."

"I killed the snake," Britt said in shock. The whole scene hadn't quite registered in her brain. She looked down at the lifeless body of the snake. Its appearance seemed almost rubberlike.

"Yes, I couldn't be freed any other way. I am Neith, high priestess of the primordial waters of the First Age." She looked at the other snakes. They had all come forward out of their corners with curiosity.

"They are goddesses too?" Britt asked, already knowing the answer.

"Yes, and they need to be freed as well. Can you do again?" Neith asked. "It needs to be done with the hand of a mortal."

Britt took in a large breath and exhaled through her mouth. "I don't know," she said. "You came after me, I didn't have a choice. I don't want to get bitten again."

"You must do it again," Neith said. "Our time has come. This needs to happen now."

"There's a fire upstairs," Britt said urgently. "Can't you just tell the others to follow you out?"

Neith shook her head. "They can't follow, they need to be free. And you must do it."

Britt thought of Skylar and all she had done to help the world. If she could do this, it would be her own small contribution.

"Oh, this isn't where your story ends, dear one," Neith said, reading her thoughts. "You have dreams of following Teresa, and that calling awaits." She smiled tenderly, like a mother, and Britt's eyes filled with tears, thinking of her own mother.

Neith said nothing more, only picked up the knife from the floor and handed it to Britt. "They will all come forward, knowing what is to take place." As her words hung in the air, the snakes drew closer to Britt, forming a circle.

Again Britt took in breath and exhaled through circled lips. "Okay," she said. A waft of smoke swept into the room.

"It has to be now. It helps if you yell," Neith said.

Britt's eyes widened. *Stabbing and yelling? This is completely unladylike.*

"Sound is a vital component for life," Neith said. "Making sounds of pleasure or of pain are vital for well-being. You've been living your life too quietly."

Britt could agree with that. "Okay," she said again. She growled softly and Neith laughed from her belly. The sound shook the walls, and the glass shards on the floor rose in the air from the vibration. When she stopped, they crashed down.

"Try that again," Neith said.

This time Britt reared up from the bowels of her being and screamed a high-pitched girl scream.

Neith winced. "Better," she said. "That one had a bit more life to it, but it was filled with fake emotion, as if it is what's expected of you. Let us hear what's not expected of you."

Britt clenched her fists, one around the knife. A low growl in her chest sank to her belly and she let out a sound that surprised her—an angry moan that quickly spiraled in a circle that consumed her. Her rage over her mother's decline, her stepfather's treachery, and her feelings of being alone all unleashed and found their voice in the moment. She screamed and cried and slashed her knife at each of the snakes that came forward. Blinded by her emotion and oblivious to how many she cut, she continued thrashing and slicing until all the snakes fell to the ground and Neith called for her to stop.

Britt collapsed to her knees. She felt a release.

A hiss filled the room, and for a moment she thought her job wasn't done. But then she realized the sound wasn't a hiss but a sizzle. The carcasses of the snakes disintegrated into fine mist and disappeared. Iridescent skins lay on the floor as the only remnants of their existence. In each of their places, a woman took form. They had all been trapped.

Another woman stepped forward. She was similar in appearance to Neith. The gold shimmer hung over her body as well. "Thank you, brave warrior princess," she said. "I am Uriela. And thanks to you, I am free of a curse that followed me from Atlantis to Egypt and all the way here." She gestured to the women all standing in a circle. "We all are free." She stepped back among the others, all of them marveling at their own bodies.

The women joined hands and formed a circle, with Britt standing in the middle. The soft glow of the serpents they'd once been still loomed in their abdomens, bright enough to shine through the gold mist. The illuminated snakes danced back and forth across their bellies as the women raised their hands to the sky. As if the ceiling had opened above, golden rays of light rained down upon them.

The energy of the circle was electrified; Britt felt the raw power run through her. She felt alive with the light tingling down her arms to her fingers. Her snakebite now had a line of gold ore running through it. The gold energy crested in her own abdomen and shot up her body like a force she'd never known. It came out the top of her head, and tiny stars could be seen around her crown.

"The Kundalini," Neith said and smiled. "Welcome to the sisterhood."

The light faded and Britt caught her breath. "Where will you go now?" she asked the group.

"We will return to the stars with our sisters of the sea," Neith said, waving her hand near Britt's hair. "We have been away from our home for far too long. Thank you again, dear one. Take to heart that you have done your part to help many worlds at once." She took Britt's hand in hers and showed her the bite. Britt's eyes widened; the bite had become a ring of three doves.

"You are a granddaughter of the Great Mother of Air," Neith said. "You now take your rightful place among us all."

They all raised their hand in farewell, and Britt watched as the gold mist around them grew brighter. It engulfed them all, and eventually they faded and were gone.

In the silence they left behind, she collapsed to her knees to process all that had happened on a normal street in New York on a Sunday morning. The thought of church services popped into her head. She remembered being forced to wear her Sunday best with her mother. When she was much younger, she'd tried to find the humor in church, convinced Jesus loved a good joke. But too often she'd been banished to the vestibule for laughing at her own silliness. She missed that girl. Somewhere in her teens, she'd lost her laughter—right around the time her mother's memory started to fade.

"It's time to bring her back, don't you think?" a familiar voice said in the corner.

Britt jumped to her feet. The image of her mother stood, radiant and luminous, before her.

"Mother!" She raced over to embrace her, only to realize that her body was a projection in the gold mist.

"This is my *subtle body*, I think they call it," Talia said.

"Is it really you?" Britt asked in wonder.

"Consider this my resurrection," Talia said. "Although my body still breathes back home."

"How is this possible?" Britt asked.

"Al used dark magic to trap my soul in that serpent. It gave him great powers to manipulate energy and control the elements. Over time, my memory left my body and remained here."

"He certainly didn't conquer the world, living in Beatrice's basement in his forties," Britt said, scowling.

Talia smiled. "Black magic always eats at the neglected parts of the sorcerer. That which hides in shadows becomes malignant."

"Now you're free," Britt said, smiling. "I can go home."

"I'm so proud of you." Talia beamed. "I can't wait to give you a hug, my divine daughter." She reached out her hand and it wafted through Britt's body.

Britt shuddered. "I felt you."

"I won't stay like this for much longer," Talia said as her image faltered slightly. "I will be waiting for you back home." She faded completely.

Britt exhaled and allowed herself to feel excited. She found her way to the front door, knowing she would never see this house again.

The front door, she thought, staring at it.

She laughed out loud. *This* was the door Suki was looking for, the one with the funny symbols; Beatrice had turned it into her front door. She couldn't stop laughing. Any concerns regarding its magical properties were unwarranted. This door was purely decorative.

She didn't know what would happen to the house, so she took the knife and put it in her massive tote bag, which she found lying on the front lawn, soaking wet—rain had found its way to Beatrice's while she was inside. Her cell phone lay next to her bag. She picked it up and found that her call with Suki was still running. The call time was over an hour.

"Hello?" she asked warily.

"What the hell?" Suki asked.

"Why are you still holding?" Britt asked. "I would have called you back."

"It doesn't matter. Is it done?"

"Yes, it's done, and it's raining, and I found your door."

Britt explained and Suki was appeased. It would seem Ocean had played a joke on her.

"One last thing?" Suki asked.

Britt huffed. "What?"

"Go stand under the tree."

32

Britt walked up to the great maple in the yard. The sound of the rain was soothing as it hit its leaves. It vibrated with energy Britt could see, similar to her mother's subtle body.

All at once, every leaf on the tree dropped to the ground.

"Did I do that?" she asked Suki.

"Wait for it," Suki said.

Britt waited. Just as quickly as they fell, the leaves sprouted anew where the old had been seconds before. In minutes, the emerald canopy was alive again, substantially more vibrant than before. This canopy shone with a new, electric light. Britt could feel the excitement of the tree filter down its trunk to its roots and spread under the shallow earth. The energy reached her and she felt a jolt. It quickly moved on, spreading across the grid to points unknown.

Britt was invigorated with life, having received a burst of fresh oxygen. She twirled in the rain like a child. She was happy and couldn't wait to get back home.

"Bye, Suki," she said.

"Bye, Britt, and thank you."

All of the Great Mothers' trees were ignited with light once the stone was returned to the well. The tree of the North, at Silverwood, felt the layers of hate and fear from the past melt away like the last bit of snow in spring. The tree was ancient and held the knowledge of the world when the curse had been placed on humanity. And now it was time to rejoice! Freedom was in the air.

The students of Silverwood played their music with verve for no other reason than to simply enjoy the moment. The tree responded to the vibrations of sound, the vibrations of joy, and did its own dance, a visible shimmy, where it stood.

Its energy pulsed down into the root system of camp, growing exponentially, connecting to all other trees through the water that they all shared, spreading the word. It wouldn't take long to reach every tree on the continent with the news: the Golden Age had arrived. Soon, every tree would awaken to its enhanced existence on the lighted grid. They would all begin to emit heightened oxygen, enlivening humanity and reversing the poor air quality plaguing the world.

Despite its appearance in the physical world, Ocean's charred tree was perfect and believed itself to be so. It had enormous capabilities as the Tree of Death—able to live in both worlds, to reach back and forth between here and the afterlife. Its roots were tied to the Underworld and it was the very first tree to become aware of the news. But it wasn't inclined to do much of anything about it. As a courtesy, it shared the news with the other Great Mothers' trees, but that was it.

It knew that death was the ultimate alchemical door, just another threshold to walk through. This tree was in a constant state of acceptance of all—life, death, good, bad, all perceptions of duality. The Golden Age was always assured by this tree. The world would soon celebrate, good had won. *This too shall pass*, the tree thought. *And I will be here, shuttling souls back and forth over the threshold of reality.*

Vivienne's kelp tree lit up like a beacon under the water when it heard the news. The pulsating filaments of light spread like the web from Skylar's heart. For miles, sea life absorbed the energy radiating from the tree, and every creature and plant took on a phosphorus glow. A nearby coral reef, once decimated, began to regenerate with the wisdom of the feminine. Around it, beautiful crystals shimmered in the water like starlight, revealing the secret that long ago, before the First Age, water had been sent to earth as a gift from the Goddess.

Giant sea horses with lit horns on their heads galloped in the crystalline water, taking their place as underwater constellations, forever blending the sea and sky. The women freed by Vivienne returned from the sky once more to swim in the magical waters. They scooped up handfuls of the glass that had once imprisoned them and had found its way to the ocean floor. They held the magical glass in their arms and all at once dissipated into the water and returned to their position in the night's sky.

Vivienne looked at the globe in the laboratory. It was different, healed. The magnetic grid lines of the dragon were complete. The melting would subside, as would the fires. Balance would be the order of the day. She was pleased.

She stepped out onto the balcony of the building; the rising water was just below her feet. She knew it would be mere moments before the sea overtook the last of this land. It had once contained the magic of human potential but had fallen to the greed of man, forsaking love for knowledge. She had always been portrayed as the coldest sister, as cold as the darkest sea. But the sea contained the yearning of the human soul. And Vivienne had carried that yearning with her for thirteen thousand years, now made visible as her trail of shadows. All of humanity's love and loss and desire and misdeeds were represented in her own. And now it was time for freedom.

"I forgive myself," she said through tears. She took off her black cloak. Underneath, her flowing, gossamer dress radiated a soft pale green in the moonlight. She held the cloak over the railing of the balcony and the wind caught it, lifting it high in the air. She watched it expand and transform into a stingray of twinkling light in the sky. It circled her once and soared high into the cloudless night. She waited but knew it would never return. All of her shadows had transformed into stars, and she felt she was finally free.

33

It rained on the planet for exactly three days and then abruptly stopped, everywhere. Suki thought she might hear from Skylar but didn't. If she were honest, though, she hadn't dwelled on Skylar too much; she was too busy loving her new job. She almost felt guilty about it, but not too much.

She stared at the door between Operation Liberty Tree and the Oval Office. "I'm creating a Life Door," she said out loud to herself. "I'm a flipping alchemist, I can create whatever I want."

"I'm hoping that's true," a voice said from behind her.

Suki turned to find Noah standing in the doorway. He looked like he had aged ten years. "Wow, look at you," she said, making no apologies for staring at him. "You made it back from the Underworld—transformed, I see." She got uncomfortably close to inspect the lines on his face, and he took one step back.

"No one told me I would age," he said angrily.

"Ahh, that would have been the ticket to stopping you," she said. "How about Milicent?"

"If you know what's good for you, you won't bring it up, or look at her too closely, or even make eye contact with her, like you're doing to me." He put his palm in her face to get her to back away.

"I may want to study you," she said, batting his hand away. "I'm experimenting with making my own door."

"I have something more pressing," he said. "When we came

back, the Quine library was in flames. I'm sorry to say the building's armored outside couldn't prevent loss from internal combustion."

She gasped. "No! All that material, gone?" She took a seat.

He nodded.

"This is terrible," she said, holding her head in her hands. "Thousands of . . ." In a flash she jumped up. "I can help. I can re-create everything." She ran to her drawing table and started to make a list. "I remember all of it, I can write it all down."

"That's why we're here," said a different voice.

Suki looked up from her list. Milicent was now in the doorway, Mica next to her.

"I've been trying to convince your new boss to give you back to me, but she refuses. So you choose."

If Noah had aged ten years, Milicent had aged at least twice that. Suki tried not to stare.

"Oh man, are you kidding me?" she asked, looking to Noah for guidance.

He shrugged.

"Thanks." She approached Milicent. "I'm happy to help you, but we're at a crucial time in the country right now. We're just about to unveil our new plan, and the judge is addressing the nation in ten minutes."

"I've invited them to stay," Mica said. "Permanently."

"It pains me to be back here," Milicent said.

"You've got nothing back in Massachusetts," Mica said. "Literally nothing. So the way I see it, this is your best offer."

Milicent huffed out of her nose but didn't say a word.

"I thought so."

They walked out on the White House lawn, now newly sodded after the fires. Mica walked up to the podium and, per her directive, the spectators who normally would have lined up along the fence were invited to sit, picnic-style, on the lawn during her speech.

Mica looked out at the sea of attendees. The majority were women, all of whom desperately wanted a female president, seeing this as the answer. But she wasn't. She was just another fallible human, trying her best in an impossible situation.

Since she didn't have a speechwriter, she had taken a run at writing a speech herself, but she'd never been good with the written word. She did better speaking from her heart.

"There are some that say our goal in America is *one color*—conform or be cast out. Some say the goal of our melting pot is sameness. But I say no: We are a diverse people. The goal is not to all become one but to embrace the paradox that we are all one, as we are different." Mica looked out at the people crowded on the lawn. "We must embrace the muddiness of life. To mistrust others because of skin color, or religion, or any differences in beliefs means we distrust the very God within them. We are all part of the whole. We like the clean lines of neat boxes labeled in a row, telling us who's who. But our hearts sense something is amiss when we look to these self-imposed walls. Our head dismisses it, judges, and shuts the heart down. But that only works for so long before our heart makes us sick from neglect. Neglecting the truth can no longer be the way of life in this country. We must embrace the unknown, in others and in ourselves. As we live and grow and raise our children together, this country will prosper through respect and cooperation."

She was met with roaring approval from her audience on the lawn. Yet again, the people of America would put their faith outside themselves. But this time, the country had a greater chance to flourish as originally intended.

Behind her, Noah trotted out a fairly large oak tree on a dolly. It was a mystery how he could maneuver something so heavy by himself, or why he had been assigned the task with so many groundskeepers present. Glaring at Milicent, who was standing with Suki behind Mica, he stopped near a freshly dug hole. Mica motioned for him to place the root ball in it. He obliged and barely got it in the hole. A few other young people on staff helped cover the roots with dirt. After a bit of work, the tree stood on its own.

One staffer began drumming a slow, rhythmic beat as Mica spoke again. Milicent shook her head but kept quiet.

"I scatter these acorns of the ancient tree in the four directions, welcoming all races to meet us here in the New America, the New Atlantis." She walked around the tree and scattered acorns behind her. "This heartbeat will call those from the four directions together in a new and unprecedented time of peace. My words are but a representation of what is buried within your hearts, waiting to be unleashed at the proper time. Now is the time. It is through the actions of your heart that our world will be transformed for good."

As if by magic, the roots of the oak tree snaked deep into the earth yet remained visible, glowing tentacles of light reaching out in the four directions. They reached deep into the core of Mother Earth and Sophia's library, connecting to the current of humanity.

"As the sap flows to each leaf of this tree, the same life flows within each person here today and to each person beyond our scope of sight," Mica said. "We are all connected by the divine water running through our veins."

Everyone on the lawn witnessed the miracle of the tree growing before their eyes. Mica knew the ideas she was voicing were planting themselves like seeds in the minds of those that were there. The most prevalent idea: compassion. She saw fifteen pregnant women on the lawn that day. She could see that each felt their own importance, carrying the future heart of America within them. They all wept, overcome with the joy and awe for life. Mica hoped this feeling would snake its way down into the cord breathing life into their unborn children, infusing the next generation with a fire to carry on the promise of her words that day.

Mica invited as many as could fit in a circle around the tree. They all joined hands.

"In a circle," she said, "there is no leader. All are equal. The truth springs from many hearts and takes many outer forms, no two ever the same. I do not wish to be a leader for a lifetime, for if I do that, I've failed you. I am a leader for a purpose: to reestablish this country as it was originally intended. I am the leader of this project, nothing more. For at the end of it, there will not be one leader, but many."

She sat down on the grass and the children in the crowd joined her. Everyone else knelt on the great lawn of the White House and felt the sun on their faces. Her staffers brought out instruments and handed them around, and together, they all began to play music.

Suki and Noah joined Mica on the grass. Milicent stood in the shade behind the podium, alone.

"You belong out there," Ocean said, walking up beside her.

"No, this is for the young ones," Milicent said. "I was never a tree hugger, and I won't be starting now."

"We all have to start somewhere," Ocean said.

"Is this how you thought things would turn out?" Milicent asked, pointing to the current president of the Unites States dancing around a tree on the White House lawn.

"More or less."

Milicent gave her a skeptical look. "What will you do now?"

"I was going to ask you the same," Ocean said. "You should

stay in DC. It will be livelier than Rosen. I really can't see you rebuilding the Quine. All of that material was burned for a reason. Walk toward the future, Milicent. Let go of the past."

Milicent nodded, and Ocean walked away.

34

Skylar and Argan stood in the great hall of Sophia's books.

"Will they be my books now?" Skylar asked. "Will this be known as Skylar's library?"

"If so, here's that glory you were looking for," he said.

She grimaced. "Argan, I don't want to disappoint Sophia, but I can't stay here for eternity."

"I don't want that either, Sky, but let's play devil's advocate. If not you, who's going to do it?"

"Well . . . Sophia," she said. "She's been doing it until now. What's she going to do, go into retirement?"

"Something like that, yes." Sophia's voice rang like sleigh bells behind them. "All souls eventually transition. Even ones like me. And Lucifer. We weren't meant to stay in this realm forever. Thirteen thousand years is quite enough."

"What happened to Lucifer?" Skylar asked. With everything turned on its ear, the fate of the prince of darkness had slipped her mind.

"Now that the stone has healed, human perception has shifted. His presence can no longer be manipulated. He transitioned."

"That's cryptic," Skylar said. "He's free without his stone?"

"Not quite," Sophia said.

"All due respect, again, but I'm not like you," Skylar said. "I didn't start out as a goddess."

"But you became one," Sophia said. "And in that process, you figured out who you are. I know you've longed for the familial connection you feel was ripped from you. But through this journey, you have found so much more. You have found your tribe. Your lineage is from the sea—it *is* the sea. You've returned to your true home."

As Sophia spoke, a rustling noise started above their heads. Against one wall, dark tentacles snaked down and wove among the books, spreading throughout them.

"Are those octopus tentacles?" Argan asked.

"No," Skylar whispered in awe. "Tree roots." She walked toward the wall as it grew dark with the black roots overtaking the books on the shelves. "Why is it so invasive? What is happening?" she asked, trying to stay calm.

"The last tree has been planted. New Atlantis has risen." Sophia smiled. The roots snaked in and out of the books and down to the floor, where they stopped, anchoring themselves.

"Suki," Skylar said, grinning. She could see the image of Suki in front of the White House. She was happy and she was helping re-create the world above. She was doing her part. She had found her purpose.

Skylar turned to Argan. "This is my part. This wild, insane ending is my part." She took his hand in hers. "I don't expect you to stay here with me, but I understand now. This is my part," she repeated, partly to reassure herself. She kissed him but he didn't kiss her back.

"I'm so glad you see," Sophia said. "Come, dear one. We must prepare for your baptism." She looked at Argan. "You will return to your sleeping quarters while Skylar gets ready."

"I didn't know I had sleeping quarters," Argan said.

Excited, Skylar followed Sophia out of the great hall, hardly noticing that Argan lagged behind.

Four turrets had been erected in the newly rebuilt castle. One in each corner; all made of sand. Sophia explained that the new structure looked nothing like her original temple. This design was intended for Skylar.

"I had no idea medieval architecture was in my DNA," Skylar said before a flurry of undines shooed her in one direction, Argan in another.

Undines were beautiful water creatures, similar to the mermaids but with legs. Their skin shone an iridescent blue and violet and like their sea sisters, they all had long hair. Most dressed in white gauzy gowns that trailed as long as their hair. These elemental beings were not prisoners of anyone. They were born of the sea, and they infused their surroundings with their love of the ocean and her creatures. They assisted those in the spirit and human realms not only with the task of purifying water but also of purifying the heart.

Skylar's room was at the very top of the turret on the opposite side of the castle from Argan's turret. Everything was decorated in silver and blue, and Skylar thought she'd have to embrace beach décor. She looked out the window into the perpetual night. *Will I really never see the sun again?* Standing in the library, she could embrace her duty, embrace her purpose, but now, standing here alone, she wasn't so sure.

She took in a deep breath as a soft knock came at the door. It opened and a delicate undine came in. Her chestnut hair carried on behind her beyond the scope of what Skylar could see.

"I've come to prepare your hair," she said, holding up a silver sand pail filled with hair supplies. She gestured for Skylar to take a seat in front of the mirror.

Skylar looked in the mirror and noticed that her curls were resurfacing. There was no hiding them in this water world. The undine retrieved a silver, jeweled comb from her pail and began to comb out Skylar's hair effortlessly. With each stroke, strands of light shot through her hair and individual curls sprang back in perfect place. Skylar was amazed.

"I must have been five or so," Skylar started a story as the undine continued her work. "My mom was so sick of my knotted hair she cut it off. We could have used a bit of this magic back then. It was short until just before I met Argan. It was about that time that I rediscovered my curls. And it was one of the things he liked about me then."

"I'm sorry I cut your hair all those years ago, that beautiful hair," the undine said. Skylar looked up through the mirror and saw Cassie's face. She continued to comb Skylar's long curls; the simple act of love shot right through Skylar's heart. All she could do was accept the pampering, accept the love of her mother through this magical creature.

When she was done, Skylar's hair was swept up exactly like Sophia's. Every color was represented—black, brown, blond, red—all in streaming ringlets. Her hair had grown exponentially since she'd been there. "It must be the water," she joked. A simple circle of udumbara flowers wove through braided green vines around her head.

She stood up and the undine's delicate features returned to their original state. She helped Skylar slip into a beautiful, white, flowing gown of lace that resembled coral lattice.

Skylar looked in the mirror and saw her reflection, then Cassie's, then Rachel's, then Sophia's.

"We are all reflections of the Great Mother," the undine said. "All unique, all beautiful."

"I'm too young to be a mother," Skylar said.

"Yes, but you embody the magic waiting, a time of life to be celebrated. All of the stages of a woman's life should be celebrated. They all hold their own magic."

Skylar thought about the nursery of souls and the evolution of a woman over the course of a lifetime.

"You are young to be burdened with such philosophy," the undine said. "Men are here to be men. They are simple, have a simple purpose. They are the protectors, the doers of the world. Women change like caterpillars to butterflies, like the sea herself. They grow as they care for others. But through these changes, one thing holds true. Women embody love."

Skylar couldn't help but be reminded that she would never change, staying here. She would be timeless, like Sophia.

The undine gave her a hug and left the room. Skylar returned to the window. She knew Argan's room was across the courtyard in the other turret. A wave of panic swept her. She would never go home, never see Joel or Michael or the horses at the barn. This would be her home now.

Skylar raced down the stairs as fast as she could in her tight lace dress. The packed sand steps were cold on her bare feet. She ran across the courtyard and back up the stairs to Argan's room. She stopped just short of the door. It was ajar. She pushed it open slowly and found Argan standing in front of his open window, bathed in the bright, full moonlight streaming through. He was luminous, bare skinned, waiting to dress.

He glanced up and shot her a smile, but it quickly faded; a look of remembering what was to come overtook him. He recovered and the smile returned, though somewhat dimmer. He turned to a shiny gold robe hanging on a hanger.

"Sophia says I have to wear this thing," he said, flipping a satin sleeve in a circle.

"It will look great," she lied.

"Nice try," he said. "I thought it was bad luck to see you before the ceremony."

"We're not getting married, Argan."

"Right," he said. "You look beautiful."

"Thank you," she said. "But help me see the bright side of this please. I understand what's been asked of me throughout all of the adventures we've had." She took his hands in hers. "You've been by my side the whole time. Thank you." She smiled. "But now, all I want to do is go home. I want to see the horses and my little house in the woods. I want to have a life . . . with you."

Argan squeezed her hand. "This is your home too, Sky, the home of your ancestors. You must feel that pull."

"Yes, I do," she said. "But it's the past, Argan. I can't feel a future here. And now Sophia expects me to embrace this but I'm scared. What will life look like on the other side of this night? It will always *be* night. There's no going back to the beginning."

"Which beginning? When we were eleven? Or when I saw you in that bar?" he asked, levity in his voice.

The memory made her laugh and she covered her mouth with her hand. "Oh, that night," she said through her laughter. "I was a hot mess."

"You weren't that bad," he said with a twinkle.

"Sure," she said.

"Everything's different. The world is completely different. You did it, Skylar." He touched her face lightly. She could see the intense love and pride in his eyes. "You changed the course of history."

"*We* did that," she said. She closed her eyes and let her face sink into his hand.

He walked away from her and put on the robe. "I will stay here with you," he said.

Her eyes brightened, but just for a moment. "Oh, Argan, I can't ask you to do that. And I'm not even sure it's possible."

"We're in the land of anything's possible, Sky," he said. "In fact . . . come with me." He grabbed her hand and led her back

down the steps. They left through the front door and walked out
to the water's edge. "We could leave right now, you and me. We
could leave Sophia a note."

"You want me to run away?" she asked.

"What do you think?" He waited.

"That doesn't sound like you, or me," she said. "If history has
proven one thing, it's that we do what's right."

"Yeah," he said, sitting in the sand.

She looked at the water and then down at her dress. "Unzip
me," she said.

"Huh?" he asked, puzzled. "Now?"

"Yes please," she said.

He obliged, and she let her beautiful dress fall to the sandy
shoreline.

"Let's take a swim," she said.

"I'm not really in the mood, Sky," he said.

"Come on. Please?"

He reluctantly took off his robe and dropped it on the shore.
They waded into the warm water, holding hands.

Skylar skimmed the waves with her fingertips and the water
responded, swelling higher and higher with each pass of her fingers.

"Sky?" he asked.

"Hmm?"

"Did you ever see us together in other lifetimes?"

She paused, quickly flipping through her mental images of
her life with him. "Yes," she finally said. "You never looked this
good"—she ran her hand over the muscles in his stomach—"but
it was always your soul signature."

"Did we ever have children?"

She collapsed under the waves to soak up the energy of the
water in her hair. She would have to apologize to the undine who
had worked so hard on it.

When she came up out of the water, Argan touched her hair, now glistening even more with the addition of fresh water crystals, and with a few shakes, he released her hair so it spiraled down around her body.

She pulled a glistening strand in front of her face and giggled. "This happens every time."

"That is pure magic right there," he said. "You're going to have to make that happen when we get back home." He looked at her with a look of assurance.

"Right," she said, looking at him briefly, then quickly away.

"I knew it," he said.

"Knew what?" she asked.

"Your eyes tell a story your words are hiding," he said. "You're staying here. Whether I can or not."

She nodded, unable to speak.

"Back to my question about children," he said.

"Why so curious?" she asked.

"The boy in the nursery, he was yours and Joshua's."

"He was," she said. "But he wasn't meant to be. He was never meant to be. He is a soul in my life that always keeps watch, like a guardian angel. We think of guardians as older than us, but he's my angel that reminds me of childlike innocence." She could see the disappointment on his face. "We did have children over the lifetimes, Argan," she said. "But the odd thing was that there was always only one. In all of our lifetimes, we only had one child each time."

"Are their soul signatures with us now, like your boy?" he asked.

"I don't know," she said. "I haven't been able to feel it, if that's what you're asking." Argan's mood changed and Skylar felt the distance creep in between them. "I bet they are, though."

"We weren't meant to have a child in this lifetime, then,"

he said. "I mean, you're not coming back to Rosen. You've made your decision. I see it in your eyes. You're time in the cycle of karma is over. No more children for you. Or for us."

He turned away from her and waded out of the water. She watched him put on his robe and walk back up the shore and into the castle.

35

L ife had been erratic in DC since the solstice. Mica's peaceful
gathering was still reverberating through the walls, but her
staff lacked concrete direction, so virtually nothing was getting
done. Suki's role had quickly morphed from mapmaker into head
of triage, and soon she was fielding questions like a veteran.

Mica stood in the doorway of Operation Liberty Tree. "You're
doing a great job, Suki."

Suki beamed at the compliment.

"Yes, I see my library is on permanent hold," Milicent said,
walking in. She had taken former–First Lady liberties with Wren
and let herself into the Oval Office. Noah was oddly absent.

"Aren't you taking me up on my offer to come back here?"
Mica said.

"Oh no, there's no way I'm coming back here," Milicent said.

"Seeing as how you haven't *left* here since you got here"—
Mica sat on one of the sofas in the center of the office and
gestured for the other two women to do the same—"I'd say you're
back here."

"Fine," Milicent said, perching on the sofa opposite Mica.
"Then give me something good, like secretary of defense or
something."

The door opened and Wren walked in. "Judge, we have more
guests."

Vivienne and Ocean didn't wait to be announced.

271

"Fire and Water together again. This must be big," Milicent said.

Mica got up. "Milicent, this is still my office. I would assume they're here to see me."

Suki bounced up. "Do you have news about Skylar?"

"We do," Ocean said. "She is alive and well. Magus is dead. Crushed by his own ego." She glanced at Vivienne, who remained stoic. "It would seem we have come to the end of our story."

"So she's coming home!" Suki was so excited that she rushed Ocean and hugged her before she could stop herself.

"Well, not quite," Ocean said.

"Why? What's left?" Suki asked.

Milicent scoffed. "Oh, please let me tell her," she said smugly. The smile on Suki's face faded.

"You see, trusting Suki, it's the dirty little secret the good guys neglect to reveal at the beginning of such quests. They tout *purpose* and *nobility* and *duty* and make the whole thing sound so sexy. Most are seduced. Most end up dead. But then there are the few like Skylar. Somewhere along the way, she actually earned my respect. Not that it helps her now. She's not dead, but her good deed didn't go unpunished." She looked at Ocean. "Tell her!" she scolded. "Tell her that our precious heroine can't come back. That she must stay at the bottom of the sea for eternity, to fulfill her *purpose*. Forsaking love for honor. Or loyalty." She spat out the last word.

Vivienne focused her attention on Ocean. "Milicent has a point, Sister," she said. "Skylar has succeeded in every monumental task given to her, and how do we repay her? By banishing her to *the bottom of the sea for eternity*, as Milicent put it? I understand that was the deal with Sophia, but it just doesn't sit well with me. I can only imagine you feel it too."

Ocean sighed. "I was waiting for you to bring this up. Sophia will not stay another moment. Her reign is over."

"Child, what would you do if you were me?" Vivienne asked Milicent. "How would you end this quest?"

Surprise washed over Milicent's face at the question. "You are asking me for the answer?"

"Yes," Vivienne said.

Milicent paused. "I would make sure everyone involved got what they deserved," she said emphatically.

"And what do *you* deserve, child?" Vivienne asked.

Milicent shook her head in confusion. "I don't understand what you mean."

Vivienne closed the gap between them and looked into Milicent's face. "You are my kin, a daughter of the sea, just like Skylar. Yet your history is tarnished with great deceit and self-fulfilling deeds. Tell me when your karma has been cleared."

Milicent stood silently.

"Right," Vivienne said. "Your worst crime? Believing you were above the rest, not taking responsibility for your actions because you thought the Universe owed you. The Universe owes you nothing, child. You get what you give."

Milicent stepped back from Vivienne and leaned on the presidential desk for support. "What are you saying, Grandmother?"

"That you should take Skylar's place," Vivienne said.

"That's absurd." Milicent's eyes widened. "I didn't think that could be done."

Vivienne looked at Ocean for confirmation. Ocean shrugged and nodded, essentially giving her approval.

"I don't need a secretary of defense anyway," Mica said casually. She tapped Suki on the shoulder and they vacated the room, leaving the other three to their conversation.

"Wait." Milicent bounced off the desk. "That's it? I don't get a say in this?"

"Why would we let you have a say?" Ocean said. "Consider this magical justice. And look on the bright side, you'll get that immortality you've been searching for your whole life."

The idea piqued Milicent's interest momentarily. While she was mulling it over, Noah burst through the door.

"I'm sorry, Mil, that damn elevator," he said. "You'd think they would fix that thing, being the White House and all." He looked around the room. "What's going on, what'd I miss?"

Ocean and Vivienne were already on their way out. "Tell him about the field trip you're going on," Ocean said over her shoulder.

"Can he come?" Milicent asked, warming to the idea by the minute.

Ocean shrugged a *why not*. "I figure you come as a set any-way." She and Vivienne left and Milicent was left alone with Noah.

"Where are we going, Mil?" he asked.

"Well, Noah, I figured out *what's next*," she said.

36

Skylar stood at the water's edge. She had redressed and fixed her hair herself. She inhaled deeply. The sea was raw magic, but it couldn't soothe away the reality of her circumstances.

She put one foot in the water; it was warm on her skin. She was now between worlds—one foot on land, one foot in the sea. The soft waves lapped at the hem of her dress. This was her baptism. A rebirth into a new way of being. Argan was yet to come back down after their fight. Although it hadn't really been a fight, if she thought about it. More of a surrender.

But she was ready to release all that had happened up to this point—all of the mistakes, all of the shame, all of the blame of others for the experiences of her life. Stepping into this water, she was stepping into the unknown and accepting her destiny. The plan that only the Great Mother, greater than the three, knew. It was planted in her heart. She had carried the stone as a representation of the light. It was an embodiment of what cannot be captured within all women, what all keepers of the flame carry—their one wild heart.

She waited for Sophia, but she didn't come. She didn't know how long she should stay by the water.

"Sky, look!" Argan shouted from his window in the turret. He pointed to a simple rowboat out in the distant sea. He left the window and raced down to the water's edge. Skylar and Argan watched in utter shock as the people in the boat materialized into

Milicent and Noah. He rowed, she rode. Once they got within earshot, they could hear the bickering.

"You know, Mil, you haven't done any of the rowing this entire trip," he said.

"I never said I was going to," she said.

They reached the shore and Milicent hopped out. She navigated the sand in her purple Louboutins as Noah collected a mountain of luggage from the boat. She was wearing a large, floppy, grape-colored hat and matching sheath dress.

"I could use a hand here," Noah said to Argan.

"You're on your own, buddy," Argan said with a wide grin.

"Nice robe," Noah said sarcastically.

Milicent walked by Skylar and started to remove her purple satin gloves. "You are dismissed," she said, and headed toward the castle without another word.

Noah lagged behind with the bags, stopping every so often to shake the sand out of his Ferragamos.

Skylar and Argan didn't say a word until they both disappeared from view.

"Holy cow," she said. "I'm free."

"Sophia is going to have her hands full with those two," Argan said.

They looked at each other with giddy smiles.

"Take me home, Argan," she said.

He picked her up in his arms and waded into the water. He kissed her softly on the lips . . . and then dumped her on her head.

She shot up out of the water, sputtering, hair dripping wet. "What the hell was that for?"

"You chose glory over me!" he said. "Don't think that little detail just magically disappears now that you've escaped eternal servitude here." He waded back to shore.

"Did it look like I had a choice to you?" she asked, following him.

"Uh, yeah." He kept walking.

"Okay, so how long are you planning to stay mad at me, so I can plan the day?"

"I don't know. Probably just five minutes, because I have to figure out how to get us out of here."

"Since when are you my savior? I've done just fine on my . . ." She stopped herself. "Okay, I'm sorry."

"Thank you," he said. "We could take their boat back to Vivienne's tree." He circled back to the shoreline to investigate the boat.

"Argan, what is that floating out there?" she asked, looking out at the sea. The moonlight was reflecting something in the water.

He squinted. "Looks like reflective tape." He shrugged and resumed getting the boat away from shore. He hopped in. "Are you coming? I'm not waiting another moment." He ditched his robe for the T-shirt and shorts underneath.

"Of course." She waded over and jumped in the boat in her long dress.

When they were about fifty yards out, they identified the floating object. It was Kyle, unconscious in a reflective life vest.

"Leave him," Argan said.

"Seriously?" Skylar asked.

"Fine, but he's not coming back with us," he said. "Take him to shore."

Skylar grabbed Kyle's vest and Argan rowed the boat close enough to drop Kyle on land. "Here's your stop," he said. He gave one strong yank on Kyle's vest and heaved him onto the sand. Kyle never woke up.

"Is he dead?" Skylar asked.

"No, he's just Kyle," Argan said. "He'll eventually come to and I'm sure Milicent will find plenty for him to do."

They left him sleeping on the shore in the bright moonlight.

"I'll never be so happy to see the sun as I will when we get home," Skylar said. She took one last look behind her at the castle that had almost been hers for eternity. Sophia stood on the shore; she had come to say good-bye. A shiny black jaguar sat regally next to her. A beautiful green stone shone from its forehead.

"Is that Lucifer?" Argan asked as he waved to Sophia.

"Nah," Skylar said doubtfully. "That would be weird."

July 25, 2021

The morning of Skylar's birthday, she stood on the porch of Ocean's house with the blue ceramic urn holding Cassie's ashes in her arms. She had agreed to bury them under the black tree now that Joshua's ashes were there alone. She had waited a half hour; she finally gave up on Ocean and made her way across the back lawn alone.

The grass had gotten high again, and she bent to swat away something that grazed her leg. She thought it was a bug, but when she looked down, she saw fur. Startled, she let the urn slip out of her hands and it crashed to the ground. The wiry grass wasn't soft enough to break its fall, and the urn cracked in half.

She knelt to salvage it but a wind kicked up. "Nana! Stop!" she shouted into the air, but it only increased. Skylar knew this was deliberate.

The ashes swirled up off the ground and sailed into the air. All she could do was watch the wind carry the remnants of Cassie's body into the sky. And watching, she understood. Her mother had never wanted to be stuck in that urn. Now she was eternally free, flying into the ethers. Skylar smiled.

She looked at the ground. The pile of gray ash was gone. Left behind was one perfect round white crystal, lying in the rubble of the ceramic urn. "This I'm keeping," she said. "My mother's heart." She walked back to the porch, leaving the ceramic for

Ocean to deal with. "I'll see you at three," she shouted through cupped hands. Ocean never came out.

All Skylar wanted for her birthday was a gathering of her friends and family in her tiny house, so that's what she'd planned. Since she'd been back home, she hadn't done much of anything except catch up with those she'd missed. Cheveyo had been waiting for her and she'd enjoyed getting back to riding. She'd been dodging the dean about a job. She fully enjoyed not knowing her next move and wanted to live in the unknown for as long as possible.

She took a break from the festivities inside to get some fresh air and enjoy the sunshine. Seconds later, Ocean came barreling down the driveway on her motorcycle. She hopped off and pulled out a bakery box from her storage seat, and as she walked toward Skylar, she flipped it open. In it was one cupcake, its candle already lit.

"Make a wish!" she said.

Skylar stood on the steps of the porch with the hum of activity behind her. She closed her eyes and blew out the candle.

"Whad'ya wish for?" Ocean asked.

"World peace," Skylar said.

"Good one," Ocean said. "I saw you this morning. Sorry about the cat."

"That was a cat?" Skylar shook her head. "It's fine. It's how things were meant to happen."

"I'm not coming in," Ocean said. "This is a gathering for family."

Skylar looked at her. "You are family."

Ocean smiled. "Okay," she said, sitting on the steps. "Is Joel still mad at me?"

"About the thymus thing?" Skylar asked. "Not sure. He's not allowed within a hundred yards of the White House, but he never goes anywhere, so I wouldn't worry about it."

"He'll laugh about it one day. I had to keep him out of trouble somehow." She took in a deep breath. "The weather is changing. Things are settling down. You'll see a fall this year."

"Oh, that's good news," Skylar said. "I'm looking forward to seeing the leaves change." She sat next to Ocean. "Boy, it hasn't been easy knowing you."

Ocean gave her a look.

"I'm just saying," Skylar said.

"I'll give you that," Ocean said. "But I'm fire, and when the student is ready, they jump into that fire, to be refined and remade into something better. I dare say, you are something better. And you are better for having known all the people in this house." She waved her hand over her shoulder. "We are all the sum of those we surround ourselves with. You add to their lives as much as they add to yours."

Skylar looked at her.

"Yes, grasshopper, you have added to my life," Ocean said.

"My parents are getting a divorce." Skylar stared out at the trees.

"I heard," Ocean said. "I'm sorry."

Skylar shrugged. "I get it. And maybe now they can find happiness somewhere else."

"Maybe," Ocean said. "Hey, how've the memories been? Getting a break from them all?"

"A break?" Skylar's mind came to life with the vivid details of important moments she never wanted to forget: Cassie brushing her hair; Joel and the horses; Argan at age eleven; Argan now. Meeting Suki, Ronnie, and Rhia; laughing with Britt in Cabin 3A; the birds in the trees of the greenhouse; all of the trees of the Great Mothers—the Silverwood tree, Beatrice's maple, Vivienne's kelp tree, and lastly, Ocean's black tree. "There are things I never want to forget." She smiled. "What will happen to you now? What will you do?"

"Anything I want." Ocean winked. "Actually, if Joel's single . . . I thought maybe . . ." She shrugged suggestively.

Skylar's eyes widened.

"What?" Ocean asked defensively. "He needs a bit of loosening up."

Skylar's forehead rose high. "You think you're the one to do it?" She laughed at the idea. Then her thoughts turned to the day she met Ocean in the Round Room at Rosen a few short years before. The Book of Sophia had been foreign to her then, but it had called for her to make a choice of destiny.

"It's gone," she said out loud.

"Yes," Ocean said. "In physical form. But it's returned to the sea, gone back to the shelves of Sophia's temple, where it belongs."

"Isn't it Milicent's temple—or should I say castle—now?" Skylar asked, and they both chuckled at the thought. "She didn't need the Quine re-created after all. Now she has all the knowledge she could possibly want for eternity." Skylar thought it would be fun to get a glimpse into Milicent's new world, but she was in no rush to return to the land under the water.

"Not all of it," Ocean said. She stood up, reached deep into her jeans pocket, and pulled out a handful of wrinkled pages.

"The last three pages," Skylar said with a smile. "I should have known you'd have them."

Ocean handed them to her. "Perfectly preserved, for the end of your story."

"There is no end," Skylar said. "It's all one big circle."

Ocean smiled again. "Now you truly know everything." She went to hug Skylar but stopped herself and patted her on the head instead.

Rhia came running outside, carrying an extremely tolerant Michael. Ronnie followed. They both smiled at Skylar and ran into the yard to play.

"There's proof of your work, right there," Ocean said. They watched Rhia dance in a circle, barefoot in the grass.

"Well, of all the endings I predicted, I didn't see this one coming," Argan said from the doorway.

"No?" Skylar asked.

He walked down the steps and sat next to her. "We're back where we started and the world isn't in ruins—in fact, it's better than ever," he said, looking at Rhia. "None of us are dead, especially me, and now we get to think about our next chapter." He looked at her.

She nodded. Joshua was dead, but she had to accept that she couldn't save the whole world. Rhia was certainly enough. "I'll start with these." She held up her pages.

Suki walked out and squeezed in next to them, making it very tight on the steps of the porch.

"When do you have to get back?" Skylar asked her.

"Tonight," Suki said. "This country needs me."

"I can't believe you're working in DC," Skylar said. "You're practically president. It's a far cry from the barn, but that place was always too small for you." She put her head on Suki's shoulder. "Thanks for making the time for me."

Rachel and Leonora peeked their heads out the door. "It's time for cake," they said as a pair.

"Be right in," Skylar said. She looked at Argan. "They've certainly hit it off." He nodded.

"Happy birthday, Sky," Suki said, handing her a small white box with a red bow.

Skylar untied it. "No way! My magic rock!" She looked at Argan. "Did you know?"

He shook his head no.

"This is amazing!" Skylar said. "You got it back from Britt? Did she come back here?"

Suki inhaled. "Funny story . . ."

Now it's your turn to write your story . . .

Page 1

Page 2

Page 3

ACKNOWLEDGMENTS

I thank all of the readers who have read this story to the very end. Thank you for taking this journey with me. I hope you enjoyed the ride.

ABOUT THE AUTHOR

Stacey L. Tucker uses the fantasy fiction genre to bridge science and spirituality in her Equal Night series. Tucker's first book in the trilogy, *Ocean's Fire*, took gold at the Living Now Book Awards. She is passionate about helping women and teens see their untapped potential and follow the voice within. She has written for *Women's World*, *Working Mother*, and PopSugar, and speaks to teen groups about self-empowerment and awareness in today's social media–saturated climate. You can find her at www.staceyltucker.com. She currently resides in Connecticut.

SELECTED TITLES FROM SPARKPRESS

SparkPress is an independent boutique publisher delivering high-quality, entertaining, and engaging content that enhances readers' lives, with a special focus on female-driven work. www.gosparkpress.com

Echoes of War: A Novel, Cheryl Campbell. $16.95, 978-1-68463-006-6. When Dani—one of many civilians living on the fringes to evade a war that's been raging between a faction of aliens and the remnants of Earth's military for decades—discovers that she's not human, her life is upended . . . and she's drawn into the very battle she's spent her whole life avoiding.

Alchemy's Air: Book Two of the Equal Night Trilogy, Stacey L. Tucker. $16.95, 978-1-943006-84-7.Now that she's passed her trial by fire, Skylar Southmartin has been entrusted with the ancient secrets of the Book of Sophia. Ahead is her greatest mission to date: a journey to the Underworld to restore a vital memory to the Akashic Library that will bring her face to face with the darkness within.

Deepest Blue: A Novel, Mindy Tarquini. $16.95, 978-1-943006-69-4. In Panduri, everyone's path is mapped, everyone's destiny determined, their lives charted at birth and steered by an unwavering star. Everything there has its place—until Matteo's older brother, Panduri's Heir, crosses out of their world without explanation, leaving Panduri's orbit in a spiral and Matteo's course on a skid. Forced to follow an unexpected path, Matteo is determined to rise, and he pursues the one future Panduri's star can never chart: a life of his own.

Ocean's Fire: Book One in the Equal Night Trilogy, Stacey L. Tucker. $16.95, 978-1-943006-28-1. Once the Greeks forced their male gods upon the world, the belief in the power of women was severed. For centuries it has been thought that the wisdom of the high priestesses perished at the hand of the patriarchs—but now the ancient Book of Sophia has surfaced. Its pages contain the truths hidden by history, and the sacred knowledge for the coming age. And it is looking for Skylar Southmartin.

Hindsight: A Novel, Mindy Tarquini. $16.95, 978-1-943006-01-4. A 33-year-old Chaucer professor who remembers all her past lives is desperate to change her future—because if she doesn't, she will never live the life of her dreams.

ABOUT SPARKPRESS

SparkPress is an independent, hybrid imprint focused on merging the best of the traditional publishing model with new and innovative strategies. We deliver high-quality, entertaining, and engaging content that enhances readers' lives. We are proud to bring to market a list of *New York Times* best-selling, award-winning, and debut authors who represent a wide array of genres, as well as our established, industry-wide reputation for creative, results-driven success in working with authors. SparkPress, a BookSparks imprint, is a division of SparkPoint Studio LLC.